Hiram's

Boy

HAZEL HART

ISBN-10: 197941372X
ISBN-13: 978-1979413725

DEDICATION

To Clayton

ACKNOWLEDGMENTS

Thank you to my great-grandson, Clayton Moreno, for giving me permission to use his photo on the cover. Also, many thanks to B.J. Myrick for critiquing my novel and designing the book cover, and to my other critique partners, Vicki Hermes-Bond and Wes Brummer, for their suggestions.

Hiram's Boy

PART I

.

ONE

Ambrose

Hidden Springs, Kansas Territory
August 21, 1859

I knelt at Ma's grave and placed a bouquet of daisies beside the marker, then slid to a sitting position and crossed my legs, getting comfortable for my talk. Closing my eyes, I imagined Ma beside me, her hand on my back, asking me what was wrong. So much was, and it had been a month since my last visit. My sister Lucy had come with me that day, so I hadn't felt comfortable or had the time to have a conversation about what troubled me.

Before speaking aloud, I glanced around the cemetery to make sure I was alone. The last thing I needed was someone telling Pa I was talking to myself. We'd had too many ruckuses the last few weeks. I hated arguing with him. I'd rather do about anything than argue when I know I can't win, and no one ever wins an argument with Pa. Well, no one ever did until Miss Carstairs came along.

I shook my head. "How does Miss Carstairs do it, Ma? How does she get her way when you never could?"

I picked up a daisy and twirled the stem between my fingers, then put the flower down and stared off toward the cottonwood trees on the north side of the cemetery. "I don't have to tell you I turned fifteen today. You always remembered my birthday and made that joke about how you were there. Pa never remembers.

I'm almost grown now, but no one sees that. They all think of me as Hiram's boy. I'm tired of being that. I want to be my own man, but I'm not sure what that means, either."

A hand touched my shoulder. "Ambrose."

Susan Hogan's touch startled me. Embarrassed that she'd caught me talking aloud and wondering how much she'd heard, I felt my face get warm.

"Hey, Sue. I didn't hear you come up behind me."

She chuckled. "I could tell."

I forced myself to look up and relaxed at the sight of her warm smile and twinkling brown eyes.

She took a step back. "I guess you were talking to your mother. I shouldn't have interrupted."

I tensed up and glanced away.

"It's all right you know." She nodded to a fresh grave three rows back. "I talk to my sister."

"She passed just three weeks ago," I said. "Ma's been gone four years."

"They're never gone from our hearts." She glanced at the half-dozen purple coneflowers in her hand. "I saw these and had to bring them. Is that what happened with you and the daisies."

"Yes," I said.

"Well, I'll leave you to your visit." She backed up a couple of steps before turning and gliding across the grass to her sister's grave.

Susan was the prettiest girl in Hidden Springs and lived on the next farm down the road from ours. I wanted to go talk to her some more, maybe walk her home, but Pa had notions about society and becoming a legislator if Kansas ever became a state and had declared Susan Hogan and her family not good enough to associate with upstanding citizens like us.

I pushed to my feet and stood looking down at Ma's grave. The feeling of communication was gone. I didn't blame Susan for interrupting, but I'd have to come back another day.

Susan looked up and gave me a wave as I headed toward the road. I waved back. There was no time for more. I had chores to do. I always had chores.

TWO

Hiram

I stared into the buffet mirror, fidgeting with my bow tie. Here it was almost time for church, and Ambrose still hadn't finished his chores. Where had the boy gone off to so early? He'd better not be fooling around with that Hogan girl. There was no way I'd allow that wench to get her hooks into my son. Ambrose was too nice for his own good, just the sort to be taken in by a pretty face.

I heard footsteps on the cellar stairs. "Ambrose, what's the hold-up? We're going to be late for church."

Ambrose poked his head around the corner of the dining room door. "Just finished with the milking."

"Well, get into your church clothes, and let's go."

"I'm on my way to do that now." Ambrose raced for the stairs.

I shook my head. I didn't like his tone these days, and getting that boy in church clothes was a battle every Sunday. Ambrose couldn't seem to grasp the importance of a good appearance for advancing in a community. I checked my clean-shaven reflection in the mirror and once again considered whether to grow a beard. If I did, I'd want a full one. No sense going halfway. But a full beard around a blacksmith forge could be a fire danger. Almost unconsciously, my hand went to my chest and touched the almost square four-inch area where the border ruffians had branded me with a blazing hot horseshoe. I shuddered at the possibility of sparks catching a beard on fire, at the pain of the burn and the

3

scarring it would leave. The puckered flesh on my chest was ugly enough.

I worried that my bride, Ava Carstairs, would be sickened by my mutilated ribcage. She had never seen it, of course, but in two weeks we would be married. Would she be repulsed on our wedding night?

"I'm ready, Pa."

Ambrose's voice startled me out of my contemplations.

"Let's go then," I said.

THREE

Ambrose

The first hymn was starting as Pa and I walked down the center aisle of the church and settled in our pew in the second row. All eyes were on us, and I imagined folks were thinking that Hiram's boy had made him late again. If they had as much to take care of on Sunday as I did, they'd be late, too. Well, maybe not. Maybe I was just bad at planning. At least, when it came to how long things took.

The choir sang the last notes. I glanced up at the chorus. Miss Carstairs frowned at me from the front row as she closed her hymn book. She was all about promptness. Once she and Pa were married, they'd both be on me about being on time.

The choir members took seats, and Reverend Sherwood began with an opening prayer. Then he began his sermon with "Honor your father and mother."

I closed my eyes and clasped my hands in my lap. He'd been over the topic so many times I had to wonder if he thought our town was full of rebellious kids. Truthfully, I didn't know any, but maybe parents saw things differently. It seemed like Pa was always on me lately, no matter how hard I worked.

While Reverend Sherwood's voice rumbled on with examples of ungrateful children and what happened to those who disobeyed the Lord's commandments, my mind wandered through the past few months, trying to pinpoint just when Pa started letting me know I was a slacker and needed to start pulling my weight. "I won't be having my boy sitting idle or running with the likes of that Hogan hooligan."

He was referring to Willie Hogan, Susan's brother. He didn't like the family because he thought Willie's father was shiftless since all he did was farm. With Pa, if you didn't have two or three jobs going, you weren't working hard enough. But Pa had only badmouthed the Hogans in passing until Miss Carstairs came along. Now that I thought of it, it wasn't until after Pa's blowup with my sisters, Lucy and Delia, that he came after me so hard. The memory of that day played again in my mind, drowning out the sermon.

I'd been working in the livery stable, cleaning the stalls when Pa started yelling and cursing next door in the blacksmith shop. He'd stomped into the stable. "Saddle my horse," he'd demanded.

I hurried to do as he said. "What's happened, Pa?"

"That little slut's back causing trouble." He pushed me aside and tightened the saddle while I slipped the halter on Red.

Given his temper, I decided not to press him on who the "little slut" was. The only person I could think of was Susan, but it didn't make sense for it to be her.

Pa mounted the horse and took off at a gallop, storming past Mr. Derryberry, the schoolteacher who was boarding with us.

Mr. Derryberry sidestepped to keep from getting run down and turned to me, his eyes round with alarm. "I mentioned your older sister had come to visit, and Hiram became enraged. I had no idea there was bad blood between father and daughter."

Mr. Derryberry could only mean Delia, and he couldn't know she wasn't truly Pa's daughter. Pa blamed Delia for every bad thing that ever happened in our family: She was Ma's bastard child, the one who ran away and worried Ma so much she went into labor early and both she and my baby brother died.

I ran to the back door to call Bob Clark, who divided his time between the blacksmith shop and the stable. "Something's happened at home," I told him. "Look out for things."

He nodded.

I raced down the street. I figured I could run home faster than I could saddle a horse and then go. Mr. Derryberry ran beside me. Mrs. Collins had heard the commotion and drove her buckboard toward our place. I ran into our kitchen just as Pa grabbed Delia's arm. Cursing her and calling her a guttersnipe, he shoved her across the room. She fell, and Pa pulled back his booted foot to kick her.

Mrs. Collins shouted at him. "Hiram, stop!"

Mr. Derryberry gripped Pa's shoulder. "Settle down. It's not worth it."

Pa shook him off, determined to kick Delia.

Two men burst through the door, one holding a pistol and the second a rifle.

"Don't touch her," the man with the pistol ordered.

Pa stopped and swiped his mouth with the back of his hand. "Get her out. Get 'em both out."

Just like that, Pa had disowned Lucy, his own daughter. Sometimes, I worried he would disown me, too, no matter how hard I tried to please him.

Pa nudged me with his elbow, bringing me back to the present.

"Stand up!" he ordered through gritted teeth, his voice low to keep others from hearing. He shoved a hymn book in my hand. "Number 140."

I stood, opened the book, and mouthed the words.

FOUR

Hiram

I flicked the reins and headed the buggy toward home, Ava at my side, Ambrose in the back seat. The boy had been woolgathering in church again instead of paying proper attention to the sermon. Exasperated, I drove in silence. What was going on with Ambrose? He had always been the light of my life. Now, he was the cause of one irritation after another. I guided the horse into the circle drive and pulled him to a stop in front of my house. The sight of my home lifted my spirits, and I took a moment to admire the spacious stone structure, the fruit of my labors and evidence of my success and standing in the community.

My mood improved as I stepped to the ground and helped Ava down while giving an order to Ambrose. "Take care of the horse."

Ambrose took the reins and drove the buggy toward the barn.

I ascended the front steps and moved to one side to open the door for Ava. She entered the hall and removed her shawl.

"Let's talk in the parlor," I said, leading the way.

We settled in the new chairs I'd placed side by side when they'd arrived the week before. It being August, there was no fire in the fireplace, but I could picture the room on a winter evening with Ava as hostess while I entertained Mayor Tompkins and possibly even Sam Wood or Dr. Charles Robinson. At last, my dreams were coming true. Or they would be if I could get my children in line.

I sat on the edge of my chair, thinking of a way to broach the topic of my younger daughters, Ella and Jennie. As soon as Ava and I tied the knot, I wanted to bring the girls home.

"Less than two weeks 'til we're married," I said, by way of opening the subject.

Ava straightened in her chair, her green eyes gleaming. "Wait until you see my wedding dress. And my cousins have planned a wonderful party for us after the ceremony."

"I'm sure it will be perfect, but I'm thinking beyond the day. Maybe we should take a trip to Westport. Bring Ella and Jennie home before that witch Hannah has any more time to infect them with her suffragette nonsense. She's already ruined Lucy, as you know."

Ava frowned, her forehead furrowing. "Are you sure it isn't too late for those girls? They've been away from you for four years, and they were so young when they left. How old are they?"

"Ella's nine and Jennie's seven."

"So they were only five and three when they left you. And you said Minerva let them do pretty much as they wanted, what with her being ill so much of the time."

I nodded. "That's all the more reason to get them home as soon as possible."

Ava slipped her hand on top of mine and squeezed lightly. "I know you want to do your best for them, but after the way Lucy behaved, refusing to consider marriage to any one of the fine gentlemen you introduced her to, perhaps it's too late for these younger girls. Besides the influence of their aunt, there's their mother's influence. I know I shouldn't speak ill of the dead, but Minerva was obviously weak in both body and morals. Perhaps her girls inherited the same traits."

I clamped my lips together. I wanted to object, to tell Ava she was wrong. The girls were my blood, too, after all. But she was right about Lucy. I was certain she had disobeyed my order to stay away from the Hogans, that she had spent time with Willie and might even now be carrying his bastard. Who knew what had happened between them. She was like her mother, even though her physical resemblance was to my side of the family.

"I suppose," I admitted, studying my hands, trying to stifle the fury in my heart that came with acceptance that my daughters would never be the young women I had imagined: wives of important, prosperous men and mothers to children who would grow up to be a part of a line of men who built the state, and yes, the country.

"Best to leave the problems they cause to the aunt raising them." Ava flashed a slight but reassuring smile and tightened her grip on my hand. "We'll have our own children, strong in body and mind, sons and daughters who will be a credit to us and the community. Let's not take the chance that Minerva's girls will influence our future children with any strange beliefs Hannah might have indoctrinated them with."

"I see what you mean." I swallowed hard. "We don't want our youngsters swayed by that kind of talk. You're right. We'll leave them to Hannah to deal with."

Ava smiled and bent closer, brushing my cheek with her lips. "I know it's hard, but you've chosen the right path for the children we will have."

FIVE

Ambrose

When I came in from the barn, I paused in the kitchen for a dipper of water and then headed for the stairs. Hearing voices from the parlor, I paused, thinking I would remind Pa that Mr. Clark had taken today off, and I needed to return to the stable in town to feed the horse left in our care the night before.

I had my hand on the parlor door, ready to push it open, when I heard Miss Carstairs belittling Ma, calling her weak in body and morals. My stomach twisted when Pa agreed with her. Ma died trying to give him sons, and he had no respect for her sacrifice. I was shaking, doing my best not to storm in and tell him what I thought. Then I heard the outcome of the talk—Ella and Jennie would stay in Westport with Aunt Hannah.

Good. If they came here, Miss Carstairs would make servants of them, just as she had Lucy. My little sisters deserved a better life. Still, how would they feel, knowing their own father didn't want them? I remembered how much Lucy had wanted Pa's love and admiration, and how sad she was when she realized she would never get it.

I shook my head. Miss Carstairs didn't want to be bothered with my little sisters; clearly, that was what was behind her conniving against their coming. And Pa fell for everything she said, never seeing her real intent.

I backed away from the door and went back through the kitchen and outside, figuring there was no sense telling Pa where I was going. He wouldn't miss me as long as Miss Carstairs was with him.

I took off at a run, passed the Hogan place, and made a turn into the cemetery. Falling on my knees beside my mother's grave, I let out my anger and misery.

"She's taken over everything, Ma. Everything. And Pa is blind. Why? If only you'd mattered to him as much as Miss Carstairs does, you might still be alive."

SIX

Hiram

Ava patted my hand and straightened on the couch beside me. "There's still our wedding to discuss. I'll make us some tea."

My eyes followed her as she stood and left the room, looking perfect as always, her pale yellow skirt swaying as she walked. Surely, she wore a hooped petticoat beneath her dress. My mind lingered on what else lay beneath the skirt and the possibilities of our wedding night, and I felt an eagerness I hadn't since my marriage to Constance, my first wife, the one before Minerva.

It had been years since I'd thought of Constance. Mostly, life gave me no reason to think of her. I had been twenty-eight when we met, working for my father in the Westport shop, my world revolving around perfecting my blacksmithing skills. And then Constance had walked in with her uncle who owned the bakery down the street. I remembered the way her brown eyes scanned me, top to toe, and the way they flashed when they came up to my face again. In spite of the suspicions I'd had of her after the marriage and the too-familiar glances between Constance and my brother, the memory of that first meeting aroused me, held me, played in my mind.

"Here's the tea," Ava said, bringing me back to the present. She set the tray on the low table between our chairs and poured each of us a cup, placed mine on a saucer, and handed it to me. Then she lifted her own and took a sip, her green eyes meeting mine over the rim. She smiled as she lowered the cup, a seductive smile full of promise.

"Since we've reached an agreement on your daughters' living arrangements, we need to plan the details of our wedding."

I set my cup and saucer on the table, not really wanting the drink, but liking the formality that signaled a serious discussion. "I've already spoken to Reverend Sherwood about conducting the ceremony. He offered the church, but I thought a wedding here in our home might be best."

She straightened, her eyes rounding. "Oh, Hiram, no."

"No?" Confused, my chest tightened. What was she saying no to? "Why not?" I had never met a woman so hard to satisfy.

"I assumed we would have a church wedding as befits a man of your social position." Her eyes widened. "Surely, we will have so many guests that even this lovely home will not be large enough to accommodate them all." She reached for her reticule and withdrew a card and a sheet of notepaper. "I hope I haven't overstepped, but I spoke with Reverend Sherwood about the church yesterday." She handed me the card. "With his assurance that it was available, I had these invitations printed."

I gazed at the fancy script, my heart swelling with pride. Ava thought of everything. After two marriages to unsuitable women, I would finally, in my third, have a true helpmeet.

Ava unfolded the sheet of paper. "I've also made this list of possible guests for your approval. Is there anyone I've forgotten?" She offered me the paper.

I set the card on the end table and reached for the list. Scanning the names, I saw the mayor, the Fletchers, Mrs. Collins, three members of the town council and their wives, and three members of the territorial legislature who lived in nearby towns.

"Would you like to add someone? I plan to address the invitations tomorrow morning. Perhaps Ambrose could deliver them in the afternoon."

"Yes, of course. Bob Clark can watch the livery stable while he does that."

"My cousin Agnes will be playing the piano for the ceremony." Her green eyes glittered with happiness. "And I am picturing you standing at the front of the church, looking handsome in your suit, waiting for me in my beautiful white wedding dress and long veil."

I was overtaken by the vision she projected. Yes, a church wedding was just the right way to mark this new and triumphant chapter of my life. "You're being married in a white dress?"

"Of course. White has been the proper color for a bride ever since Queen Victoria's marriage to Prince Albert." She sighed. "I realize a man doesn't have time to keep up with society like a woman does."

"I shall depend on you for all things social." I handed her the card and list.

She returned the items to her reticule and laid it on the side table. "And I shall do my best not to fail you. Which brings me to our attendants and your choice of best man."

"Ambrose, of course."

Her forehead wrinkled. "I understand your choice, but he's just a boy. Perhaps someone more mature, an indication of your stature in the community. You and Mayor Tompkins are close, aren't you? You often have your heads together about civic plans, and I imagine he will be a frequent guest in this house."

The mayor as my best man? What a marvelous idea.

***

While I was driving Ava home, we passed the livery stable. The door stood open, and I realized the afternoon had passed into evening with no sign of Ambrose. Ava and I had been so deep in plans for our wedding and for completing the furnishing of the house that I hadn't noticed my son's absence.

After dropping Ava off, I returned to the stable and entered by way of the open door. "Ambrose! You in here?"

"Yes, Pa." The boy's voice came from the stall farthest from the door.

Walking toward him, I asked, "You been here all afternoon?"

Ambrose leaned a shovel against the wall. "Wanted to get some cleanup done, and you and Miss Carstairs seemed focused on your plans for the house, so I figured I'd stay out of the way."

"Out of the way? Son, you've never been in the way. You're my right hand. I couldn't get along without you."

Ambrose smiled. "I'm glad to hear that, Pa. These days, I sometimes feel like an extra wheel."

I grabbed Ambrose by the shoulder and gave him a little shake. "Let's go home."

SEVEN

Ambrose

Regardless of what Pa said about me being his right hand and how he couldn't do without me, I doubted him. Ever since he'd sent Lucy away, I'd felt the bond between us weaken. And today, hearing Miss Carstairs say my mother was weak in body and character and how my sisters probably inherited that from her made me wonder what she was saying to Pa about me.

I was mad at Pa for not defending my mother and went to bed stewing about the hateful things Miss Carstairs had said about her. I fell into a troubled sleep and a dream that came often and haunted me: the night my brother Mark died.

Mark was born on Christmas Day, 1854. He died one week later on New Year's Day, 1855. When he was born, the whole family laughed and celebrated. He was the perfect Christmas gift, tiny but healthy, or so we thought. But he started spitting up his milk and crying a lot. Ma, Delia, and Lucy took turns walking the floor with him. Nothing seemed to help.

Then came New Year's morning. Ma looked pale as she set about making breakfast. She'd been up most of the night with Mark, but for now, he was quiet in his basket beyond the curtain that separated the bedroom from the rest of the cabin. We were all doing chores except Jennie, who was only three. She disappeared, and when I came in from milking, Ma asked me to check on her.

I found her curled up in the cradle beside Mark, a blanket wrapped around them. She was hugging him.

"What are you doing, Jennie? You shouldn't be in the bed with Mark." I reached down to lift her out. "Let go of the baby."

"He's cold," she said. "I want to make him warm."

That's when I noticed how still he was. I reached down and pressed my hand against his still chest. My heart clenched. "Ma! Ma! Come now!"

"What is it?"

I heard her rushing toward us as I pulled Jennie out of the basket.

Ma yanked back the curtain and rushed in, Pa right behind her.

Jennie was crying and asking, "Did I do something wrong? I just wanted to make him warm." She stood clutching one corner of the blanket to her chest.

Ma fell to her knees and lifted Mark's lifeless body from his bed.

Pa turned to me, his eyes were wild. "Get Doc Sloan," he ordered.

I ran from the house toward town. I knew it was too late to save Mark, that he was already gone, but I was only ten years old, and I didn't know what else to do, so I ran.

As it always did, the dream woke me. I tossed in the bed, kicking off the sheet and sitting up, breathing hard. Six months after Mark left us, Ma and another infant boy born too soon both died. That's when my sisters went to live with Aunt Hannah, and I was left alone with Pa, a man broken in body and spirit.

EIGHT

Hiram

I tossed aside the thin blanket and tramped down the stairs to the kitchen where I poured whiskey in a tin cup. I settled in a chair at the table, tilted the cup to my mouth, and took a swallow, then stared out the window into the dark night, a pale moon revealing the dark hulk of the old cabin. Sights and sounds from four years ago, ending with that witch Hannah stealing my girls, haunted me.

Minerva had been next to death when Hannah showed up with Delia, the two of them forcing Min out of bed while they washed sheets. They should have left her alone to rest like Doc Sloan had ordered. Min hadn't complained, though, and what could I do, laid up with broken ribs and a healing chest burn. My hand went to that place below my heart and rubbed the rough, puckered scar.

Delia, the little slut, had brought Hannah to destroy my family. They'd succeeded. I gulped another slug of whiskey, the cries of that night echoing in my head. Lucy's cries for help, the little girls sobbing, Ambrose running out the door for the doctor, Hannah taking control while I lay helpless in bed, straining to sit up, pain from my broken ribs gouging every move.

I should never have let Hannah take my girls. I had imagined such fine lives for them, married to professional men, raising strong, smart children (preferably sons). Although their sons wouldn't bear my last name, they would carry my blood, and everyone would point to them and say what fine grandsons Hiram Pierce had. The girls might have honored me by naming their boys Hiram or Pierce.

I slumped in the chair, my hands circling the cup. That possibility was gone now. Ava had been right this afternoon when she had said they were tainted with Minerva's bad blood. Lucy looked strong in body; she resembled my side of the family. But she was obviously morally weak like her mother. I knew she'd met with that Willie Hogan. I could imagine what they had done alone in the fields. Surely, Ella and Jennie would follow in her footsteps and come to a bad end. Better to start anew, as Ava said, with our own children, who would have strong blood from both parents.

September first and my wedding to Ava couldn't come quickly enough.

NINE

Ambrose

The next day I was at the back of the livery stable putting fresh hay in my horse Butter's stall when the palomino nickered and nudged me with her nose. I laughed. "What?" Then I heard voices. Pa and Mayor Tompkins came strolling in the front of the building, both men laughing.

The mayor slapped Pa on the back "Hope your boy will be all right with this arrangement. You sure he won't feel left out?"

"He'll be fine." Pa called out, "Where are you, Ambrose? I've got great news."

Wondering what had Pa in such a good mood, I leaned the pitchfork against the wall and stepped out of the shadows and into the sunlight coming through the open front door. "I'm here, Pa. What's the news?"

"Mayor Tomkins has agreed to be best man at my wedding."

He stood there with such a big smile on his face that all I could say was "That's great," even though I didn't feel that good about it.

"Didn't I tell you he'd be just fine with it?" Pa said to Mayor Tompkins.

"You did," the mayor responded. "Stop by the newspaper office after work, and we'll have a drink to celebrate. I have to get back to work now."

"I'll be there." After the mayor left, Pa turned to me. "Bob will be over to take care of the stable. You're to pick up the wedding invitations from the Emporium and deliver them." With that, he strolled out the door to the adjoining blacksmith shop.

I went back to feeding Butter and set a bucket of fresh water in her stall, all the while thinking about why I was in a bad mood about Mayor Tompkins being Pa's best man. I reckoned it had something to do with the mayor referring to me as Pa's "boy." I'd been doing the work of a man for the past four years, but when it came to anything official for a man to do, I was still a boy. I didn't even like Miss Carstairs, so I should be happy I wouldn't have to be part of her wedding. Watching it would be hard enough. And why was that? I didn't have anything real against her, only a bad feeling.

"Ambrose," Bob Clark said.

Startled, I looked up to see Bob, his arms folded over the top rail of the stall.

Bob chuckled. "You seemed pretty lost in thought."

"Just thinking about Pa's wedding, wondering who all Miss Carstairs invited. Guess I'll find out today. Pa wants me to deliver the invitations."

"That's why he sent me. He says there're guests in Junction City and Ft. Riley. It's nearing noon, and with all the ground you have to cover, you'd better get on it."

I groaned. "I'll run over to Fletcher's Emporium and pick up those invites now."

"Want me to saddle up Butter while you're gone. Save you some time."

"I'd appreciate it." Brushing hay from my trousers, I headed for the door. The Emporium was straight across the street. As I crossed, I saw their door was wide open to catch what little breeze there was on this blazing hot August day. I stepped inside and stood for a moment, letting my eyes adjust to the dimmer light within. Blinking, I looked around. No one was at the front of the store. There were some thumps and voices from the back, though, so I figured they were unloading freight and headed back through the long center aisle. I was perhaps five feet from the door to the loading dock when I heard Mr. Fletcher's raised voice. "We've got a good life here. I hope Ava's not going to mess it up for us like she did back in New York."

I stopped dead still. How had Miss Carstairs messed things up for them? Maybe my not liking her was some kind of recognition that she wasn't the good person she pretended to be. I remembered how upset I was with Lucy over her matchmaking between Pa and Miss Carstairs. All I could say then was that we didn't know anything about her. We still didn't. So I stood holding my breath, listening for Mrs. Fletcher's reply to her husband's worry, but her voice was too soft for me to make out the words.

Not wanting them to know I might have heard something they wouldn't want me to, I backed up to the center of the store and called, "Hello. Anyone here?"

Mrs. Fletcher bustled through the back door. "Ambrose. I suppose you've come for the invitations."

"Yes, ma'am," I said.

She opened a drawer behind the counter and withdrew a stack of sealed papers tied with string. "Here they are. Ava put the out-of-town ones on top, figuring you'd deliver them first."

"Yes, ma'am," I said again, unable to think of anything else when my mind was still spinning with questions about the trouble Miss Carstairs had caused them in New York City. I accepted the invitations and looked at the fancy handwriting on the outside of each sealed sheet of paper. I guess I stared overlong because Mrs. Fletcher cleared her throat. I looked up.

"If you're going to get those delivered today, you're going to have to move."

As I headed for the door, I wondered how I could find out more about New York City and what Miss Carstairs had done. Was there something Pa should know before he married her?

TEN

Hiram

I closed the shop at six and, seeing Ambrose hadn't returned from delivering the invitations, decided to have that drink with Mayor Tompkins before eating supper at Mrs. Collins's boardinghouse. Ambrose might be back in time to share the meal with me.

Mayor Tompkins had started the newspaper after the previous publisher had moved to California instead of staying in Hidden Springs. I considered myself one of the newspaper's biggest supporters since I ran a weekly advertisement for my blacksmith and livery businesses. I also wrote the occasional letter to the editor in support of Kansas becoming a free state. I refused to let the border ruffians who'd attacked me and branded my chest four years ago scare me into silence.

The bell above the newspaper's door jingled as I entered. Mayor Tompkins, seated at his desk, glanced up, and then stood in greeting. "Ready for that drink, are you?"

I blew out a breath. "I am.

"Have a seat, then." Mayor Tompkins pulled two small glasses from a shelf and removed a bottle of whiskey from his desk drawer. While pouring the drinks, he said, "I've been meaning to ask how preliminary planning for the city building is coming. Any idea when construction will start?"

I relaxed in a chair across the desk from Tompkins. "Ambrose has talked to Mayfield, the stone mason, about finding workers for the job and acquiring the rock. Ambrose learned the trade from Mayfield, who has done first-rate work in Junction City."

24

Tompkins handed me a filled glass, returned the bottle to the drawer, and sat in the chair behind his desk. "We're coming to the end of summer. If the construction can't start soon, it may be best to delay until next spring. We'll have more time to raise money, and we won't have to worry about rough winter weather interfering with the building."

"I'll speak to Ambrose and have him set up a meeting with Mayfield. See if we can get a commitment."

"With business out of the way," the mayor said, lifting his glass, "let's have a toast to your upcoming marriage."

ELEVEN

Ambrose

It was dark and the cow was impatient to be milked by the time I got home from delivering the invitations.

When I saw lamplight coming through the library window, I figured Pa was probably going over the day's business, recording income and expenses in his ledger. My stomach growling, I set about the milking, my mind on the kitchen and what I might find to eat. Miss Carstairs had begun bringing by baked goods, mostly biscuits and cookies. I had my doubts about whether she actually baked them herself, but I would be glad if either was available.

While I milked, my thoughts wandered to the conversation I'd overheard between the Fletchers. What had Miss Carstairs done in New York City? If there was something Pa should know, I had to be the one to find it out. He was so under her spell, he'd never see anything suspicious on his own. He was always calling Aunt Hannah a witch, but in my opinion, Miss Carstairs was more like one than my aunt.

I finished the milking, carried the full bucket to the cellar and strained its contents. When I was finished, I skimmed a cup of cream from the morning's milk and took it upstairs, thinking to cook oatmeal and top it with the cream if there were no leftover baked goods in the house.

In the kitchen, a look in the pie safe revealed empty shelves, so I stoked the fire and set a pan of water on the stove.

Pa came in while I was working and stood with his arms folded across his chest. "You get all those invitations delivered?"

I glanced at him as I waited for the water to heat, wondering why he looked so out of sorts. "I did."

"What have you done about the city building? Have you spoken to Mayfield? "

I blinked. I had not expected the question, at least not tonight. "I talked to him about three weeks ago. He said he'd get back to me or to you."

"He hasn't, and now the mayor says we may have to postpone construction until next spring if we can't start soon." He slammed his fist on the work table beside me. "I recommended you for this job, Ambrose. I'm going to look bad if you don't do your part."

"I'll get on it tomorrow, Pa." I dumped oatmeal in the pot of boiling water and stirred it. My head ached. I needed food. I needed sleep. I didn't need the job he'd recommended me for. I already had more than I could do. I was always running—the stable, the house, errands for Miss Carstairs, and now, running this job of constructing the city building. I hoped Pa didn't volunteer me for any more jobs.

***

In spite of being worn out, I found sleep hard to come by. Mr. Fletcher's words about Ava causing trouble kept whirling in my mind.

I turned on my side and reached for the drawer of my bedside table. Opening it, I removed the book of Aesop's fables and other fairy tales Ma had made for me. It had been my fifth birthday present, but I had watched her putting it together for weeks before I knew it was to be mine. She had embroidered thick cream-colored cloth with the tortoise and the hare in bright colors and glued the material onto a thin wood cover. The inside pages each contained one of her drawings of the characters in the fable and the hand-lettered story that went with it. She'd said there were lots more stories than what she'd put in the book, but it was already three inches thick, so she'd had to stop with the ones she liked best. I remember lying on my cot at night while she read one of the stories to me. If I had misbehaved, she would choose a story that would point out the right and honorable path to take.

It didn't matter that it was too dark now to see the pages. I had each one memorized. I lay back with the book pressed to my chest, thinking about the morals that fit my current situation, morals about who could be believed and about the ills gossip could cause.

Would Ma consider me asking around about Miss Carstairs's past as gossip or as a necessary investigative tool into knowing whether she could be trusted? I closed my eyes and thought on the fables and their morals. Miss Carstairs gave the appearance of an educated, religious woman. She attended church and sang in the choir. Pa thought she was wonderful. But many of the fables warned that appearances were deceiving, and Mr. Fletcher's statement about her causing them trouble in New York hinted that she was not what she seemed. On the other hand, Ma said the Bible viewed gossip as destructive, but the only way I knew to find out what had happened was to listen to gossip.

Who might know something? Maybe Mrs. Collins. With her boardinghouse right next door to the general store, she might have overheard something. She'd be honest and wouldn't tell anyone I was asking questions if I asked her not to. She'd always looked out for us kids.

With a course of action decided on, I returned the book to the drawer, closed my eyes, and took long, even breaths, willing myself to sleep.

***

The next morning, I told Pa I was going to Mr. Mayfield's job to find out when he could start work on the city building, and I needed Mr. Clark to watch the livery stable for me. Before riding out, I headed over to the boardinghouse. Most of the breakfast crowd had left, and the place was quiet. Mrs. Collins was clearing dishes from a table. I stood a moment, not wanting to interrupt her and thought of what I might say.

Mrs. Collins looked up. "What's got you biting your lip, Ambrose?"

I cleared my throat. "I don't know how to ask this?"

"Then it must be important."

"Yes, ma'am. Otherwise, I wouldn't ask."

She walked behind the counter and propped the broom in a closet before turning, resting her arms on the countertop, and giving me her full attention. "Whatever has you searching for words, saying it straight out is the best way."

"It's about Miss Carstairs."

Mrs. Collins raised an eyebrow. "Go on."

"When I went to pick up the wedding invitations yesterday, the Fletchers were out back unloading a wagon, and I overheard Mr. Fletcher say something about hoping Miss Carstairs wasn't going to cause trouble for them here like she did in New York." I paused and studied my boots for a second before meeting her eyes. "I just wondered, you being next door to them and all, if you ever heard them say what Miss Carstairs might have done. I wouldn't ask, but, well, she's new in town, and we know next to nothing about her. I thought if there was anything Pa needed to know before they permanently tied the knot, I should find out and tell him."

Mrs. Collins sighed and shook her head. "Ambrose, I haven't heard a thing. I understand it must be hard to see someone take your mother's place in your father's life, but he has a right to move on and be happy."

"I guess so." Disappointment flooded me. She thought I was just a dumb kid missing his mother and not wanting a stepmother taking her place. I backed toward the door. "Well, I got to go see Mr. Mayfield about the city building." Then a worry cropped up. "Please don't say anything to anyone about me asking. It would only cause trouble."

She smiled. "I understand, Ambrose. I promise I won't say a word."

"Thank you." I hurried out the door and crossed the street to the stable where Butter stood, saddled and waiting for me. I pressed my face against the palomino's neck and hugged her before mounting and riding out of town.

TWELVE

Hiram

I had just finished settling up with a farmer for two new axes when Ambrose returned that afternoon, a hangdog expression on his face, riding past me into the stable without a word. I glanced around my now-empty shop and followed him.

"Out with it, boy," I said while Ambrose was dismounting.

He led his horse to a stall and began loosening the saddle. "Mr. Mayfield says he can't get the stone or the men to do the work until at least the first of October."

"That's too late. The mayor wants to break ground right away."

"Mr. Mayfield said he'd understand if we wanted to go with someone else."

"Mayfield's the best. We don't want less."

"Then I guess we'll have to wait, make a time for him to start in the spring, like you said last night."

"Did you tell him that?"

"Yes."

"Did he give a date?"

"The first week of April. He said the bad weather will be over by then—except for rain, of course. Figured to be done by late summer."

"What did you tell him?"

"That I would check with you, but to put the building on the schedule for April unless he heard different from you or Mayor Tompkins."

I shook my head. "Humph! I suppose this serves me right for thinking you could handle the job. Next time, I'll know better." I turned and stomped back to the smithy.

THIRTEEN

Ambrose

In the coming days, I tried to think of some way to find out more about Miss Carstairs and her time in New York.

Finally, on the Sunday before the wedding, August twenty-eight, we were having a pot luck dinner at the church, and I felt brave enough with the crowd around us to ask her a question about her church in New York. Was it a big church? Were folks as friendly there as here? What about the abolitionists? Were they as active there? Did she ever get letters from her friends letting her know about what was happening back east?

She gave me one of those calculating looks she often did when I spoke and then brushed me off like I was a mosquito. "I haven't heard from anyone for some time. The mail's not very reliable."

That was not a good answer since the mail delivery here was fairly good. Sure, letters from back east would take longer, but they'd get here. My letters got to my sisters just fine, and Lucy wrote every week. Of course, now that Pa had disowned Lucy, she sent her letters to the boardinghouse, and Mrs. Collins passed them on to me. I didn't say so, though, because I didn't want Pa to know I was in touch with Lucy and Delia.

Then I realized my mistake. I had asked Miss Carstairs about her life in New York, but she'd never mentioned living there to me. I wondered if she'd said anything to Pa and might think he'd told me. Surely, she'd mentioned the places she'd lived to him.

Wouldn't that come up in conversation with someone you were going to marry?

I looked up to see Susan across the way with her brother Willy. I wished I could join them and listen to Willy's fishing stories and Susan's jokes. Instead, I was stuck here with Pa and Miss Carstairs, listening to wedding talk and worrying that I'd let her know I'd learned something I wasn't supposed to know.

***

It was September first, Pa's wedding day. I got up and did the usual chores, thankful that Mayor Tompkins was the best man. I wished I had time to visit Ma's grave, but Pa had me busy with chores until the last minute.

The wedding was at eleven. It was ten-thirty when I came down the stairs dressed in the new black suit and white shirt Miss Carstairs insisted was correct for weddings. I stopped to check my reflection in the buffet mirror and adjusted my bowtie, another "must wear" according to Miss Carstairs.

Realizing that today I was going to have to quit calling her that, I tried out Mrs. Ava in my mind and settled on it.

Mayor Tompkins had come by earlier and picked up Pa. I was to bring our buggy so Pa would have it later to drive him and Mrs. Ava to Junction City for a four-night stay at the hotel there. Pa planned to meet with the livery stable owner there to talk about our horse exchange contract and meet with some territorial delegates about the Wyandotte constitution, so it wasn't all a pleasure trip. Nothing with Pa was ever purely pleasure.

I hurried to the wagon, worried I might be late. Pa would complain I was dragging my feet, and I was. It seemed like he was doing the worst thing he could for both of us. I had talked to Mrs. Collins when I'd picked up my letter from Lucy and Delia on Monday.

Although Mrs. Collins understood my feelings, she said Pa seemed to truly love his bride the way he listened to everything she said and took her opinions into consideration. Mrs. Collins didn't realize those were the very things that worried me. Pa seemed to be under some kind of spell, doing everything Miss Carstairs wanted. That wasn't the Pa I knew. But Mrs. Collins thought I might be jealous of her influence over him. She seemed to have forgotten my questions concerning what Miss Carstairs might have done in New York to shame her cousins.

When I got to the church, the street was crowded with wagons and a couple of other buggies. I set the brake, tied the reins to a post, and hurried inside. Miss Carstairs and Mr. Fletcher stood in the vestibule. Miss Carstairs gave me a hard look and hissed, "You're late." I apologized and rushed in, everyone's eyes on me as I scurried down the central aisle to the second pew and took a seat beside Mrs. Collins. Pa was standing in front of the altar with Mayor Tompkins at his side. Mrs. Fletcher sat at the piano, fingers on the keys, staring toward the back of the room.

Mrs. Fletcher must have gotten a signal to begin playing because she turned her attention to the piano and began pounding out some kind of march. Pa had told me it had been played at the wedding of Queen Victoria, and Miss Carstairs was set on doing as much like that wedding as she could. She desired to copy all the best of society and what could be better than copying a royal wedding?

About five chords into the march, there was a rustle at the back of the room and all heads turned to see the commotion. Then everyone stood while Mr. Fletcher, Miss Carstairs on his arm, took small mincing steps as they proceeded down the aisle toward the front of the church. Miss Carstairs's face was covered with a white, lacy veil, her white, floor-length skirt swaying slightly with each measured step. I heard little whispers about how beautiful she was, and I glanced at Pa.

He was staring at her, his eyes wide and this big grin on his face. I guess he looked the happiest I'd ever seen him. Maybe he'd been that happy when Mark was born, but that had been followed with crushing pain a week later when Mark died in his cradle. Now I feared his happiness might be crushed again if it turned out Miss Carstairs wasn't what she seemed.

Miss Carstairs made it up the aisle, Reverend Sherwood began the wedding ceremony, and Mr. Fletcher said he was giving the bride away and took a seat. The vows were next, and finally Reverend Sherwood said they were man and wife, and "what God has joined together, let no man put asunder."

With those words, Miss Carstairs became Mrs. Ava to me. I swallowed hard, thinking of Reverend Sherwood's last words of the ceremony. My throat hurt with the knowledge that it was too late to look for what Mrs. Ava had done in the past. She was Pa's wife.

I forced a smile as the two started up the aisle toward the back of the church. I needn't have bothered. Neither of them paid any mind to me as the wedding guests called out congratulations and filed in behind them as they paraded toward the door.

FOURTEEN

Hiram

The heat in the church was oppressive. I resisted the urge to swipe sweat from my forehead. It wouldn't do to fidget in front of the wedding guests. I slanted my eyes toward the first pew where Ambrose sat, having slithered in late.

The boy was getting less dependable by the day. The trouble with Ambrose had all started with my engagement to Ava. The boy was too old to be concerned about stepmothers, but still, he'd shown resentment toward Ava and our coming marriage. Well, I didn't care what Ambrose thought. I finally had a chance at the life I had always envisioned for myself, and I wasn't going to let a boy's foolish resentments stand in my way.

Now that Ambrose had arrived, the ceremony could begin. My eyes fixed expectantly on the double doors at the back of the sanctuary. They cracked open. A white hanky fluttered. Mrs. Fletcher began pounding the piano keys, playing what Ava had said was the song used in Queen Victoria's wedding.

The doors at the end of the center aisle opened. There stood Ava on Mr. Fletcher's arm. My heart swelled with pride at the sight of my bride, a vision in white. I heard a slight gasp from the guests and knew it was because she projected wealth and status. I was a tradesman, a blacksmith, but I was going to be more, and Ava would be by my side, her instincts for society elevating me.

I felt a smile spread across my face as she inched closer with tiny steps. I wanted to shout "Hurry up! I've waited long enough!" But, of course, I stood stock still, waiting.

At last she was in front of me, lifting her veil, her green eyes shining, looking up at me through half-lowered lashes, her lips slightly turned up in a smile.

The vows were a blur as the heat in the room mounted. Sweat trickled down my face as Reverend Sherwood pronounced us man and wife and directed me to kiss the bride. Afterward, he introduced us as Mr. and Mrs. Hiram Pierce. Then I took Ava's hand, and we strode down the aisle toward the door and fresh air.

We stopped on the steps just outside the church, the noonday sun beating down on us as we greeted our guests and reminded them lunch would be served immediately at the boardinghouse, a joint arrangement between me, the Fletchers, and Alice Collins.

Ambrose meandered out, gave what I considered an insincere smile, and mumbled "Congratulations!"

I clamped my mouth shut, telling myself I wouldn't start anything here on my wedding day, but I was definitely going to have a talk with the boy about his attitude. Like it or not, Ava was now Ambrose's stepmother, and he was going to have to do as he was told and be polite about it.

I patted Ava's arm. "Shall we join our guests for lunch?"

"Of course," she said, smiling up at me.

With Ambrose straggling behind us, we crossed the street and walked the two blocks to the boarding house.

All was going well. The food was delicious, and then the cake was brought in, three tiers with white frosting. Everyone gathered round for the cutting. When all the guests had been served, Ava and I stood to one side, dessert plates in hand.

Ava nodded. "I wonder what's going on there."

I looked in the direction of her nod. My jaw tightened. Ambrose was standing with that Hogan tart. What was she doing here?

Ava leaned toward me, put her lips to my ear, and whispered, "They seem exceptionally friendly. In fact, he seems smitten with her."

That was just what I'd feared for close to a year now. I looked around and saw Alice Collins overseeing the placement of a newly-filled bowl of punch on the refreshments table. She turned and glanced about the room.

I raised my hand and, frowning, pointed toward Ambrose and the Hogan girl.

Alice Collins's eyebrows lifted questioningly as she came my way and stopped in front of me. "Is something wrong?"

"What's the Hogan girl doing here? She wasn't invited."

"She's the best baker in town, and she works for me now, doing the baking for the boardinghouse. She made your cake, and she's helping serve refreshments."

"Some help she is! She's been yapping with Ambrose for a good ten minutes." I took a deep breath, considering what to say next. Alice didn't take kindly to orders. "Maybe you could tell her to get back to work and tell Ambrose I want to speak to him immediately."

She squinted at me. "Of course, Hiram. I'll do that right now."

She looked a bit huffy as she walked away, but I didn't care as long as my boy got separated from Hogan.

Alice stopped beside the young couple and put a hand on Ambrose's back. A moment later, the Hogan girl nodded and disappeared into the kitchen. Ambrose turned toward me, his face stony as he crossed the room.

"What do you want, Pa?"

"I want you to stay away from that girl like I've told you more than a dozen times."

Ambrose shook his head. "She made your wedding cake. I was just paying her a compliment on how good it was."

"She was paid to make it, which makes her the hired help. No compliment necessary. Stay away from her. I don't want my boy getting tangled up with her lowlife family. Now go talk with our guests like the son of the groom should be doing."

"Yes, Pa," Ambrose replied and walked away.

Ava gripped my arm. "He didn't say that like he meant it," she murmured.

"No, he didn't," I agreed. Ava and I would be out of town for four nights, more than enough time for Ambrose to go sneaking around with that girl. There was nothing to be done about that. I could hardly cancel the wedding trip. I'd just have to hope nothing came of Ambrose's willful actions and have a long talk with the boy next week.

FIFTEEN

Ambrose

Shaking with anger, I walked away from Pa and Mrs. Ava. So Susan didn't deserve a compliment because she got paid to make the cake and was just the hired help? That was something coming from Pa. He perked up every time someone said something good about his blacksmithing work and bragged about how he made the best axes in the territory, and that was all based on what his customers said about him. Yet he thought Susan didn't deserve to hear good words about her baking skills.

I wandered through the dozen or so guests, but I couldn't find any conversations to join, so I sought out Mrs. Collins. "Will you tell Pa I've gone to change so I can open the stable?"

She offered a weak, sympathetic smile. "I will."

I slid through the crowd toward the front door. The Fletchers were standing facing the windows, and I was almost even with Mrs. Fletcher when she spoke to her husband in a low voice. "We'll know soon enough if she's fooled him."

Mr. Fletcher looked up, his face paling when he saw me, and he flashed his palm at her as if to say "Stop."

She turned and stared at me.

I continued out the door, not knowing which was racing faster, my heart or my mind. Surely, the "she" Mrs. Fletcher was talking about was Mrs. Ava and the "him" was Pa.

I was so mad at Pa right now that I was telling myself if she'd fooled him, good for her. He deserved it. Then my heart did an about face, and I reasoned that Pa was smitten with her, so he really wasn't in his right mind. She was managing him, making him believe her choices were his own. Look at the way she had convinced him to leave my little sisters in Westport, saying they were born with a weak character inherited from my mother. Then there was the smirk on her face just now as Pa said I was his boy and needed to act like it. I knew he didn't like Susan, but Mrs. Ava was taking advantage of that to make Pa mad at me. Did she want him to send me away, too?

I unlocked the stable door, banged it shut behind me, and stomped toward Butter's stall, pulling my bow tie from the collar and unbuttoning my shirt on the way. Butter must have sensed my bad mood because she nickered and shuffled about, tossing her head.

"Hey, it's okay," I said, calming voice. But it wasn't okay. I removed my work pants and shirt from a peg and undressed quickly, shoving the tie into the pocket of the suit jacket, yanking off that jacket, stripping out of the dress shirt, tossing both shirt and jacket onto a stack of hay. I had just shucked out of my dress trousers when the front door cracked open, letting in a patch of daylight.

"Ambrose," Susan called. "Ambrose, are you in here?"

"Stop right there!" My face flushed hot. I was standing in nothing but my unmentionables. Why hadn't I gone into one of the stalls to change? "I'm not dressed for company."

She giggled. "Should I leave?"

"No, just stay there. I'll be with you in a minute." I stepped one foot into my work trousers and pulled hard, not seeing that my other foot was on the cuff. I stumbled off balance, letting out an "Ahhh!" before steadying myself.

"What's going on?" Susan asked. "Do you need help?"

My face was burning hot by this time. "I'm fine. I said I'd be with you in a minute."

She giggled again. "No need to be snippy."

I fastened my work trousers and grabbed my shirt. After slipping my arms into the sleeves, I pulled the front closed across my chest and started buttoning while I walked toward the door. "I wasn't expecting you," I said.

Her eyelashes fluttered, and her cheeks puffed out like she

wanted to laugh, but her lips were pursed tight to keep from making a sound. Finally, she allowed herself another giggle. "Obviously not."

"So why have you come?"

"Your pa and his new wife are getting ready to leave. Mrs. Collins said someone needed to tell you to bring the buggy to the front of the boardinghouse. I said I would and ran out the door before she could tell me no." She paused and then asked, "How long will your pa be away?"

"Five days," I said. It came to me then that one of those days was Sunday. The livery stable and blacksmith shop would be closed. With Pa gone we could—.

Pa barreled through the door, eyes blazing. "What are you doing, standing there with this wench and your shirttail hanging out?" He grabbed Susan's arm, whirled her toward the door, released her, and gave her a shove. "Out!"

My hands balled into fists. "Leave her alone." My whole body was shaking.

Pa faced me, fury in his eyes, his hands also clenched, ready to strike. "I'll do what I want in my own place of business."

Behind him, Susan turned and gave me a quick, tearful look, shaking her head before running from sight.

The door adjoining the smithy opened, and Mr. Clark stepped in. "What's all the commotion? Everything okay in here?"

Pa stepped back, still glaring at me but uncurling his fingers, flexing them. "Promise me, Bob, that you'll watch out for my boy while I'm gone. If he sees that girl again, I want to know about it."

Mr. Clark's eyes shifted away from me. "Will do."

Pa gave me a slow, calculating onceover. "Put my trunk in the buggy and bring it around to the boardinghouse." He turned on his heel and stomped out of the stable.

Mr. Clark stepped back into the smithy and closed the door, leaving me alone.

I stood for a moment, shaking off the tension, relieved that Pa and I hadn't come to blows, but knowing it was going to happen, sooner rather than later. And strong as I was from all the work I did, Pa was stronger. I could not win a physical fight with him, but it was becoming clear to me that someday soon I would have to fight one for the sake of my self-respect.

SIXTEEN

Hiram

I slammed out of the livery stable and stomped across the street to the boarding house, fuming over what had just happened with Ambrose. What was going on with that boy? He'd looked like he might actually throw a punch at his own pa.

I paused at the door of the boardinghouse to take a deep breath and tamp down my rage. This was my wedding day. I was about to leave on a trip with my new bride. I wasn't going to let Ambrose's rebellious actions spoil the day for me. I entered the boardinghouse determined to put on a smile for my bride, but a glance around the dining area revealed she wasn't there.

Joe Fletcher caught my eye, gave a signal of recognition with his finger, and crossed the room toward me. "Agnes has stepped next door to our living quarters with Ava to help her change. As soon as they're back, I'll bring Ava's trunk down."

I nodded.

"Something wrong?" Fletcher asked.

"Just my boy messing with that Hogan tart again. I've warned him to stay away from her, but do you think he listens to his Pa anymore? Not likely."

"That's pretty much the way boys his age are."

The man had some nerve, making light of my boy's behavior. "Easy for you to say when you don't have kids," I shot back.

Fletcher blew out a breath. "True, but I see a lot of what goes on between fathers and sons every day in the Emporium. As an unbiased observer, I can tell you Ambrose's actions are normal."

"Humph." My eyes were focused on the window. A horse and carriage came around the side of the stable onto the main street with Bob Clark driving. Ambrose was nowhere to be seen.

"There's the buggy," I said. "If you're collecting the trunk, you might tell Ava it's time to go."

"No telling necessary. There she is."

I took another look. Ava in a yellow silk traveling dress, parasol open to protect her skin from the sun, was approaching the carriage. "About time." I walked toward the door to join her on the boardwalk.

Fletcher followed. "I'll get that trunk."

We stepped outside, and Fletcher hurried off to the Emporium.

Ava gave the handle of her parasol a twirl and smiled. "Time to begin our first trip as man and wife."

My heart lightened. This new part of my life as a married man promised to be the best yet. I assisted Ava as she climbed into the buggy, then went around to my side as Fletcher appeared with Ava's trunk and stowed it in the back. With everything settled, Ava and I waved goodbye to the small group of well-wishers, I cracked the whip, urging the horse in motion, and we were off.

Before a mile had passed, my cheerfulness faded. The steady movement of the buggy and sound of the horse's hooves pulled me out of the present moment with my bride at my side and into the memory of my ugly, final confrontation with Ambrose. What was going on with that boy? I realized that I kept repeating the question. It had taken hold of me the past few weeks, coming up every time Ambrose defied me or failed in his duties. I flashed back to the child who had given me so much joy and pride. Ambrose had tagged after me from the time the boy had learned to walk. Over Minerva's objections, I'd taken Ambrose to work in the shop when he was five, feeling proud every time I introduced my son and men remarked on how well behaved he was and chuckled when he struggled to bring me a heavy hammer. Then there were the years we'd spent alone together after Minerva's passing and the girls had gone off to Westport with Hannah. No one could have taken better care of me and those hellish injuries the slave hunters inflicted on me than Ambrose. And he'd run the shop, too, overseeing Bob Clark, who was new to the town, and bringing home meticulous records every night.

When I'd finally been able to ease back into my blacksmithing tasks, Ambrose had introduced me to a new customer, Mayfield, the stonecutter. Mayfield needed his stonecutting tools kept sharp and in good repair, but pay from his clients was sporadic. Was there a trade to be made?

There was. My lifelong dream of a magnificent house would be realized at last. With not enough work at the shop to keep me, Ambrose, and Clark busy, the obvious solution was to trade stone for my house in exchange for keeping Mayfield's tools in shape. And to sweeten the bargain even more, Ambrose could become Mayfield's apprentice. By learning to cut and build with stone, Ambrose could do much of the actual construction work on the house that would one day be his. Together, Ambrose and I were building a life and a legacy. And now—.

"Hiram." Ava's voice broke through my musings.

I blinked. "What?"

"You haven't said three words since we left Hidden Springs. Something is obviously troubling you. What is it?"

I stared straight ahead, my mind a jumble of concerns.

Ava cut through the silence. "It's Ambrose, isn't it? It's the disrespectful way he's been behaving these past weeks."

I sighed, relieved that she understood as she so often did. "He was such a good boy, and now—I don't know what's happened. He refuses to see how dangerous that Hogan girl is to his future."

Ava's eyelashes fluttered. "Oh, Hiram, it's his age. All those urges young boys have are stronger than any father's wisdom."

I flicked the reins. "Not forever, I hope."

"We'll see," Ava replied. Then, sounding reluctant, "It could be more, I guess."

"More? What more?"

"Me." Her voice quavered. "He hates me."

Alarmed, I glanced at my bride and saw her dabbing tears with a handkerchief. "I don't think he hates you."

"Resents me then, for coming between the two of you." Head bowed, she dropped her hands in her lap and twisted her handkerchief,.

"I'll have a talk with him, Ava. He'll come around."

"There's also the matter of the children."

"What children?"

"Ours, of course. The ones we will have to fill that wonderful home of ours." She sniffled and brought the handkerchief to her nose. Wiping, sniffling, wiping, and letting her hand fall back in her lap before she went on. "He must resent even the thought of them, how they might decrease his inheritance."

She shifted in her seat, turning toward me, eyes imploring. "I know he's the oldest with the right to inherit everything, but you won't forget our children, will you?"

I pulled on the reins and stopped the buggy. Looking her full in the face, I saw the worry in her moist, green eyes. "Oh, Ava. Never doubt I will take care of our children and see to it they have a fair portion of my property. As I've told you, I was the third son in my family and passed over, receiving no share of my father's business even though I worked harder and with more skill than my brothers."

She gripped my arm. "It's a relief to hear you say so." She leaned against me and pressed her cheek to mine.

I took a deep breath, inhaling the sweet scent of her perfume.

She drew back, straightened but kept her hand on my arm. "I'm so sorry I've come between you and Ambrose."

I picked up the reins and the whip. With a snap, the horse got going again. "Don't worry. I'll have a talk with Ambrose." Of course, we both knew that would come to nothing. These days, Ambrose wasn't listening.

.

SEVENTEEN

Ambrose

It was Sunday, and church was over. I finally had some time for myself before Pa and Mrs. Ava returned from their wedding trip tomorrow night. After my standoff with Pa just before he left, I was worried what would happen when they got back.

The previous night, I had spent hours flipping through the pages of the fables and fairy tales book, searching for answers, imagining the sound of Ma's voice reading to me and her pausing to explain the lessons in each story, finally going to sleep with the book open on my chest. I had found no answers. So today I had come to the cemetery, the place where I felt closest to her now that Mr. Derryberry, the schoolteacher, had moved into our old cabin.

I knelt beside Ma's grave, the book she'd made for me clutched in my hands. "I've been looking for answers, Ma, but I can't find any. I go back and forth. I don't know what's going to happen. Mrs. Ava has already convinced Pa my sisters aren't worth his time. I think she wants to get rid of me, too, so there will just be her and the kids she has someday in the house."

Of course, that idea was based on gossip. Should I dismiss what I overheard the Fletchers saying as idle talk? Was my fear of being driven out of my home coloring my understanding of those snippets of conversation? And wasn't eavesdropping rude and unseemly for a well-mannered person?

I slid off my knees into a sitting position, folded my legs, and crossed my ankles. Holding the book with one hand, I fingered the image of the turtle. "Slow and steady wins the race," I said aloud. "But what is the race, Ma? What am I trying to win?"

I thought back to the day of the wedding and my argument with Pa. What had happened to the man who'd loved me, the man I'd spent my life admiring. True, I never wanted to be the kind of husband and father Pa was, but from the first time I'd stepped foot in Pa's smithy, I'd known he was proud to have me for a son.

I remember I was five that first time Pa took me to work with him. He'd said I could help him by handing him a hammer. When one of his customers came in, he'd put his hand on my shoulder and say, "This is my boy Ambrose. He's a big help to me."

When he'd said "my boy Ambrose," my chest had puffed out. Now when he said "my boy," my chest sank in because those words were always followed with what I'd done wrong or how I'd disappointed him. "My boy was late," he'd say. Lately, it wasn't even "my boy." I had become "the boy." And his disappointment had started after Mrs. Ava became part of our lives.

"What should I do, Ma?" I knew I was asking a question that had no answer until Pa did something I could react to. I gripped the book in my hands, remembering how Pa had taken Ma's comb from Lucy that day in the cabin, and how he'd let Mrs. Ava toss it in the trash. Trash was all that a broken, fake tortoiseshell comb was to her. But to Lucy, it was an important keepsake. It was my job to empty and burn the trash, so I rescued it and sent it off to her. Now I worried about my fables book. If it was in Pa's sight when he got mad at me, he would certainly destroy it out of pure meanness.

"Where can I put this for safekeeping, Ma?"

Footsteps rustled in the dying grass, bringing me back to the present.

"Ambrose."

It was Susan. She stopped beside me. "I thought you'd be here. I hope it's okay that I came."

"I'm glad you did," I said. "I been wanting to apologize to you for the way Pa acted the other day, but he asked Mr. Clark to report any Susan sightings when he got back to town, so I've stayed away."

"Then maybe I should go." She took a hesitant step back.

I reached for her hand, grasping her fingers. "No, it's okay. There's no reason for Mr. Clark to show up at the cemetery today." I gave her fingers a slight tug. "Sit for a minute."

"I thought you'd never ask." Her voice was light and teasing. She sank down beside me and smoothed her blue gingham skirt. Her brown eyes turned serious. "I overheard you say you needed something kept safe. What is it?"

"This book my mother made. Want to see it?" I offered it to her.

"Your mother made this?" She squinted at the images on the front cover. "It's wonderful. Such fine, even stitches. She must have been a wonderful seamstress."

"And artist," I said. "Look inside at the drawings."

Susan turned the pages, remarking on the pencil drawings of the ant and grasshopper, the lion with the thorn in its paw, and Cinderella sitting among the coals. "These are so fine, Ambrose. I can see why they mean so much to you. But why are you worried about keeping them safe?"

"Because when Pa gets mad, he rips apart anything he thinks someone cares about." For just a second, I thought about telling her about how Pa had turned on Lucy and kicked her out without letting her take her clothes or any other belongings. Then I changed my mind. Such happenings would fuel town gossip if they got out. According to Ma, even people you trust can let slip secrets they swore not to tell. Better to limit what others knew. It was one of the few things Pa had agreed with her about. I'd probably said too much already.

"I could keep it for you," she offered.

"No, Pa would be furious if he ever found out. He shoved you the other day just for being in the stable with me."

She studied her hands. "I suppose you're right." Her forehead furrowed as she handed the book to me. "What about Mrs. Collins? I bet she'd keep it for you."

"Maybe. She's always been a good friend. She brought food and helped Lucy around the cabin when Ma was sick and Pa was laid up from the beating he took from the slave hunters."

Susan brushed her skirt again. "Speaking of Mrs. Collins, I need to get over to the boardinghouse. It may be Sunday, but folks still eat, and I'm working in the kitchen this evening." She stood. "I guess with your Pa coming back tomorrow, I'll only be seeing you at a distance. Take care."

"Bye," I said.

She turned and walked away, leaving me alone with Ma and my unanswered question: What should I do about Mrs. Ava?

I stayed another half hour or so before the lowering sun reminded me it was time to do chores. But before going home, I took a turn past the boardinghouse for a piece of chocolate cake to eat after supper. When I got there, I found Mrs. Collins behind the counter of the glassed-in dessert case.

She was busy cutting a pie when I walked up.

"Hello," I said to get her attention.

"Ambrose, what brings you by?" She slid the dish with the cut pie into the glass case before looking up at me. "What do you have there?"

"A book my ma made for my fifth birthday."

"May I see it?"

"Sure," I said, handing it over.

She studied the cover for a moment before opening to the drawings inside. Her eyes widened, and she smiled. "Did your mother make these sketches?"

I felt that little burst of pride in my chest that came whenever anyone saw how talented Ma was. "She did."

"They're amazing." She slowly turned the pages, studying the pictures on each one. "I had no idea your mother was an artist."

"Like I said, she made the book when I was little. She wanted to make one for each of my sisters, but she didn't have time for drawing once they came along."

"That's a shame. I know they would have treasured such a gift."

That's when I made my decision. I glanced around to make sure we were alone before speaking. "Please don't repeat what I'm going to tell you."

She looked up from the book, frowning. "Of course, whatever you say is just between us. What is it, Ambrose?"

"Well, Mrs. Ava gets upset when she sees anything that reminds her of Ma. I had to rescue Ma's comb from the trash, the one I sent to Lucy. I'm worried she might throw this away, too, if she runs across it. Would you consider keeping it here for me?"

She nodded. "I will. I suspect you are worried about something that would never happen, but if it eases your mind, I will keep it here."

"Thank you, Mrs. Collins. Now, can I get a piece of that chocolate cake to take home?"

She put the book aside on the counter behind the case. "You can," she said. She wrapped the cake for me, accepted my payment, and handed me the package. "Now, I'll go put away this wonderful book."

"Thank you," I said, relieved but sad. I wouldn't have Ma's gift to hold on sleepless nights.

EIGHTEEN

Hiram

The wedding trip had been a success, a round of social activities and political meetings that had me elated at my choice of wife. Ava had presented the perfect picture of grace and domestic skills, joining the ladies of the town for a quilting bee and stunning them with her fine stitches and knowledge of the latest fashions from Paris and New York. I, on the other hand, had spent an informative Friday evening with a number of Junction City's town council members and an elected representative to the territorial legislature. The stimulating discussion centered on the Wyandotte Constitution and the upcoming October fourth vote to ratify it.

In spite of all my satisfying memories, the closer the buggy took me and Ava to Hidden Springs, the more my mood darkened. Had Ambrose kept his distance from the Hogan girl as I'd ordered? Would Bob Clark give an honest account of any meetings between the two young people? Clark had always leaned toward Ambrose's side in personal matters. I wouldn't have tolerated it except for the fact that the man was good at his job, giving me freedom to be away for a few days, as I had been for this trip.

My gaze shifted from the trail to Ava, who sat quietly beside me, holding a parasol to keep the sun from ruining her complexion. She preferred the parasol to a bonnet while traveling, saying a headpiece was hot and caused her to perspire. I was dressed in work trousers and shirt. To passersby, I might be taken for a hired driver instead of the husband to this elegantly-dressed woman.

Seeming to feel my gaze upon her, she met my eyes. "What?" she asked.

"We're almost home. Our lives together truly begin now. I've decided to take the side road to our house instead of stopping in town first. Less commotion that way."

"You'd like to check on Ambrose without giving him advance warning?"

I smiled at the way she was in tune with my thoughts. "Yes."

When I guided the horse into the circle drive and stopped in front of the entrance, I glanced about. "Everything seems in order. Go on in. I'll bring the trunks."

Her trunk being larger than mine, I carried it in first and led the way up the stairs to what was now our bedroom, where I placed it on a chair. Ava followed me.

"You'll have to rearrange everything," I said.

"That will be my pleasure."

"There'll be my things to put away as well."

I left to retrieve my trunk. When I returned, she'd already opened the wardrobe and was hanging her afternoon dress. There was also an evening dress, two house dresses, a church dress, and the traveling dress she was currently wearing. I had never seen one woman with so many dresses. My first wife had three and Minerva only two for daily wear. Each had had a dress for church.

She threw a glance over her shoulder as I entered. "We'll need a second wardrobe."

"I'll speak to Ambrose about building one." I set my trunk on the floor. "I'll be leaving for the shop now."

She closed the wardrobe door and approached me, placing a light kiss on my cheek. "Supper will be ready when you return, my first official home-cooked meal as your wife."

I hardly knew what to do with Ava's easy familiarity. I gave her a brisk nod and headed for the door.

I climbed into the buggy and headed for town, eager to see what Ambrose was doing and to learn how business at the shop had fared in my absence.

NINETEEN

Ambrose

I had just finished writing a receipt for a horse being left by a rider from Topeka when Mr. Fletcher poked his head in the stable door. "Saw your pa and Ava pass by on the side road maybe half an hour ago. Reckon he'll be in soon. Wonder how the wedding trip went."

My throat tightened. What was Mr. Fletcher's point? Was he trying to figure out if Mrs. Ava had really fooled Pa like I'd heard Mrs. Fletcher say?

"I reckon Pa or Mrs. Ava will tell how the trip went if they want to and in their own time." I knew I sounded abrupt, maybe even disrespectful, but I didn't have time for speculating on Pa's trip. "Is there anything else? I have to take care of this horse." I took the reins of the animal left in my care.

"Just being friendly. Sorry to keep you from your work. We'll talk to Ava later, see how it went."

"Sounds like a good idea." I led the horse toward the back of the stable, leaving Mr. Fletcher standing alone.

After a second or so, he left.

Pa arrived a few minutes later. I had unsaddled the stallion and taken him to the corral to drink from the water tank when Pa drove up. He pulled the buggy to a stop, set the brake, and hopped down.

"How'd everything go while I was gone? You keep up with the accounts?" he asked.

Just like that. No hello. But that was Pa.

"I did. The book is in on the stand. I knew you'd want to see it first thing."

He strode for the back door of the stable, then stopped and turned toward me. "Anything happen while I was gone."

"Regular stuff. Chores, mostly. Sunday, I put some flowers on Ma's grave." I figured I wouldn't say anything about Susan being there. Maybe no one had seen us. "I bought a piece of cake from Mrs. Collins."

He came toward me, hands clenched at his sides. "That Hogan girl sell it to you? Can't leave her 'cake' alone, can you."

"What?" Then I remembered that Susan was doing the baking for the boardinghouse now. "No, I bought it from Mrs. Collins, like I said. Ask her if you don't believe me."

He stood for a moment, glaring at me. "I will," he said before turning on his heel and heading for the back door.

Shaking my head, I blew out a breath. Pa had as much as called me a liar. I couldn't think of a thing I had done to cause him not to trust me.

I took care of the horses and buggy, puzzling over Pa's attitude the whole time. In spite of the big faceoff we'd had just before he left town, I'd expected him to calm down while he was gone. That hadn't happened. My work outside done, I ambled toward the back door, wondering what I would get inside. More accusations?

I heard voices coming from the side door near the front of the building. Pa was talking to Mr. Clark.

"You keep an eye on things like I asked you to?" Pa asked.

I figured I was first on the list of "things" Pa was asking about. I guess Mr. Clark thought so to because he said, "Ambrose didn't have any special company while you were gone. Leastways, not here."

I stepped forward and cleared my throat. "You have any questions about the books, Pa?"

He squinted at me. "Not yet."

With that, I mucked out some stalls while Pa studied the accounts, occasionally shouting a question at me.

At last, it was closing time. I saddled Red for Pa and Butter for me. We rode home side by side, but our hearts couldn't have been farther apart.

TWENTY

Hiram

I was fuming on the ride home, knowing by the way Ambrose was talking that he was lying to me. His stories of what had happened the past five days were clipped and shy of details. He told no tales, funny or otherwise, about what had gone on, which wasn't like him. He usually boasted about his successes and laughed as he recounted odd occurrences. I cut a sideways glance at him. Who was this boy? I hardly recognized the closed, angry youngster. I figured it had to be that Hogan tart that changed him. Ava had been right. Ambrose was at the age to get bodily urges, and those urges were aimed toward Susan Hogan.

I knew he was lying, so I couldn't talk to him either. There had been a time when I would have been filling Ambrose's ears with stories about my trip, my meetings with important men and our discussions of the impending vote to ratify the constitution, but not now. The rift between us was growing. If I was going to save Ambrose from himself, I'd have to find some way to get him to see my side of things.

The house was in sight, and I remembered the meal Ava had promised to have ready.

"Ava's preparing a fine spread for our first meal as a family," I said.

"Really." Ambrose sounded like he didn't believe it.

"Really." I set Red at a gallop, leaving Ambrose and his horse in the dust. Ava was right about the boy. He was mad because I'd found a wife to replace his mother. Well, he could be mad, but he'd better be respectful of Ava or he could find a new place to bunk.

TWENTY-ONE

Ambrose

Four weeks later

I had to admit Mrs. Ava was a good cook, but cooking, along with sewing, were the only woman's work she was willing to do. By the end of September, she had wheedled Pa into hiring a maid. She was a grown woman with no children and no infirmities, weaseling out of her job by saying it wasn't proper for a lady in her position to be scrubbing floors. And Pa bought it.

The new girl, Missy Phelps, was about my age. Pa was thorny about paying wages for something he was used to getting from the women and girls of the house for free, but now there was just Mrs. Ava, and her only interest was in being a lady and making Pa look like a prominent member of society. He puffed up every time she planned a meeting or meal for the mayor and city council. When the State Constitution was adopted on October sixth, she began including candidates for the new legislature to the guest list for her Saturday formal dinners. Pa practically popped his vest buttons with pride. Anyway, Mrs. Ava's value as a society lady was worth more to him than money, so he agreed to pay Missy three dollars a week, which was cheap for the work he got out of her, but all he paid me was two dollars a week for running the livery stable, and I worked harder, longer, and had a lot more skills. Of course, Pa said I was building the family business, so I was investing in my future by earning less in the present. But remembering how he had so easily tossed aside my sisters at Mrs. Ava's suggestion, I worried what she might convince him to do in regards to my place in the family.

I found out late one afternoon. Pa told Mr. Clark to take over the stable so I could go home and put together the new buffet that had arrived the previous day. Ma's buffet had been moved back to the cabin for Mr. Derryberry's use. As much as she could, Mrs. Ava was getting rid of every trace of Ma in the house. I was glad I had put my book of fables in Mrs. Collins's hands for safekeeping.

The two crates containing the unassembled buffet were stacked in the dining room. Before prying open the first one, I toted in a couple of sawhorses and planks and made a bench to work on. Then I got to work unpacking the pieces, looking for a part sheet as I went. I'd helped Reverend Sherwood assemble enough furniture-in-a-box projects for the church to know pieces might be missing. Usually, it was easier to make the missing part myself than wait for one to come from the factory, but not always. Drawer pieces were scattered everywhere on the floor when Mrs. Ava swished into the room.

"Ambrose, do you have to make such a mess?"

I looked up from a drawer I was assembling. "If you want a whole piece of furniture, I do."

I heard the front door close and figured Pa was home. Good. Maybe he'd tell Mrs. Ava you have to have all the pieces of something in plain sight before you can figure out how it goes together. I went back to work, fitting a drawer bottom to the sides.

Mrs. Ava let out a yelp. I looked up to see her stumbling toward me, off balance, about to fall. I reached out to catch her, and she tumbled into my arms.

Immediately, she shoved me backwards, screamed, and shouted "How dare you?" She slapped my face.

Shocked by her attack, I touched my cheek, and my mouth fell open. "Why?"

She swiped away tears with her fingers, all the while shrieking at me. "I told your pa what you were about, but he defended you. How could you take such liberties with your own father's wife?"

I shook my head, confused.

Pa filled the doorway, his eyes flashing with anger. "What's going on here?" He glanced from me to Mrs. Ava. I looked at her, too, noticing for the first time that the top buttons of her bodice were open, like someone had ripped at them.

She swirled around and ran to Pa, threw herself in his arms, and choked out her complaint between sobs. "It's like I told you. He's been making improper comments, looking at me in suggestive ways, and you didn't believe me."

"I believe you now," he said, his eyes hard coals, his face purpling with rage, his hands clenching into fists. He moved her aside and came toward me.

"I didn't—" I shook my head and took a step back, my brain foggy, trying to make sense of what was happening. His fist came up, and I raised my arms. He swung at me with all the strength he used to hammer iron and knocked me aside. I fell against the wall, straightened, and raised my fist to strike back, a weak punch compared to his, only an effort to clear the way so I could get out of the house.

My fear was no match for his rage. He knocked me to the floor with his second blow and kicked me with his heavy boots three times: in my ribs, my side, and my stomach. Then he hauled me from the floor by my belt and shirt collar and half-dragged me to the kitchen door. He opened it and shoved me out.

I fell to the ground, pain shooting through every inch of my body.

"Get off my property and don't come back," he roared.

Opening my palms, I pressed them flat against the ground and tried to push up, but the pain was too much. I fell and my fingers dug into the dry autumn grass.

Pa reached for a piece of firewood, picked it up, hefted it, drew it back as though to strike. "I said to get your sorry self off my land."

"Hiram. What's going on?" It was Mr. Derryberry.

The schoolteacher's voice brought me relief. His presence would stop the beating. Physically, he was no match for Pa, but Pa respected his opinion and position in the community.

"No one takes what's mine," Pa said, his voice hard. "You want to keep him from getting another licking worse than the one I just gave him, take his thieving hide out to the road and dump him." He threw the piece of firewood back on the pile. Then he stomped his foot down within an inch of my hand. "Don't come back if you know what's good for you." He spun around and tramped toward the house.

Mr. Derryberry squatted beside me. "Do you think you can stand?"

I groaned and pushed up on one elbow. Blood dripped on the ground. I hadn't noticed before that my nose was bleeding.

The schoolteacher removed a handkerchief from his coat pocket and handed it to me.

"I said get him out of here," Pa roared.

I looked toward the doorway and saw him framed in the light, Mrs. Ava slightly to one side and partly behind him. I imagined she was smiling.

Mr. Derryberry helped me to my feet. I leaned against him.

"I have to get my horse," I said. "I can't leave without Butter. Pa will never let me get her once I'm gone."

Mr. Derryberry called out to Pa, "We're getting the boy's horse."

"Get her then," Pa shouted. He slammed the door.

Leaning on Mr. Derryberry, I limped to the barn. I rested on an empty crate while he saddled Butter. "What does Hiram think you took from him?"

I shook my head and momentarily lifted the handkerchief from my nose. The bleeding had almost stopped. "I don't know. You'll have to ask Mrs. Ava." There was no use telling my side because hers and Pa's wouldn't match it, so the town may as well have just one story to talk about.

"Mrs. Ava, huh." Mr. Derryberry frowned and brought Butter around to my side. "Let's see if you can get on."

With him at my back, I manage to get a foot in the stirrup, pull myself up, and then work my other leg across the saddle. Finally mounted, I clung to the saddle horn as he led Butter out of the barn.

When we got to the road, he kept walking, leading my palomino toward town.

I said, "I can make it from here."

He glanced at me. "I'm not taking a chance on you falling off the horse, hitting your head, and dying out here on the road. I'm taking you to Doc Sloan."

I shut up then and started thinking. What was I going to do now that I didn't have a home or a job? I remembered how Lucy had begged me to come to Westport, and I had promised to come when the time was right. I figured this was that time.

TWENTY-TWO

Hiram

Ava's comforting arm rested on my shoulder as I turned away from the closed door.

"I'm so sorry," she murmured. "I'd hoped my instincts weren't true. I know how much you love your son."

"Loved," I said. "He has betrayed me." I turned to her, touched the dangling button on her bodice, and saw a scratch at the base of her throat. "He did this?"

Her green eyes glistened with tears. "Yes." She squeezed her eyes closed When she opened them, they were moist, as though she might cry. "I don't know what set him off. I went to see what progress he was making on assembling the buffet. I was standing next to him when he suddenly grabbed my arms and declared he was attracted to me. "It's your perfume," he said. "It announces your arrival in the room and makes me imagine what could be."

She bowed her head and pressed her palm to my chest. "I can't ever wear this scent again. It will always be a reminder of this ugly night."

"We will find a new scent," I said, knowing what she said was true, but regretting the loss of the lilac fragrance I connected with her presence. I could imagine how the perfume that excited my own need for her might also affect Ambrose. Still, that was no excuse for his betrayal.

I put a finger under her chin, lifted her head, and gazed into her sad eyes. "He'll never have a chance to touch you again," I vowed. "I no longer have a son."

"But you will, perhaps sooner than you imagined." She took my hand and pressed it against her belly. "I think. Well, I can't be certain yet. But there are signs we'll have a little one by next June."

The news was heartening, but it didn't give me the joy I had often imagined it would. My mind had played over this possible announcement many times while I was doing some routine work at the forge. My loss of joy was Ambrose's fault. His actions had spoiled this moment for me.

Anger filled me as I looked again at the torn bodice and the scratch on Ava's neck. "I'm clearing the house of him now." I put her at arm's length and rushed from the room.

I ran up the stairs to the second floor, flung open the door to Ambrose's room, and crossed to the dresser. In the bottom of one drawer, I saw the comforter Minerva had made for Ambrose's cradle before he was born. I spread it on the bed and dumped his clothes on it. A piece of iron landed on top of the clothes. I recognized it as first flower Ambrose had made. He had given it to Minerva for her birthday one year. Well, it was going in the fire, too, even though it would withstand the heat. I would cover it with ashes, shovel dirt over the top, and bury it deep. Bringing up the corners of the comforter, I carried the load downstairs and out to the fire pit in the yard.

I piled kindling and dried grass on the side and struck a match. The grass and baby quilt caught fire and soon the entire pile was blazing. I stared at the flames until they consumed the clothes, then got a shovel and buried the remains.

There. It was done. My son was gone. Reminders of him were gone. I turned as the moon peeked out from the clouds and hit the limestone walls of the house—the house that Ambrose built.

TWENTY-THREE

Ambrose

By the time Mr. Derryberry tied Butter to a post in front of the boardinghouse, there wasn't any part of me that didn't hurt.

Through swollen eyes, I looked in the window of the dining room. Two people were finishing meals. Susan was behind the pastry counter.

"I thought you were taking me to Doc Sloan," I said.

"He'd likely be at home now, and you need somewhere to lie down. Let's see if Mrs. Collins has a room available. Then I'll get the doctor." He tied Butter's reins to the hitching post and then came around to offer me a hand down.

I dismounted, stumbling backward into him. He steadied me by sliding his arm around my waist. I limped forward, groaning as I took the single step up onto the boardwalk.

Through the window, I saw Mrs. Collins join Susan behind the counter. A bell jingled as Mr. Derryberry opened the door. We shuffled inside.

"Ambrose!" Susan slid through the opening between the pastry case and the cash drawer and ran toward me. "What happened?"

Mrs. Collins was right behind her. "Was it border ruffians? We're usually too far west for them to bother with us."

I shook my head, the slight movement sending a bolt of pain along the back of my neck.

Susan's eyes hardened. "It was your Pa, wasn't it? Is it my fault? Did he find out we'd met?"

"No. I mean yes. I mean it was Pa, but it wasn't because of you. It was . . . ." My voice trailed off, shame and uncertainty leaving me without words. "Pa says I took something from him. I don't know what. It wasn't true. I don't know." My head fell forward. I gasped and squeezed my eyes shut.

Mrs. Collins called, "We're closing," to the two customers. "Susan, see our guests to the door and turn the sign."

Shifting glances at us as they moseyed toward the door, the two men left. Susan turned the sign to "Dining Room Closed" and headed for the table to clear the empty dishes.

Mrs. Collins stopped her. "Susan, leave those for now and go get Doc Sloan." She turned to Mr. Derryberry. "Let's get this boy to bed." She led the way down the hall toward the stairway to the rooms for rent and bustled right on by it. "Don't see you making it to the second floor. I've got a small room down here. Not much, but it'll do."

She opened the door on what appeared to be a combination storage and sleeping room. Sets of shelves holding canned food lined two walls. The third wall was bare except for a window. A cot and small table lined the fourth wall. Mr. Derryberry eased me onto the cot.

"You get his shirt off," Mrs. Collins said, "while I open this window. It won't let in much air since the Fletchers put up a high fence between our establishments, but it will help some."

She rustled through a basket of clothes. "Here's a nightshirt for you." Glancing toward me, her kind eyes turned to shock when she saw the bruises on my chest. "Damn Hiram! What's wrong with that man?" Then she flushed red at having used such language. "Here, put this on. I'll get some water to wash away that blood." She wiped her eyes as she hurried from the room.

Mr. Derryberry unbuttoned the nightshirt and slid it over my head. The front had buttons almost to the waist, and the shirt was big on me, which I was thankful for. I didn't have to lift my arms much to get them in the sleeves. He pulled off my heavy work shoes.

"Off with the pants," he ordered.

I blushed. "The ladies will be back soon."

"That shirt has everything covered. You need out of those pants so Doc can examine your injuries."

I stood with his help, unbuttoned my trousers, and pushed them down before easing onto the bed and reaching for the cuffs. I scrunched my face in pain at the stretch.

"Sit back," Mr. Derryberry ordered. Bending over, he grabbed the bottom of the pants and pulled them free of my legs.

I eased back on the bed and tried to relax my muscles. I thought about the time Pa had broken ribs and how long he'd been laid up. Were my ribs broken? What was I going to do if they were?

Mrs. Collins returned with a basin of water and a washrag. "Let's get you cleaned up." She shooed Mr. Derryberry back and pulled a stool to the side of the cot. After wetting the washrag, she washed my face, wiping gently across the cuts and bruises. Then she started on my hands, scrubbing them like I was four years old and they were covered with mud instead of blood. I closed my eyes and imagined it was Ma cleaning me up like she had so often when I was a little kid back home after working with Pa at the shop.

"Why, Pa? Why?" I moaned. "I didn't do nothing. Nothing."

I didn't realize I was saying the words aloud until Mrs. Collins asked, "What does he think you did?"

"I don't know. Mrs. Ava said I did something, took something. I don't know."

I heard footsteps in the hallway, Susan's quick, light taps on the floor and Doc Sloan's less frequent, heavier thuds. The door swung open.

Doc took one look at me and cursed. There was agreement all around about where Pa's soul should go when he left this life. Doc motioned for Mrs. Collins to move aside, and he took her place on the stool. Cupping his hand under my chin, he studied my face. "The cuts on your forehead and left cheek may leave scars, but they don't need stitches." He held up two fingers and moved them slowly in front of my face. "Follow with your eyes."

I did as he asked.

He nodded. "The injuries look worse than they are. We'll patch those cuts and put cold compresses on the bruises to take the swelling down. Now, let me see your chest."

"Ummm." I grabbed the neck of the nightshirt and darted a glance at Mrs. Collins and Susan.

Doc smiled. "Why don't you ladies leave the room while I finish examining my patient?"

Susan pressed her fingers to her lips and looked away. I figured she was holding back a giggle.

"I'm going to need some thick cloths and a bucket of cold water from the well," Doc Sloan said.

Mr. Derryberry moved toward the door. "I'll get the water."

I raised my head from the cot and took a breath, my brows knitting with pain. "Will you take care of Butter?"

Mrs. Collins said, "Mr. Derryberry can put her in my barn."

"Thank you." I lay back.

After the ladies and Mr. Derryberry left, Doc unbuttoned the nightshirt, pulled it open, felt around on my chest and pushed here and there. "Yell when it hurts," he said.

"That would be anywhere you touch me."

"What about your back?"

"There, too. I fell across a drawer I was putting together. With any luck, the drawer broke." Pa would have to fix it. He would have to put the buffet together, and wood wasn't something he liked to work with. It was a sour thought that didn't give much comfort, but right now, I would take what satisfaction I could get.

"Try to sit up." Doc held out his arm.

I grabbed hold, pulled myself to a sitting position, and slid my legs over the edge of the bed.

Doc slid the nightshirt off my shoulders and did more poking and prodding. I yelped every now and then. Then he held the cups of a stethoscope to my back and told me to take deep breaths.

"Hmmmmm." He straightened and pulled the nightshirt up over my shoulders. "You'll feel better in a day or two, but it's going to be at least a couple of weeks, maybe more, before all the pain goes away."

Someone knocked. Doc glanced at me before calling, "Come in."

Mr. Derryberry and Mrs. Collins filed into the room. Mr. Derryberry set a bucket of water on a stand near the window.

Mrs. Collins eyed me. "Susan wants to come in, too."

"Okay," I said.

Susan slipped around the edge of the door. "You're going to need some help with those cold compresses," she said. "I've taken care of injuries for just about everyone in my family. I know what to do."

"That's right," Doc said. "Susan took care of her brother when he fell and banged up his knee and elbow last summer."

Susan chimed in again. "Mrs. Collins has her hands full with the boardinghouse, and Mr. Derryberry has school to teach, so I'm the best one to help out."

I ducked my head, embarrassed that a girl would be taking care of me, but she was right. "Okay," I mumbled.

She chuckled. "Just okay?" She set some white cloths on the stand beside the pail of water, then came to stand beside Doc Sloan. "Besides his face, where do the cold compresses go?"

Doc raised his eyebrows at me. "You'll need to let go that shirt front so I can show her."

I looked past Doc and saw Mr. Derryberry and Mrs. Collins exchanging amused looks. "I know you have things to do," I said, stalling, "so before you go, I'd like to ask you not say anything about me being here or what happened unless someone has already said something to you. Let Pa and Mrs. Ava tell their story. Let folks believe what they will."

Mrs. Collins nodded. "If that's what you want, that's what I'll do."

"And I as well," Mr. Derryberry said.

I felt the need to explain. "It's just I want to know Pa's thinking on this. Why did this happen? He and Mrs. Ava will talk more freely if they think you don't know much about what happened."

"Very well," Mrs. Collins said. "Those last two diners who left when you came in were strangers from the trail. With your horse in my barn, I think your presence here should be unknown, at least for a few hours tomorrow. We'll see what your father says about you not opening the livery stable." She stepped forward and laid a gentle hand on my head. "We'll leave you in Susan's good care, and I'll check on you in the morning."

Susan spoke up. "Mr. Derryberry, on your way home, will you stop at my place and tell my family I'm staying the night at the boardinghouse, doing some special work for Mrs. Collins. I don't want them to worry about me."

"Of course," he said.

When Mr. Derryberry and Mrs. Collins had left, Doc Sloan

sighed and shook his head. "Like I said before, lie back and let go that nightshirt. Susan needs to see where to put those compresses."

I obeyed, groaning as I lay my body down on the straw mattress and let go the shirt.

Doc Sloan opened the front of the garment.

Susan's eyes rounded. "Oh!"

I figured my bruises must look pretty bad. Doc Sloan confirmed that assessment. "As I told you earlier, I don't think anything is broken, but the swelling is going to get worse before it starts going down. The cold compresses will help." He turned to Susan. "Fold the cloth until it is several layers thick, wring the water out good, maybe hold the material to the window for a few seconds to let the night air chill it even more. It won't take long for his body to warm them up, but he doesn't need constant cold. Change them about every hour or so." He reached in his bag and withdrew a small pouch. "Here's some willow bark. Make it into a tea. Steep it for five to ten minutes and give him some every couple of hours. It's bitter, so you can add some honey to sweeten it, not that it'll improve the taste much." He glanced at me. "Drink it anyway."

"Yes, Doc," I said.

"You're talking like a patient at last. I now leave you in capable hands. Good night." He picked up his bag.

Susan smiled and pursed her lips, looking mischievous. "Let's get to those compresses."

I groaned and shook my head.

TWENTY-FOUR

Hiram

Ava, exhausted from the ugly experience with Ambrose, slept beside me, but I lay staring up in the darkness, wondering what had happened to make the boy behave in such an ill-bred manner. It must be as Ava said, some fault in the blood from his mother. It was there in Delia, who had no blood of mine, and in her sisters. Now it had shown itself in Ambrose.

I had always been so proud of my son, taught him everything I knew, set him up in a business that would be his someday, and he repaid me by putting his hands on my wife. Well, he was no longer welcome in my home or my life. Ava was right. We were starting over with a new family. She was certain there was already a child on the way. A son. At least, I hoped so. We were both sturdy, not frail like Minerva. Ava and I would have children strong in body, mind, and morals.

But that was a long time off, and morning was only hours away. Where had Derryberry taken Ambrose? To Doc Sloan? Alice Collins? They were the likely ones. What had Derryberry and Ambrose said about what happened? Surely, Ambrose hadn't told the truth about his lewd actions.

Beyond what to say about Ambrose, there was the problem of the livery stable. Bob Clark would have to take over until I could find someone else. I didn't like to think of the high cost of hiring someone, not when I had reached into my savings to furnish the house. Ava was right. We needed our home to match our standing in the town, but quality furnishings from companies like Tiffany's were more costly than I had expected. I should have known quality pieces would cost more. It was the same in my shop. I might have to raise prices.

This was all Ambrose's fault. What had possessed him to make advances toward Ava? She had warned me this might happen, had told me how he stood too close to her, brushed against her when there was room to pass by with no contact, made comments that made her blush. I hadn't wanted to believe her, but there was no mistaking what I saw tonight.

I sighed and turned on my side to face the window. A faint beam of moonlight filtered through the new lace curtains. Maybe I shouldn't have kept Ambrose from seeing the Hogan girl. If he'd fixed his manly urges on her, maybe he'd have left Ava alone.

I threw back the covers and tread quietly from the room. A shot of whiskey might help me sleep.

TWENTY-FIVE

Ambrose

I awoke to the sound of Susan snoring. It was a soft sound, like a cat purring. She was sitting in a chair by my bed. I grinned and reached out to shake her arm but was stopped by Mrs. Ava's sharp voice. It was coming from the other side of the fence that divided the boarding house property from the Fletcher's.

I hadn't made out what Mrs. Ava said, but I was all ears to hear more because she could only be fussing around, looking to find out where I was and what I'd said.

"What's going on, Ava?" Agnes Fletcher demanded. "What's got you out so early of a morning? Now that you're the lady of the manor, you usually don't show up in town until mid-morning."

"What have you heard?" Mrs. Ava screeched.

Susan jerked, eyelashes fluttering, and she straightened in her chair. She looked at me, her mouth opening.

I touched a finger to my lips and shook my head.

She nodded, her forehead furrowing as we listened in silence to the conversation between Mrs. Ava and Agnes Fletcher.

"Heard about what from who? Joe's just now opening the store. We haven't spoken to anyone except each other since yesterday evening." A pause, and then Agnes asked, "What have you done? This isn't something that's going to come back on Joe and me, like your New York foolishness, is it?"

"You worry too much. Or should I say Joe worries too much. You never made such a fuss over what I did before you married him. Joe's too sensitive. No one blamed him for what happened to Gerald."

"We like life in Hidden Springs, but Joe won't stay if we become the target of gossip and suspicion. I'm asking again. What have you done?"

"What have you heard about Hiram's boy?"

"Ambrose?" Agnes sounded puzzled. Then her voice changed, alarmed, demanding. "Have you done something to Ambrose?"

"What could I possibly have done to the little prince? But I'll tell you this. He's been dethroned."

"Why? What happened?"

"Hiram gave him a sound thrashing and the boot." She laughed. "And he *did* use his boot."

"How bad was it? What happened to the boy?" Agnes sounded alarmed.

Mrs. Ava let out a long growl. "That's what I'm trying to find out," she snapped. "What have you heard?"

"Nothing. Absolutely nothing. What did you do?"

"Ambrose and Hiram did it all. Hiram came home to find Ambrose's arms around me, the buttons on my dress torn open, and this scratch on my neck."

Susan squinted at me. I shook my head.

"Ambrose assaulted you? I don't believe it," Agnes said.

"Hiram believes it. That's all that matters. Well, not all. I need to know what Ambrose told everyone."

"I haven't heard anything, Ava, but we've barely opened. There hasn't been much time for folks to come in. What story is Hiram going to tell?"

"It depends on what the boy says—wherever he is."

"Do you think Ambrose might have died from the beating?"

"No, when Hiram tossed Ambrose out of the house, Derryberry showed up. He stopped the beating and took Ambrose away. If he'd died, Derryberry would've had the sheriff out."

"Agnes!" Mr. Fletcher called. "Agnes, we've got customers. Get in here."

"In a minute," Mrs. Fletcher called back. "I have to go," she said to Ava. "This had better not end up like that thing with Gerald and his family complaining about the man's untimely death.'"

"His family was just upset because I tried to get part of Gerald's estate, for all the good that did me."

"Are you in Hiram's will?"

Susan's eyes widened, and she clapped her hand to her mouth. I signaled once again for her to remain quiet. The two women were obviously getting ready to leave, and I wanted to learn all I could before they were gone.

"Of course. Oh, don't worry Agnes. I expect he'll have a long life. We're having a new addition to the family, so he'll soon forget about Ambrose."

There were footsteps and their voices faded.

"Close the window," I whispered.

Susan hurried to the window and closed it. Then she turned to me, frowning. "You made advances on her?"

"Of course not. She must have staged the whole thing to get rid of me. She wants Pa and everything he owns for herself and the children she's planning to have." I closed my eyes, remembering how I'd predicted what might happen when Lucy was playing matchmaker with Mrs. Ava and Pa. "She got rid of my sisters and now me. Everything's for her now."

"Are you going to tell your pa what we heard?"

"And get another beating? No, not until I have proof. I have a name now, Gerald Ward. And the Fletchers came here from New York City. I have to go there. Maybe I can find the man's family. If she killed him, she might be wanted by the law."

"How will you get there?"

"I have Butter—and some money in the bank." I congratulated myself on putting it there; then I got worried. Would the bank hand my money over to Pa? I struggled to sit up. "I have to get to the bank before Pa does."

"You're not well enough," Susan protested.

"I have to go anyway. Hand me my clothes."

She got the trousers and shirt from a shelf where they had been laid out to dry and handed them to me. The bloodstains on the shirt were faded from washing, but it was clear what made them.

"You should wait for Doc Sloan."

"I'll come back after I have my money. If Pa knows about the box Mr. Shaw is keeping for me, he might get there first."

"When people see you, they are going to ask what happened. What will you say?"

"I'll say, 'Ask my pa.'" I sighed. "Susan, you have to leave so I can get dressed."

"Promise you'll come back. You won't leave without saying goodbye."

"I promise."

After she left the room, I pulled the stool close, pushed on the seat, and stood, every muscle in my body shooting pains through me. I let the nightshirt fall to the floor, then eased back onto the cot. I comforted myself with the thought that my body would heal. I wondered if this thing with Pa ever would.

TWENTY-SIX

Hiram

Bob Clark was building a fire in the forge when I arrived at the shop. He looked up. "Where's Ambrose? These days, he usually gets here before you."

His question puzzled me. In a town where gossip spreads faster than a prairie fire, I expected people to already be buzzing about what had happened to Ambrose and why I'd given him a sound thrashing. I'd already exchanged "Good morning" with both the mayor and Alice Collins. Neither one had said a thing about Ambrose—although I did think Alice had frowned when she greeted me. I hadn't pressed to learn the reason for her chilly attitude because I didn't want to hear what she might say.

Derryberry had left for the school before I was out the door of my house, so I'd had no chance to talk to him about where he had taken Ambrose.

A man entered the shop. "Where's the stable boy? I need my horse."

I turned to Bob. "Take care of this fellow. Ambrose won't be in. You'll have to work the stable today."

Bob's brow wrinkled. I could see he wanted to ask something, but the man was fidgeting, obviously anxious to get his horse and be on his way, so Bob didn't take time to question me.

Alone, I used the bellows to build heat in the fire. Instead of setting to work on the axe heads I was making, I walked to the front door. Ava came out of Fletcher's Emporium and hurried across the street toward me. I was glad I'd sent Bob next door, anxious to have a private word with my wife.

The moment Ava was in the shop, I took her arm and walked her to the back. "What did Agnes say?" I asked, keeping my voice low.

"She hasn't heard a thing. But she's stirred up now, worrying about what Joe's going to say. You know how he hates gossip."

"What did you tell her?'

"That Ambrose had tried to take advantage of me, and you had done what any husband would do. You gave him a sound beating."

I drew back at that. "I thought we were going to wait to learn what his story was before telling our side."

She fussed with her sleeve. "Yes, I told her that was our plan, but she's my cousin. I had to tell her the truth, and she's good at keeping secrets."

"Humph. I hope so."

"There he is." Ava slipped past me and scurried to the door. She peeked around the corner, staying out of the sight of any passersby.

I came up behind her, my breath catching in my chest. Ambrose was hobbling toward the corner, leaning on a walking stick. Seeing him creeping along, his slow steps reminded me of the time my ribs were broken and how hard it was to get around. Did he have broken ribs? Fatherly concern threatened to take over. I pushed it away. Ambrose had betrayed me in the worst way a son could, and he had gotten what he deserved.

"Did you see where he came from?" I asked.

"No, but I'm guessing the boarding house. Your friend, Alice Collins, is probably harboring him."

I remembered Alice's frown from earlier. "Probably," I agreed.

As Ambrose limped across the street, a wagon veered around him. Glancing down the street, I fastened my gaze on the sheriff's office. If he was going to complain, it wouldn't do him any good. I was within my rights to punish my own son for theft. It was a family matter—even though he was no longer family to me.

TWENTY-SEVEN

Ambrose

I grimaced with every step, clamping my teeth, determined not to yelp in pain. The bank was at the end of the next block, a minute to reach on a regular day. But it was no regular day with me shuffling along like an old man. I reckoned in a race, the old man would win.

Mayor Tompkins poked his bald head out of the newspaper office. "Ambrose! Good lord, boy, what happened to you?"

I leaned on the walking stick I'd borrowed from Mrs. Collins and focused on him with my right eye, my left eye being too swollen shut to see much. "You'll have to ask my pa."

The shock on his face gave me some satisfaction. While he was still thinking on what to say next, I turned my face forward and continued inching my way down the boardwalk to the bank next door.

I pulled the door open, and a bell clanged overhead. Mr. Yates, the banker, looked up from his stand behind the counter, eyes rounding when he saw me. I braced for the question I knew was coming.

"What happened to you?"

Every time I heard that question, it got harder to stick with my plan. I wanted to spill out my anger and tell how Mrs. Ava had lied about me, but then it just became my word against hers. Let Pa tell his story, whatever falsehood he believed or lie he had thought up to justify what he'd done. Then he could see what folks believed.

"You'll have to ask my pa," I said. "I've come for the box you're keeping for me."

"Of course." He ducked his head, looking below the counter and coming up with a key. Sneaking glances at me, he hurried to the back wall and opened a wood door. Beyond that was a door made of iron bars, like a jail cell. He unlocked it and went inside the limestone-walled room.

He emerged a few seconds later with the iron box I had left with him and set it on the counter. "Check the contents. You'll have to sign for it."

I unlocked the box and shuffled through the gold and silver coins, reluctant to count the money in front of him, not wanting anyone to know how much I had. It looked right, one-hundred-five dollars and twenty-five cents.

"It's all here," I said and signed the paper he laid out in front of me. I put the small box in the leather bag that hung from my belt. "Thank you, Mr. Yates."

I turned and limped toward the door, the weight of the box causing pains to shoot up my side and back.

"Take care of yourself, Ambrose," he called after me.

That was exactly what I intended to do.

I headed back to the boardinghouse. There were more people on the street now, staring at me as I passed. When I came even with the livery stable, Bob Clark dashed across the street.

"What happened to you, Ambrose?"

I looked toward the blacksmith shop and caught a glimpse of a fancy dress and figured Mrs. Ava and Pa were watching from the shadows. Rage filled me. Eyes misting and body shaking, I ground out the words, "You'll have to ask my pa."

His eyes narrowed. "It was Ava, wasn't it?"

"Like I said, ask my pa." My stomach churned. I tightened my grip on the walking stick, weaving a bit, my head pounding.

"You're supposed to be resting." It was Doc Sloan's voice. He came up behind me, put a steadying hand on my waist, and shooed the gathering crowd out of my path.

"I had business," I protested.

"Your business is getting well. You fall and healing will take longer." His voice deepened with concern. "You're wobbling. Put you free arm around me."

I did as he said. We shuffled forward, the leather bag with my money box bumping my leg with each step.

When at last we reached the boarding house, Susan rushed to open the door for us.

Doc Sloan scowled at her. "Your patient got away."

She scowled at me. "I told him not to go. He wouldn't listen."

Doc shook his head and frowned. "How about now, Ambrose? Are you going to listen now?"

"Yes, sir," I said.

With Susan following, Doc Sloan helped me to the storeroom and deposited me on the cot. "I'll go get my bag and have a look at you. Susan, more cold cloths on those bruises."

"Yes, sir."

The minute he was gone, she frowned and said, "I told you so."

I groaned.

She checked the temperature of the water in the bucket. "I'll get fresh water. Do you want the window open?"

"Not now. Wait until after Doc finishes examining me. I think the fence is where Mrs. Ava and her cousin exchange confidences. I don't want them to find out I'm here."

"Okay." She picked up the pail and left.

I closed my eyes and was drifting toward unconsciousness when the door opened. I lifted the lid of my good eye, thinking Susan was back, but it was Mrs. Collins.

"What were you thinking, going out like that?" she scolded.

"I had business," I said.

"What you have is the whole town talking."

Her voice was raised. I glanced toward the window, hoping that being closed was enough to keep anyone on the other side of the fence from hearing.

"I know," I said.

She squared her shoulders, took a deep breath, and blew it out. "Doc wants you to stay put. Can I get you anything?"

"The fable book Ma made that I gave you for safekeeping."

Her face softened a bit at my request. "Sure. What about some breakfast?"

"Not now." The room seemed to be fading. "Just the book."

"Be right back with it."

My eyes closed before the sound of the door told me she had gone. I was half asleep when she returned.

She touched my hand. "Here it is."

I gripped it with both hands and laid it on my chest. "Thank you."

I heard her leave again. I ran a hand over the book cover and said a silent prayer that some story in the book would guide me down the right path. "Oh, Ma," I whispered, "show me the way."

I awakened to a cool cloth being pressed lightly on the bruised left side of my face. Opening my good eye, I saw Susan's sweet face studying me.

I groped for the fable book, brushing my chest where I had laid it and felt a damp cloth. "My book?"

"I put it to the end of the bed so it wouldn't get wet," Susan said. "Doc still wants cold compresses on your chest to take the swelling down."

I noticed her voice was hushed, so I glanced at the window. It was open.

"Have you heard any more?"

She shook her head.

"How long was I asleep?"

"A couple of hours. It's past noon. Can you eat something?"

Could I? My chest, back, and shoulders hurt so much I hadn't thought about food. The mention of it brought my attention to an empty ache in my gut. I hadn't eaten since noon yesterday.

"I think so," I said. "But not much."

Susan smiled. "I'll bring chicken soup. My mama swears by it." She put a fresh cool cloth on the side of my face and left.

I wanted the fable book, wanted to pick it up and look through the pages, but I couldn't risk Ma's drawings getting wet. My mind ran through the stories, remembering her favorites, searching for a moral that best fit my current situation when Mrs. Ava's sharp voice carried through the open window.

"Did you see him?" she said. "The way he was hobbling down the street he was obviously trying to stir up trouble."

"I didn't see him," Agnes said. "From what folks tell me, he went to the bank, so he didn't pass by the store."

"People are looking at Hiram like he did something wrong,"

Mrs. Ava complained. "It's all because that boy won't say a word beyond 'Ask my pa.'"

I balled my fingers into a fist, my breath catching in my chest. Saying nothing had been the right plan. It made Pa have to justify what he'd done all on his own.

"So what is Hiram telling folks?" Mrs. Fletcher asked.

"There's hardly anyone to tell. Mayor Tomkins usually stops by a few minutes, just to talk about the latest news on the upcoming election. So does Reverend Sherwood and Doc Sloan. Not today. It's like Hiram's been condemned when it's Ambrose who should be on the receiving end of bad opinion. This isn't going the way I planned it."

"What are you going to do?" Agnes asked.

"It's you who are going to do something," Mrs. Ava replied.

"Me?" Agnes raised her voice. "I can't be in on this. Joe won't stand for it." Susan came in with a tray as Agnes was saying the thing about Joe. She stepped quietly to a shelf and set the tray on it, then stood listening, her eyes widening as Mrs. Ava told Agnes what she should do.

TWENTY-EIGHT

Hiram

Doc Sloan was the only council member who had stopped by the shop this morning. He came to tell me about Ambrose's injuries.

"In case you're interested," he said, "there are no broken bones. That's a miracle, really. Were you trying to kill the boy? What did he do?"

"What does he say he did?"

"He doesn't. What he says is 'ask my pa,' so that's what I'm doing."

I had planned to use whatever Ambrose said and shape it like a piece of hot iron, pound out his excuses and sharpen the guilt in his story for all to see. But without a story from him, I had nothing to work with. I didn't want to say the truth, that he had taken liberties with Ava. A son attempting to cuckold his father was not a story I wanted going around, but I had expected Ambrose to twist the tale and deny what he had done. But he hadn't, leaving me searching for words.

"Well?" Doc was looking at me like I was a bug under his microscope.

"Ambrose stole from me."

"What did he steal?"

"Something precious," I snapped. "Something he's obviously ashamed to say, so I won't either."

What he had stolen was my good name in this town. I realized no one was going to believe Ambrose had tried to force himself on Ava. I wouldn't have believed it either if I hadn't seen it with my own eyes.

In fact, when Ava had warned me about Ambrose's overlong looks and brushes against her when they were alone, I had thought she must be misreading his actions. But that was before last night when I had walked in to see his hands on her, her bodice ripped, and a scratch on her neck. Just thinking about it made my breath quicken and my blood pump harder.

Doc closed one eye and studied me. "You're turning red right now over whatever it is. Better calm down, Hiram. You'll give yourself a heart attack." He turned and left.

Shaking with anger, I returned to the forge and pumped the bellows to fan the fire, building the heat. Picking up a bar of iron with tongs, I thrust it into the flames.

"Hiram!"

It was Ava, back from a second attempt to get information from Agnes.

"What did she say?"

"The town's on Ambrose's side, and they don't even know what he did."

I removed the iron from the fire, thrust it into a pail of water, and then placed it on the anvil and began pounding, fury feeding the force of my blows.

"I saw Doc Sloan leave," Ava said. "What was his reaction?"

"The same as the rest of the town." I brought the hammer down on the iron with all my might. "Ambrose's silence has stolen my good name."

"You have to say something to counteract that," Ava said.

I stopped pounding and stared at her. "What can I say? I told Doc that Ambrose stole from me. He didn't say so, but I knew he didn't believe me."

"Ambrose will leave town, and all this talk will blow over. You've been here almost five years. People know what a good man you are, how you stood up to those border ruffians when they came hunting for the runaway slave, how you bear that mark on your chest. This thing with Ambrose will pass."

I looked down at the iron on the anvil and took another swing.

"I hope you're right."

"I have errands to run," Ava said. "We'll talk later at home."

I nodded and stuck the iron back in the fire. Perhaps an hour passed after Ava left before Reverend Sherwood came by.

"Hiram, do you have time to talk?"

I laid my hammer aside and reached for a rag to wipe away the sweat from my forehead. "Sure," I said, glad for the chance to talk to someone who would be sympathetic to my plight as a father whose son had betrayed him. Then I took a good look at the reverend's stern face, his lips drawn together, his eyes glaring at me, and I knew convincing him of Ambrose's guilt would not be easy.

"Let's sit." I pointed at a wooden bench along one wall and led the way. Once we were settled, Reverend Sherwood continued his solemn stare.

At last, I could take it no more. "So have you judged me without hearing me out?"

"I've come to hear you out, Hiram, but I've seen your boy. I've seen the seriousness of his injuries. What could he have done to justify a beating like that?"

My fingers curled into fists, and I pressed them into my thighs. I was shaking with anger. "He attempted to take what was mine. He betrayed me. That's all I'll say."

Reverend Sherwood's mouth straightened into a line, and his eyes seemed less hard, more concerned. "Mr. Derryberry said he feared you might have killed the boy if he hadn't stopped you."

"Derryberry needs to mind his own business or find another place to live."

"Surely, the punishment was more severe than the crime, whatever it was," Sherwood said.

"Spare the rod and spoil the child," I reminded him.

"Wouldn't it help if you told me what Ambrose did? You know I would never repeat anything you tell me."

"It's a private matter between me and God. I don't need a middleman."

Reverend Sherwood stood. "Very well, but if you feel the need to talk, you know where I am."

I stood and met his eyes. "I do."

He shook his head. "By not telling how Ambrose betrayed you,

you are only making the rumors and judgment of the townspeople worse."

"What people think is no concern of mine," I said, stepping away and taking up my tongs, thrusting another piece of iron in the fire.

TWENTY-NINE

Ambrose

I had just finished a dinner of beef stew and biscuits when Doc Sloan stopped in to see how I was doing.

"Better, Doc," I said in answer to his question. "I was even able to eat a big meal without my stomach churning."

"Let me have a look at that eye."

His hand cupped my chin and turned my face one way and then the other. Then he let go, held up two fingers, and had me follow them as he moved them back and forth in front of me. "You are on the mend."

"How long before I can ride?"

"Anxious to leave Hidden Springs, are you?"

"I got business to see to elsewhere," I said.

"Oh?"

"Just my sisters." I said, realizing I had almost given away my true intentions. "Lucy, in particular."

Doc's eyebrows shot up. "She left in a hurry. I never heard what that was about. I remembered how happy she was to be home and thought her abrupt leave-taking strange."

"She thought Pa was in too big a rush to marry her off." Not the whole truth, but not a lie either.

Doc nodded. "I see."

"So you didn't say when I could ride."

"Give your body another day. Then ride slow. No fast galloping down the trail."

When he left, I lay back on the cot and planned my trip, first to Westport, and then east to New York City.

THIRTY

Hiram

It was time to close the shop. I had tried all day to put Ambrose out of my mind, but he wouldn't go. Reverend Sherwood, during his visit, had further impressed on me the low opinion in which the citizens of Hidden Springs held me after the brief appearance of Ambrose hobbling down the main street on a makeshift cane. Speculation ran high on my reason for punishing him. No one accepted the story I told of the boy stealing from me, particularly when I had no specific item to point to as stolen.

Business had been light all day, as though all tools remained sharp and no wagon wheels broke. I had kept myself busy pounding out new axe heads, fulfilling an order from a shop in Junction City.

Bob Clark came in through the side door to the stable. "I'm ready to lock up for the day. Is there anything I need to know about tomorrow?"

"If you mean is Ambrose coming back, he is not. If the boy knows what's good for him, he'll leave town."

"Alice says he'll be leaving soon as he can ride."

"I suppose she's got that palomino hidden out somewhere."

"No need to hide it. The horse belongs to Ambrose. As I remember, it was a birthday gift some years ago from his family in Westport."

My temper flared again. Bob seemed to think I would claim the animal as my own. "You remember correctly," I snapped.

"Yes, but Alice says when you're angry, you sometimes forget things like that." Bob paused. "The two of us aren't enough to run both the stable *and* the smithy."

Riled by the news of what Alice, someone I had considered a good friend, really thought of me, I growled, "I'll hire help. I'll post a sign out front in the morning. There are plenty of youngsters around needing work."

"None as skilled as Ambrose."

My fists clenched. It was all I could do to stop myself from taking a swing at him.

He took a step back. "Okay. I've tied your horse out front. See you in the morning."

Bob closed the door separating the businesses. I heard him lock the front door to the stable.

I blew out the candle by the smithy entrance, locked up, and stood for a moment, staring across the street at the lighted windows of the boardinghouse dining room. Somewhere in the building, Ambrose was holing up, getting ready to leave town. I supposed he would join his sisters in Westport. Hannah would soon have all my children.

Well, not all. I had a new family now: Ava and our coming child, surely a son. Shoving away thoughts of Minerva's offspring, I mounted my horse and headed for home.

THIRTY-ONE

Ambrose

On the fourth day after Pa lit into me, I was preparing to leave Hidden Springs.

Doc Sloan had come by to check on me one last time, letting me know he thought I should wait another day or two. "Riding is going to hurt. Just getting in the saddle will be painful."

"Lying on this cot, doing nothing but thinking all the time hurts more." I eased up on one elbow. "I got to be going somewhere."

"I can see there's no talking you out of leaving, so take care of yourself on the trail. Rest often. Where are you heading?"

"To see my sisters. I don't know after that. Find work."

"Nothing heavy for a bit," Doc advised.

"I figured you were going to say that."

"Write and let me know when you get settled. Folks in this town care about you."

After Doc left, I slipped my arms into the new shirt Mrs. Collins had bought for me at Fletcher's Emporium. I didn't like giving them business, but there wasn't anywhere else to buy clothes in this town, and even after three scrubbings, my old shirt was still stained with my blood.

There was a knock at the door. I quickly fastened two buttons and called out, "Who is it?"

"Me," Susan called through the door. "May I come in?"

"Sure."

She entered the room. "Doc said you were leaving."

"Yeah." I stood like an idiot, not knowing what to say or do next. A week ago, when I still had a home and a job, I had thought about courting Susan. Of course, we couldn't marry or anything for a long time. We were both still kids. But I liked her better than any other girl in town, and I could tell she liked me, too. But now I was leaving. Unless I found out what Mrs. Ava had done that caused her cousins to leave New York City, I probably wouldn't be back.

"Were you going to say goodbye?" From Susan's sharp tone, I knew my long silence wasn't pleasing her.

I swallowed hard and gazed into her brown eyes. "I wish I didn't have to."

Her face softened. "Will you write to me?"

"Yes." I laughed. "With all the people I've promised letters, I won't have time to do anything but write."

"I expect to be first on your list," she said.

I glanced toward the window, my face warming. "You will be."

Then I met her eyes again, feeling awkward.

She solved everything by stepping forward and kissing my right cheek, just a smidgeon from my lips. Quickly moving back, she reached for the leather bag containing my belongings that lay on the bed. Hefting it, she said, "I'll walk you to your horse."

She turned and was out the room in a flash. I shuffled behind her, still leaning on my walking stick.

Mrs. Collins looked up as we entered the dining room. "I guess this is goodbye," she said. "You'll write, won't you?"

I groaned. "I will."

She smiled at me and handed a cloth bag to Susan. "Here are some treats for your journey. Two muffins, two biscuits, and a nice slice of ham."

"Thank you," I said.

We walked outside. Butter nickered when she saw me. I stroked her neck and gave her a hug. I had missed her. Susan handed me my bag of belongings and the one of food. I hooked them over the pommel. Then I looked at the huge step from the street into the stirrup.

"I'll lead Butter around sideways to the walk so you can mount from there," Susan said.

Why hadn't I thought of that? I'd remember to look for a step up from the ground in the future.

She led Butter around, and I mounted, taking the reins from her. She handed me my walking stick.

"Goodbye," I said.

Just as I was about to knee Butter to get moving, I looked up and saw Mrs. Ava come out of the Emporium.

She raised her chin and gave me the slightest, smirking smile, letting me know she had won.

For now, maybe, but not for long. I vowed again to learn what she had done that caused a scandal so bad her cousins had been forced move from their home.

Before I left Hidden Springs, I had one more stop to make. I turned Butter toward the cemetery.

It was a cool autumn day. The leaves were turning red and gold, and a slight breeze rustled those still clinging to the trees. I stopped by a large flat rock at the edge of the cemetery, eased off Butter onto it, and then off the rock, using the walking stick for leverage and balance. I retrieved the fable book from my bag and carried it with me to Ma's grave.

I wanted to kneel and spend some time talking to her, but I knew standing again would take my strength, so I stood and looked down, clutching the book to my chest, my throat tight.

"I guess from where you are, looking down at me, you know I'm leaving town. You know about the lies Mrs. Ava told on me, lies Pa believes. You know about him beating and disowning me. I'm mad at him, but I know it's because of Mrs. Ava's falsehoods. He just can't see the truth about the dishonest woman she is.

"I shouldn't care after what he's done, but I want him to know the truth. I want him to know I'm not the one who betrayed him. She's done something in New York City, something bad, I think. I've got to find out what that is and bring back proof. Without proof, Pa will never believe me.

"See what I've got here?" I raised the book of fables. "I thought I'd pick one at random and see if it might give me a message, a way to go. I'm going to do that now, Ma. I hope you'll guide my hand."

I tucked the walking stick under my arm, closed my eyes, felt along the side of the book, and opened it. There was "The Farmer and the Fox." I frowned. I knew the moral of the story. Ma had read it often, and I didn't see how it applied to me. The story was about a fox stealing chickens from a farmer, and how the farmer tried to get even by catching the fox, soaking the animal's tail in oil, and lighting it on fire. That part always made me shiver. Burning a living thing like that seemed worse than the crime of killing chickens, which was just what foxes do. Anyway, the fox got away, ran through the farmer's ripening wheat, setting the whole field on fire. The moral of the story was about how revenge could bring the avenger to ruin. I always thought the story was incomplete. I wanted to know what happened to the fox. Maybe he ran into a creek and put out the fire. Maybe he'd survived, just like I would.

Anyway, I stared at the words on the page and the picture Ma had drawn of the farmer covering his nose with his handkerchief against the smoke curling up, hazing the air, as he looked out at his blazing field, shock and heartbreak on his face, watching his crop being destroyed, and the fox in the distance, running out the opposite side of the field into the woods, flames still shooting from his tail.

Why had Ma guided me to this page? I wasn't planning revenge against Pa or Mrs. Ava. I didn't blame Pa for what he did. I blamed Mrs. Ava for fooling him with her lies. All I wanted was to find out the truth about her and warn Pa, make him see that she wasn't right for him. I knew he might not listen to me, but I had to try.

"It's not about revenge, Ma," I said. "It's about the truth. You always said the truth is important."

I closed the book, disappointed that the message had not fit the future I faced. "I'll keep the story in mind, and if I don't make it back here, I know you're looking down on me from heaven, no matter where I am."

I stepped back and gave a last, long look at the headstone before turning and hobbling toward Butter, ready to face the unknown, my determination to find the truth stronger than ever.

Hiram's Boy

PART II

Hazel Hart

THIRTY-TWO

Ambrose

Doc Sloan had been right about taking the ride slow. It was ten days before, exhausted and in pain, I arrived in Westport. I went immediately to the hotel. Weary, I eased off Butter, a hand on my aching ribs, and trudged onto the walk. When I pushed open the heavy hotel door, the bell overhead rang.

Aunt Hannah stood behind the desk. She barely interrupted her conversation with a tall, dark-haired man who faced her to glance toward me and call out a hello. The man turned, straightened, and raised his eyebrows as I limped toward them. He said something I couldn't hear.

Aunt Hannah shot a longer look in my direction, and her eyes widened. "Ambrose? Dear Lord, child. What happened to you?"

"Pa," I said, giving the same answer I had to everyone else. Only this time I was ready to tell the whole story and ask for help. Of course, whether Aunt Hannah would want to help with anything that might aid Pa was questionable, but I had to try.

I scanned the quiet room, disappointed. I had pictured my sisters being present when I came in. I realized now that was silly of me. This was just a hotel entrance lobby, not a family parlor.

"Are my sisters sleeping?" I asked.

Aunt Hannah came around the side of the check-in counter and sped toward me, stopping short in front of me and stroking my chin with her fingers. "Cordelia and Lucy are putting Ella and Jennie to bed." She glanced toward the man. "Ryan, will you let the older girls know their brother is here without disturbing the little ones."

He nodded and disappeared into the nearby hallway.

Aunt Hannah turned to me. "As soon as my desk clerk returns, I'll take you to my suite where we can talk." She touched my hair and peered at the fading bruises on my cheek. "When did this happen?"

"Two weeks ago."

An elderly man shuffled into the room.

"Here's Wesley now," Aunt Hannah said. "Wesley, this is my nephew, Ambrose, who has come to visit his sisters. When they come down, please tell them to join us in my suite."

"Yes, ma'am," he replied.

Lightly touching my arm, she said, "This way."

I crept forward, slowed by my sore ribs. Doc had said it would probably be at least four weeks, maybe longer, before the pain completely went away. Aunt Hannah was such a whirlwind, I was slowing her down considerably. Thankfully, her rooms were on the bottom floor, so there were no stairs to climb.

The short hallway was lighted by two small lamps attached to the walls. I stopped short as we entered. "Butter. My horse is tied out front. I need to take care of her."

"I'll send Jake as soon as I get you settled."

She opened a door and guided me inside.

Unable to wait for the others, I told her what I needed. "Will you help me?"

THIRTY-THREE

Cordelia

Lucy and I had tiptoed out of Ella and Jennie's room, determined not to wake them, when Mr. O'Rourke came for us.

Nodding toward the closed door, he asked in a low voice, "Are your sisters asleep?"

Lucy rolled her eyes and nodded. "At last," she mouthed.

Mr. O'Rourke beckoned us away from the door. We followed him down the hall until we were far enough from our sisters' room to speak without waking them.

"Your brother's here," he said.

Lucy's face lit up with joy. "Ambrose!" she squealed. "Here? Where?"

Mr. O'Rourke chuckled. "In your aunt's parlor."

In spite of Mr. O'Rourke's smile as he watched Lucy streak down the stairs, a sadness around his eyes said all was not well.

"What is it you haven't said?" I asked as we descended the stairs.

"Someone has recently given your brother a sound beating. His face bears bruises, and from the way he moves, I'm guessing his ribs do to."

I quickened my pace. Fury choked me. "It was Hiram, wasn't it?"

"If Hiram is his father, yes. What made you think of him first?"

"We've had only one letter from Ambrose since his pa married, and from what he wrote, it was doubtful the new wife wanted him around."

We were just outside Aunt Hannah's parlor when we heard Lucy's cry of dismay.

"Ambrose, what happened?" she asked.

Mr. O'Rourke and I stepped into the parlor.

Lucy's eyes were overflowing with tears. Swiping at them with her fingers, she declared, "This has something to do with Miss Carstairs, doesn't it?"

"Yes, but, she is no longer Miss Carstairs. I wrote you that she and Pa got married September first." Ambrose blew out a breath. "I call her Mrs. Ava now."

I hurried toward him, squeezed his hand, and aimed a light kiss at the cheek with no bruises.

Aunt Hannah said, "All of you come in and sit." She motioned to Mr. O'Rourke. "You, too, Ryan. We may be asking your advice. While all of you are getting settled, I'll get someone to take care of Ambrose's horse."

She slipped past our little group and hurried down the hall toward the registration area. The rest of us found seats, Lucy on the sofa on one side of Ambrose and me on the other. Ryan took a seat in an upholstered armchair.

Reaching for Ambrose's hand, I said "From what you wrote and Lucy has said, Mrs. Ava may be a more respectful name than she deserves."

Ambrose blinked. "You're likely right, but it's the one I chose, given I sure wasn't going to call her ma or Mrs. Pierce. I reserve those names for our mother."

Aunt Hannah returned with a leather bag containing Ambrose's belongings, set it on the floor beside his feet, and took a chair beside Ryan's. She clasped her hands in her lap and leaned forward. "Tell us what happened."

Ambrose's Adam's apple bobbed as he swallowed hard. "She said I—I tried to—tried—"

I frowned and finished with what I thought had happened given the trouble he was having getting the words out of his mouth: "To make unwelcome advances toward her."

Ambrose blew out a breath. "Yes."

Lucy face reddened with outrage. "Why would Pa ever believe such a thing?"

"Because she set a trap for me. And now I look back, I can see she was hinting that I was doing such things ever since they got back from their wedding trip. There were times Mrs. Ava would call me into a room to do some chore for her, then after sidling up to me, she'd suddenly step back and say she was shocked by my bad manners and how I must learn to keep a respectful distance. Then I'd hear Pa ask what was going on. She must have known he'd come into the room every time. I don't know how. I'd just say I was doing the chore, whatever it was. I can guess now what she must have told him in private."

Ambrose paused and stared at his hands a moment before going on. "Then ten days ago, Pa said the new buffet she'd ordered had arrived. He ordered me to go to the house and put it together."

"But they had a buffet," Lucy protested. "Ma's."

"It's back in the cabin with Mr. Derryberry. Mrs. Ava doesn't want anything in the house that reminds Pa of our mother—that includes us. Remember, I told you in my letter that Pa was going to send for Ella and Jennie after he and Mrs. Ava were married. She talked him out of it. What I didn't tell you is that she said Ma's children were physically and morally weak, just like Ma."

Lucy pounded her fists on her knees. "Our sisters are lucky they didn't have to go, but they're not going to see it that way. They'll think it's our fault, just like I blamed Aunt Hannah and Cordelia for keeping me away from Pa."

"We'll talk about that later," Aunt Hannah said. "Ambrose, continue with your story."

"Well, I did as he said. The cartons containing the buffet were in the dining room. I opened them and got to work. Then Mrs. Ava came in and complained about the mess I was making, which peeved me some. I heard the front door open and close, and knew Pa was home. That's when Mrs. Ava got up close to me and stumbled. I reached out to catch her and keep her from falling. She steadied herself, screamed 'How dare you?' and slapped me hard on my cheek. Then Pa roared into the room and believed what he thought he saw."

Lucy's face was all puffed and angry. I was shaking. I clamped my lips to keep from interrupting Ambrose.

Aunt Hannah shook her head. "Then what?"

"Pa slammed his fist into my face. I fell backward over the packing boxes and pieces of the buffet. All I could see was Pa's boots coming at me. I covered my face and turned on my side, but there was no escape. He kicked me in the ribs and shoulders, hauled me to the kitchen, and threw me out the back door."

Ambrose paused, shaking. We waited until he was able to take up his story again. "Pa told me to get off his land. When I couldn't get up, he grabbed a piece of firewood and was about to beat me with it when Mr. Derryberry stopped him. Mr. Derryberry likely saved my life. I never saw Pa so mad.

"Mr. Derryberry took me into town, and Mrs. Collins let me stay in a storage room in her boardinghouse. Doc Sloan patched me up, and Susan looked after me, putting cold cloths on my bruises."

Lucy, tears running down her cheeks now, swiped at them with her fingers and sniffled. "Susan, huh?" She managed a faint smile. "I guess you know she's sweet on you."

Ambrose's face flushed. He ducked his head. "Maybe. Anyway, the storage room window was next to a fence running between the boardinghouse and Fletcher's Emporium. Their freight unloading area is just on the other side, and that's where Mrs. Ava and Mrs. Fletcher hid away from Mr. Fletcher to talk about what happened. I overheard Mrs. Ava say it was all her plan and had worked well, but Pa was upset because people were looking at him like he'd done something wrong, those folks being the mayor and Mrs. Collins and Doc Sloan."

I let out a scoffing laugh. "Their bad opinion probably hurt Hiram more than the beating and branding he took from the slave hunters did."

"Probably," Ambrose agreed. "Mrs. Fletcher also mentioned how Mrs. Ava had done something bad that caused Mr. Fletcher to leave New York City over the gossip. I've got to go there and find out what Mrs. Ava did. It sounded like she stole something or cheated someone or even something a whole lot worse. I need to find out what it was and warn Pa."

Lucy's mouth dropped open. "Warn Pa? After what he did to you?"

"But he only did it because she fooled him," Ambrose said.

"Seems like she can make him do whatever she wants. I don't understand how. Ma could never get him to do anything."

Just then, the door swung open and Jake, the boy who did odd jobs around the hotel, stood holding Jennie by the collar of her robe. He gave her a nudge into the room.

Aunt Hannah frowned at Jennie. "You're supposed to be in bed. You haven't been sleepwalking again, have you?"

Jennie scrunched her face into a pout. "No, I haven't been sleepwalking. Who can sleep when secrets are going on?" Her eyes filled with tears, and she visibly shivered. "I thought something bad had happened?" She broke from Jake's grasp and threw herself in Ambrose's arms. "And it has, hasn't it?" She pressed her face against his chest.

Ambrose winced and drew back. "Whoa," he said. "Careful."

Jennie stared at his face, tears now freely rolling down her cheeks. "I'm sorry."

Ambrose gave her a gentle hug then held her at arm's length. "Jennie, you've grown."

"Well, of course I have. I haven't seen you in forever." She curled her fists, pressed them against her hips, and demanded, "Why didn't someone tell me and Ella you were here?"

Ambrose ducked his head. Then he said, "We had some serious things to talk about. I was going to see you and Ella tomorrow before I left."

Jennie's mouth dropped open. "You're leaving? Tomorrow! You just came, and now you're leaving. You spend the evening with Delia and Lucy, but all Ella and me get is a goodbye in the morning? I guess when you're all grown up, little sisters aren't worth your time." Sobbing, she turned and ran from the room.

Lucy stood. "I'll see to her," she said and followed Jennie.

Ambrose sat staring at the door and looking miserable.

To distract him and get the conversation back on track, I leaned forward. "I know what you mean about some women always getting their way when others can't. When I ran away, I watched several women and was amazed by what I saw. I spent a good deal of time trying to figure out how they did it, but I never quite got the hang of it." I flicked a glance at Mr. O'Rourke. He was on his way to New York to visit his family. I had been pressing him to allow me to travel with him so that I might learn more about photography. He had talked about a new type of photograph, the tintype, and about meeting with Matthew Brady, who now and then offered classes in photography. Of course, now that it was established that I was a woman, he was refusing to let me travel with him. But if Ambrose traveled with us, we would have a chaperone. Did I dare I make that suggestion now when I knew from experience that I was not one of those women who knew how to get a man to do her bidding.

"The city is big—how many people?" I looked to Mr. O'Rourke for an answer.

He raised an eyebrow. "About eight hundred thousand or so. Why?"

"I was just wondering how Ambrose was going to find out what one person among all those people might have done. In a tiny place like Hidden Springs or even a town the size of Westport where everyone knows what's happening, finding out what someone did wouldn't be too hard. But eight hundred thousand people? What chance does Ambrose have without help?"

Ambrose's shoulders fell, and he studied his hands. When he looked up, I saw tiredness in his eyes and the hope that he could achieve his goal sinking. "I have to try," he said. "It's all I can think to do. I don't have anything else now."

"So how will you get to New York?" I asked.

He gave a little laugh. "On Butter, of course. She'll get me there."

"That's a long way to go on your own." I shifted my gaze to Mr. O'Rourke. "And it's the middle of October. Cold weather is coming."

Mr. O'Rourke frowned. Obviously, he had figured out where I was going with my talk. Well, he was smart. What did I expect?

There was no use hinting around anymore, so I came straight out with it. "You're going that way, aren't you, Mr. O'Rourke? To visit your family for Christmas."

"I am," he admitted.

Ambrose perked up at this news. "I have money. I can pay for my food and Butter's if you'll let me travel with you."

Mr. O'Rourke frowned at me. "As I've told your sister more than once, I'm not running a transportation service."

Ambrose's shoulders fell again. Head down, he rested his

elbows on his knees and stared at the floor. "I just want to do what's right. Get the truth for Pa. Show him I wasn't the one that did wrong."

"How much money do you have?" Mr. O'Rourke asked.

Ambrose sniffed and sighed. "Ninety-five dollars. I spent ten dollars coming here."

"It's more than twelve hundred miles to New York City. You don't have enough money to get halfway, let alone take care of your needs once you arrive," Mr. O'Rourke said. His face had softened, and I could tell he had sympathy for Ambrose's situation.

It was time for me to press my plan and see what happened. I put my hand over Ambrose's and squeezed. "Grandmother's sister, our great-aunt, Gertrude Oaks, lives on Long Island. She's alone now and has invited me to stay with her while I attend Mathew Brady's photography classes. I have a horse and a bit of money left over from my Denver trip. We can travel together."

Ambrose raised his head and smiled. "Really?"

"We both want to go to the same place for different reasons. As far as I'm concerned, I think Hiram is getting what he deserves. I wouldn't lift a finger to help him. You, on the other hand, are my brother, and if this investigation will bring you some peace, I will help any way I can."

Aunt Hannah interrupted our plans. "It isn't wise for the two of you to travel alone. You would be on the road for well over a month, possibly two, since Ambrose will have to take it slow until his bruised ribs completely heal. Anything could happen."

"Anything can happen anywhere," I reminded her. "I remember Ma telling about how she saw a boy drown when the river flooded just below the Westport wharf. And I traveled alone all the way to the Denver gold fields and got back just fine."

"And almost got run down by a stampeding buffalo herd," she retorted. "You've barely been home three months, and you want to go off and put yourself in danger again." She turned to Mr. O'Rourke. "Talk to her. Talk to both of them."

Mr. O'Rourke frowned at me, probably guessing I was using Aunt Hannah's concern to get my way. I still wasn't sure how close their friendship was, but from what I had seen, he would do almost anything for her.

He shook his head. "Talk to Cordelia? When has that ever done any good?" He ran his tongue along his top lip. "Okay. The two of you can travel with me. I'll take fifty dollars from you, Ambrose, for your expenses on the trail. I want the same amount from you, Cordelia. And I need you to accept that I am not a transportation company. I've said that before to Cordelia, but I want both of you to listen. We will go at the pace I want to go on the roads I choose. There will be no argument about that. Do you both understand?"

Ambrose and I glanced at each other and said "yes" at the same time.

"We'll leave tomorrow by noon. That will give you time to gather what you need and say your goodbyes." He stood and abruptly left the room, brushing past Lucy as she returned.

Her eyes widened as she looked after him. "He seems upset. What happened?"

Aunt Hannah flicked a speculative glance at me. "Cordelia got him to agree to take her and Ambrose with him on his trip home to New York."

"*You're* going with Ambrose? Why not *me*?" She turned to our brother. "Why Cordelia and not me?"

So I was *Cordelia* to Lucy again, which meant she was really mad at me. My sisters called me Delia when all was well between us, but Lucy's opinion of me rose and fell depending on whether she was getting her way.

Aunt Hannah stepped in with an explanation. "Because your sister is older and has some money to pay her way. She also has her own reasons for wanting to travel to New York."

Lucy raised her chin, sniffed audibly, and stuck her nose in the air. "Like her traveling companion," she declared. She turned on her heel and stormed from the room.

"What did she mean by that?" I asked.

Aunt Hannah rolled her eyes. "Think about it," she said.

THIRTY-FOUR

Ambrose

Lucy was at war with Delia again.

There was nothing I could do about that. I hoped they would work it out before we left, but there were no guarantees with Lucy. When she felt wronged, she held on to the feeling.

Aunt Hannah gave me a room on the second floor. She said my grandmother was next door and not to be surprised if I heard moaning during the night. She suggested I look in on Grandmother True in the morning. If she were having a good day, my presence would bring her joy. However, it would be a good idea to prepare a story other than the true one about how I got the bruises on my face. Perhaps I fell from a scaffold while doing stone work. That story would do as well as any other.

***

If Grandmother True made any sounds during the night, I didn't hear them. The featherbed mattress provided the most comfortable rest I'd had since being tossed out of my home. The combination of the comfortable bed and my bone-weary tiredness from the long trip to Westport were enough to have me asleep the moment I closed my eyes.

I woke to a gentle nudge on my shoulder and a whispered "Ambrose."

"Good morning, Lucy," I mumbled. I opened my eyes and

blinked at the brightness of the candle flame she was hold near my face.

Moving the candle to the bedside table, she said, "It would be if you weren't leaving today."

"I don't have much choice," I said. "Mr. O'Rourke has his own timetable, and he's made it clear traveling with him means I must abide by it."

"Cordelia gets her way again."

I eased into a sitting position. "What do you mean?"

"They would deny it, but it's there for everyone who is paying attention to see."

"Who are 'they' and what's 'there' for anyone to see?"

She let out an exasperated sigh. "Cordelia and Mr. O'Rourke and their feelings for each other. Weren't you paying attention last night? No one is talking about it, but it's there. I can't believe Aunt Hannah is letting her travel with him. As her brother, you'd better keep an eye on them." She picked up the lighted candle, walked to the dresser, and touched the flame to the wick of the candle there. "I won't leave you in the dark," she said. "Please get dressed and come spend a few minutes with me before everyone joins us."

While she left me enough light to get dressed by, I was in the dark about many things regarding my family. The latest was this idea of something going on between Mr. O'Rourke and Delia. Was it true, or just Lucy imaginings?

THIRTY-FIVE

Cordelia

Since Lucy and I shared a room, there was no way to avoid her. The night before, she had blown out the lamp, so when I entered, I had only moonlight and my own sense of where things were to keep from stumbling as I moved cautiously across the room to my bed.

Lucy, in her own bed, had lain with her back to me, but I was betting she wasn't sleeping. Still, I hadn't wanted to get into an argument with her, so I undressed as quietly as I could, my mind buzzing with what Lucy could have meant about "my traveling companion." Surely, she meant Ambrose. She was jealous because she considered herself closer to him than the rest of us girls. She was, after all, closer in age than Jennie and Ella and his full sister. I was older, almost eighteen, and only his half-sister. I loved Lucy, but there were times when she was jealous beyond all reason. This was one of those times. I willed myself to sleep, taking deep breaths and clearing my mind of thought, settling on an image of Ma in my mind, brushing my hair and humming a tune. I refused all other thoughts and was soon sleeping.

Morning came quickly and rudely with Jennie jostling my shoulder and shouting, "Where is he? Where is he?"

I squinted at her, the thin light of dawn coming through the window barely illuminating her face. "He? You mean Ambrose?"

"Of course, I mean Ambrose. Where is he?' Brown eyes narrowing, she doubled her fists and planted them on her hips, making herself as defiant and threatening as a seven-year-old in a ruffled flannel nightdress could be.

Behind her was Ella, also still in nightclothes. Two years older than Jennie, she was less judgmental, but as Jennie's big sister and self-appointed caretaker from the time Jennie was born, Ella couldn't help backing her up. "Lucy says you and Ambrose are leaving this morning—leaving us behind and going off to have adventures. We haven't seen our brother for four years and all the time we get with him is this morning—if we can find him."

I groaned, pushed up on my elbow, and cast a glance at Lucy's bed across the room. It was empty, the bed made. How could I have slept through the usual commotion of her getting dressed and doing her hair? None of us girls had a large wardrobe, but Lucy, influenced by Aunt May, a banker's wife, was all about style. She changed her appearance daily with a ribbon here, a pin at the neck of her dress, or sometimes a flower, although it being mid-October there were fewer of those now, a lingering rose.

"What time is it? Aren't you girls supposed to be getting ready for school?"

"We're not going." Jennie crossed her arms and scrunched her face. "We're going to spend every minute with our brother—if we can find him. Where is he?" She ended her assertion with a louder tone than when she started.

"You needn't shout," I said. "I'm right here."

Jennie's eyebrows drew together. "But not for long." She added, "Lucy got up early to help in the kitchen since you're running away again."

I pushed my blanket back and sat up. "I am not running away. I am taking a planned trip with everyone's knowledge." Wanting to end this useless discussion which was quickly leading to a listing of every time I had disappointed them, I added, "If you want to spend time with Ambrose, go find Aunt Hannah and ask her. She's the one who assigns rooms around here."

Ella gave Jennie's arm a tug. "Let's go."

Jennie gave me a last scowl before following Ella out the door.

I got up, opened the curtains, and gazed out at the brightening day. I was usually up at least an hour before now, working in the kitchen, cooking bacon, sausage, and biscuits for the hotel buffet line. Apparently, Lucy was going to take over my job. Well, she would be happy to earn more spending money than she was currently paid for dusting and sweeping. Likely, she would spend it on new fashions.

I turned away from the window and set about packing my own meager wardrobe. I traveled light by choice. Having taken two long trips across Kansas Territory, I knew too many belongings could weigh a person down. When it was time to escape danger, an over-attachment to clothes, or anything else, could mean death. And while there were people I would die for, no possession was worth my life. Well, maybe one. I touched the locket containing the lock of my mother's hair, considered, and then rejected that idea. Ma would have wanted me to save my life. She was always in my heart.

I spread two skirts and matching bodices on the bed and rolled each into a tube. I did the same with a petticoat. I would wear two at the beginning of our journey and judge when and if the other would be necessary. I added a heavy cape and gloves since we would be traveling well into December. I also packed the shirt, vest, and trousers Mr. O"Rourke had bought for me when I was passing for a boy in order to travel safely through the territory alone.

I smiled, remembering how I had deceived his sharp eye when others had quickly found me out. I still didn't know exactly how that had happened, but he was surely angry with me once he realized I had fooled him. I set the boy's cap on top of the pile and began packing the items into the leather bag I would tie to my horse's saddle. I added my box of letter paper and a pencil. While I preferred to write with pen and ink, bottles were easily broken and ink was almost impossible to wash out.

Leaving my packed satchel on the bed, I went down the stairs to the check-in desk and exchanged a greeting with Wesley, the elderly clerk. "I'm leaving today," I said.

"I've heard that," he replied.

"I need to retrieve my money from the safe."

He stepped aside, and I lifted the key from a hook beneath the desk and unlocked the safe. I removed a small bag and shoved it into my pocket. Then I was on my way to the dining hall to go through the buffet line and fill a plate with my breakfast. When I entered the large room, I saw that the breakfast crowd of travelers had thinned. At the far end of one long table sat my sisters, along with Aunt Hannah, Ambrose, and Mr. O'Rourke. Tin coffee cups were in front of Ambrose and Mr. O'Rourke. The girls had almost emptied their glasses of milk, and Aunt Hannah was sipping her morning tea. Jennie and Lucy were on either side of Ambrose with Ella directly across the table from him. It bothered me that Lucy had deprived Ella of the seat next to Ambrose. After all, Lucy had spent the summer with him, and the younger girls were seeing him for the first time in four years.

Determined not to cause a stir about that, I took a deep breath and crossed to the table, taking a seat next to Aunt Hannah.

Mr. O'Rourke cast me a frown. "Looks like we will be getting off to a late start."

"I'm ready," I said. "Jennie and Ella woke me, so I took time to pack before coming downstairs." I forced a smile at Jennie. "I see you found your brother."

"No thanks to you." She leaned against him and clutched his arm.

His lips formed a grimace, and I wondered what he thought of our being so at odds with each other when we were about to be parted.

Aunt Hannah glanced around the table at our dispirited group. "Are you really going to let your last morning together for who knows how long be so sour and full of discontent? You are brother and sisters. Find some joy in each other's company or you may someday regret your petty disagreements."

This from a woman who could barely stand to be in the same room with her own sisters. I clamped my lips together to keep from smiling.

She slid a sideways glance at Mr. O'Rourke. "Ryan has agreed to take Ambrose and Cordelia to New York City, a journey that will take some time and will no doubt be fraught with obstacles. While we know both Ambrose and Cordelia are determined and resilient, we need to wish them well. I want each of you girls to give a wish for them on their travels. Lucy, let's start with you."

Lucy sighed and stared at her empty milk glass. "Somebody else go first."

Ella took up the challenge. "Good weather."

"And good food," Jennie added.

We all chuckled.

"I'm for that," I said.

Aunt Hannah turned to Lucy. "Your wish for your brother and sister?"

Lucy reached for Ambrose's hand, her eyes teary. "I hope you find out what Ava's hiding and that Pa believes you when you tell him." Her face grew sulky as she turned to me. "I wish you would stop running away."

Exasperated, I asked, "Why do you keep saying I'm running away? I'm going to stay with Great-aunt Gertrude while I study photography with Mathew Brady."

"Well, then," she said, "I wish you a safe trip and that you might one day return to your family."

Aunt Hannah, apparently deciding that answer was as good as Lucy was likely to give, said, "There you are. Good wishes all around."

Mr. O'Rourke thumped his empty tin cup on the table. "I'm going to check the supplies and hitch the wagon. I should be leaving within the hour. If you two are coming, you'll have your horses saddled and be ready to go when I am."

THIRTY-SIX

Ambrose

My two older sisters were clearly on the outs with each other, and I couldn't figure out why. I was glad when Aunt Hannah suggested that each make a good wish for us to ease the tension, but whatever Lucy was angry about, she was not able to completely put her feelings aside.

When O'Rourke stood to go hitch his wagon, I followed. When we got to the stable, Jake had already fed Butter and taken her to the water trough. As I walked up to my horse, she raised her head and nickered.

I stroked her neck, then pressed my cheek against it.

"Good horse," O'Rourke said. He put leads on two mules and led them toward a wagon topped by a huge black box of a room. Maybe ten by fifteen feet. The words "O'Rourke Daguerreotype" were painted in a white arc on the side. Underneath them in a straight line was the word "Saloon."

"Butter was my tenth-birthday gift from my aunts," I said. "That was just before we moved from here to Hidden Springs. I named her Butterscotch, but that was too long, so I took to calling her Butter."

O'Rourke waved a hand in the direction of a black stallion. "That's Shadow. He was also a gift."

"Well," I said, "now that I see Butter has been fed and watered,

I'll be getting my belongings." I nodded and left, feeling awkward. All I knew about O'Rourke, Lucy had told me, which wasn't much. Delia had caught a ride with him when she ran away to persuade Aunt Hannah to come help Ma. She'd passed as a boy, wearing my clothes. Later, it turned out he was already a friend of Aunt Hannah's. As a photographer, he traveled back and forth over the same trails, taking pictures of people and places. I supposed that with all the folks heading west, there were plenty of new prospects every time he passed through.

Runaway. Lucy was focused on that, like she never forgave Delia for taking off. I thought she had last summer when Delia's friends showed up to stop Pa from kicking Delia. Then Pa had disowned Lucy. Just before Delia and Lucy left, we three had stood and hugged each other, and I thought all was right between us, but after the scene last night and the one at breakfast this morning, I figured I was wrong. Lucy held on to grudges.

I picked up my pack and hurried down the stairs as fast as my healing ribs would allow, meeting Delia on the way. She was wearing some getup with a skirt that stopped at the knees and trousers with puffy legs gathered at the ankles.

"What do you have on?" I asked.

Delia laughed. "You've never heard of bloomers?"

"I reckon I have. I just never saw any before. No woman in Hidden Springs would wear something like that."

She gave me a sideways glance as she walked, leaning toward one side as she struggled with her satchel. "How do you know that? Did you ask them all?"

"No." Seeing how aggravated she was, I decided to back off. "I'd carry the bag for you, but it's all I can do to carry my own with my sore ribs. What do you have in there? Bricks?"

She wrinkled her nose. "Don't you just think you're funny?" She rolled her eyes. "If you were a girl, you'd be weighed down by clothes, too."

"Well, if you're thinking of being a boy again, my trousers are too big for you now, and I don't have any spares anyway."

"Your old ones would still fit me, but I tossed them long ago. They were ragged by the time I got to Westport from the gold fields. You and my sisters keep growing, and I'm basically the same size as I was at thirteen."

115

"You're Ma's size," I said, "which isn't a bad one to be."

"Your pa thought it was. He called her puny, scrawny, and weak, and those were his nice words."

Obviously, Delia was in a bad mood and was going to find fault with anything I said. I could see she was working herself into a fit about the way Pa had treated our mother. I tended to agree with her, but I didn't want to start our trip on a bad note, so I tried changing the subject.

"Tell me something about O'Rourke," I said. "Lucy mentioned you traveled with him before."

"I met him on the wharf at St. Marys. He was drawing a picture of a steamship coming in. I was wearing your clothes, so he assumed I was a boy." A pleased smile crossed her face. "That thing he said last night about having his own timetable. He meant it. That's why I had to leave him and find a faster way to get to Aunt Hannah."

We went out the back door of the hotel. Across the yard at the stables, O'Rourke had finished hitching the team of mules to his wagon and was leading the black stallion to the back. "It's been four years. How come he's still hanging around?"

"Turns out he and Aunt Hannah have been friends for years."

"Oh?"

I guess Delia caught the drift of my question.

"Nothing romantic. Just friends." She sighed. "I guess she's never getting married. Maybe that's a good thing."

"Maybe," I agreed. "Pa says she's a suffragette."

Delia plunked her bag onto a bench. "You say 'suffragette' like it's a bad thing to be. I guess you learned that from your pa."

There I was, setting her off again. I should have known better than to mention Pa, but I was getting tired of her peevishness, so I decided to blow up the whole conversation. "Well, those women act like marriage is the worst thing that could happen to them, that's all."

"Well, marriage wasn't such a great thing for Ma, was it?" Delia shot back. She disappeared into the stable while I started fastening my bags behind Butter's saddle. Then I led the horse over to where O'Rourke was walking around his wagon, making sure everything was secure.

I looped Butter's reins around the pommel and reached into my pocket for the gold pieces that would pay for my travel. "Here's the fifty dollars for my fare." I handed the money to O'Rourke.

"A prompt payer. Just what I like to see." He took the coins and put them inside his black suit coat.

It seemed to me he was dressed awfully formal for traveling, but then, I thought about the itinerants that had passed through Hidden Springs and realized most of them were dressed the same, like they needed an extra respectable look.

Delia walked up then, leading her horse, a red stallion. Butter shuffled and nickered. Delia's horse answered. Then O'Rourke's horse joined the chorus with a whinny.

O'Rourke laughed. "One female and two males. This should be an interesting trip." He cocked an eyebrow as he took in Delia's clothes. "Bloomers?"

She cast him a chilly look. "It's either bloomers or I turn into a boy again." She rustled in a small bag tied to the saddle and brought out some money. "Here's my share of the money."

"I see prompt payment runs in the family." O'Rourke took the money and deposited it into the inside pocket of his coat.

Just then, the hotel's back door opened. Ella and Jennie raced out, followed by Aunt Hannah carrying a large tray covered with a heavy cloth. Lucy followed behind with a smaller, deeper pan.

"We brought you food for the trail," Ella said as she and Jennie came to a stop in front of us.

"Guess what we made for you," Jennie added.

As Aunt Hannah and Lucy drew closer, it wasn't hard to figure out. "I smell fried chicken," I said.

"And cookies," O'Rourke added.

"And fresh bread," Delia said.

"You have excellent noses for food," Aunt Hannah said. "Ryan, I expect you to return these pans on your next trip through."

"That'll be next spring," he said.

Jennie tugged at my hand. "Can we get a last hug goodbye?"

"For both of us?" I asked, sliding a glance at Delia.

Lucy let out a big breath. "Yes, both of you." She grasped Delia's hand and the little ones followed her lead. We circled and hugged, holding on for just a bit, until Lucy stepped back, wiped her eyes, and said, "Someday, I hope we can stay put with each other for a while. It seems like we're always saying goodbye."

THIRTY-SEVEN

Cordelia

We'd been on the road for an hour or so when I urged Flame to go faster until he came even with O'Rourke's wagon so we could talk.

"What's our first stop?" I asked him.

"Independence. We should be there by nightfall," Mr. O'Rourke replied. "A friend will let us stay the night as guests in his house." He slowed the mules to an amble. "The Parkers are pro-slavery. I know you have strong feelings against slavery, and I'm counting on you to hold your tongue. For myself, I figure out what my friends and I agree on and stick with those topics. Can I count on you to do the same?"

I felt a little twist in my gut, remembering Gabe, the runaway ten-year-old I'd met on the trail and later seen being towed back to his master by slave hunters. He'd stand and be pulled off his feet and dragged a yard or so before they let him stand again. I hadn't done anything to stop them, and Aunt Hannah had tried to reason me out of feeling guilty, telling me the law let the men treat him that way and would be against us if we tried to help him. She said we needed to change the law, but now, four years later, the laws were the same.

I sighed. "You can count on me."

"What about your brother? He seemed pretty proud of the way his pa stood up to slave hunters who came to your town."

"He is, but I'll talk to him."

"Best do that now. No telling who we'll meet on the road or how they'll challenge us."

"I will."

Mr. O'Rourke gave the reins a flip and urged the mules to speed up. I pulled Flame to a stop and waited for Ambrose to catch up. He was about twenty yards behind me.

When he came even, he asked, "Is something wrong? That talk between you and O'Rourke looked serious."

The wagon disappeared around a bend. Although the area was heavily wooded, there was no reason to fear losing Mr. O'Rourke. The road was well-worn, and he would stay on it.

"It was serious. He's planning to stop for the night with his friends that are pro-slavery, and he wants to make sure we won't say anything that will rile them."

"In other words, we can't speak up for what we believe."

"He'd like us to steer clear of politics, regardless of where we are or who we're with."

Ambrose's face had gone from worried to grim. "I can do that. Keeping thoughts to myself is something I got pretty good at last summer. I always thought Pa and I were on the same side in most everything. Then Mrs. Ava came along."

"We didn't have much of a chance to talk before. Tell me more about Mrs. Ava, as you call her. Lucy regrets introducing her to your father. She said so even before you showed up covered in bruises."

"That's because right after Lucy introduced them, Mrs. Ava, then Miss Carstairs, began taking over the house. Lucy had asked for help with the decorating, but she hadn't expected to be pushed aside and given no opinion at all in the matter. It was like Lucy was just the housekeeper in Pa's mind, unless, of course, he was finding a husband for her. That's what caused the problem to start with. Lucy was trying to distract Pa from finding her a husband."

"Lucy's told me as much," I said. "What else?"

"That's right. I forgot that you don't know the Fletchers. They run the Emporium. They're Mrs. Ava's cousins. Well, the wife is. Like I said last night, I overheard her and Mr. Fletcher talking about how Mrs. Ava had caused such a scandal in New York that Mr. Fletcher packed them up and moved them to Hidden Springs to escape the gossip. Mrs. Ava followed them. Later, I overheard Mrs. Fletcher telling Mrs. Ava she'd better not cause a scandal here. Mrs. Ava said not to worry, that Pa would do anything she wanted. She got that right."

Ambrose stopped for a breath.

I shook my head in wonder. "I wouldn't have thought any woman could tame Hiram."

"Well, she did. She talked Pa out of bringing Jennie and Ella home. Said they were morally weak like Ma and they'd bring down the children she and Pa would have. They were best left where they were. Then she started in on me."

"Your pa thought *you* were morally weak?" That was hard for me to believe. Hiram had always acted like Ambrose was a young god. "How could she have made him think that?"

"She tricked me, tricked both of us. She kept finding ways for me to be alone with her, sometimes just for a few seconds. Then Pa'd walk in, and she'd step back and say something like "Really!" in a huffy voice, like I'd said or done something wrong. I didn't know what. Then the night he tossed me out, she accused me of trying to force my attentions on her. Just as he came in the door, she shrieked and stumbled like she was going to fall. I reached out to catch her, but she shoved me away with one hand and yanked her bodice open with the other. There was a fresh scratch on her neck. Pa came running. That's when she accused me."

"He didn't listen to your side?"

Ambrose shook his head. "He just started cussing and swinging. Then he tossed me out the back door. He'd have kept hitting me except for Mr. Derryberry, the schoolteacher who is living in the cabin."

"I met him." I said.

"He's a good man. The best one Pa introduced Lucy to."

"Lucy's not interested in marrying any time soon."

"I know. That's why she was so interested in finding Pa a wife. So he'd have someone else to occupy his time and thoughts."

"Well, now he has."

"Yes, and now that Mrs. Ava is rid of all Pa's children, I wonder what she has planned next. I overheard a name—Gerald Ward. He's supposed to be somebody Mrs. Ava knew, maybe worked for. Anyway, his death was suspicious, and she tried to get some of his money after he died. Maybe she killed him. Maybe she'll kill Pa too after she gets him to make out a will giving her everything. Maybe that's what getting rid of me is all about."

That seemed more like the plot of a novel than real life, but I agreed with him. If Ambrose was right, Hiram was getting what he deserved, but Ambrose was losing everything he'd worked so hard for, and losing the father who once adored him. I had no sympathy for Hiram, but I hurt for my brother. He deserved so much more—and so did my sisters.

THIRTY-EIGHT

Hiram

It had been two weeks since Ambrose had made a pariah of me with his silence and slithered out of town. Only the Fletchers knew the whole story. Ava had told them, and they had spoken well of me to others. Not telling the whole truth, mind you, but telling enough that the townspeople knew I had just cause for giving the boy a sound thrashing and tossing him out.

Mayor Tompkins came around first. I expected it. After all, we worked together on the council and had the construction of the new city building to consider. That, at least, was on hold until next spring. I had talked with Mayfield, the stone mason, and he assured me he would take over Ambrose's role in the job. But Alice Collins refused to greet me when I patronized the dining room in her boarding house at lunch times. She sent that hateful Hogan girl to wait on me. And Doc Sloan gave me the cold shoulder at city council meetings. Reverend Sherwood preached a prodigal son sermon and looked directly at me.

Ambrose's sudden absence made problems for my businesses, as well. As Bob Clark had said, there was too much work for the two of us. I needed to hire someone fast. Wouldn't you know that suddenly all the boys I would have preferred to hire were busy. That left me with one applicant, Willie Hogan.

Why Willie wanted to work for me, I couldn't figure, but I hired him. He was usually five minutes late, but he did show up. He took over the livery stable with Bob's supervision. I wanted as little to do with the boy as possible. I had to pay him more than I had Ambrose even though he knew less and did less.

I missed my son. But I would soon have another. My heart swelled with pride every time I thought of the child now growing inside Ava. We would have a family to be proud of. The feelings of the town would pass as more people moved in and Ambrose became a faded memory.

THIRTY-NINE

Ambrose

I was used to rolling hills, open skies, and prairie except for trees mostly lining the Kaw and smaller streams in Kansas Territory. Here in Missouri, the trees were denser. The roads had more twists and turns, and O'Rourke's wagon sometimes disappeared as I went at a slower pace because of my injured ribs.

O'Rourke did stop frequently. When he wasn't talking to folks, he was taking a picture or drawing one. I had to admit, he was good at picture-making.

Delia spent a lot of time hovering around him while he worked, asking questions, clearly wanting to learn all she could about photography. There was something else in the way they huddled around the camera, something neither of them seemed willing to recognize. Lucy was probably right. They were attracted to each other. He was too old for her, around thirty, I reckoned, and she wouldn't be eighteen until next May. Still, there had been a wide difference in age between Ma and Pa. Of course, Ma and Pa hadn't had a love match. It was a marriage of convenience, and except for me, Ma hadn't lived up to her end of the bargain, which was giving Pa sons. She'd died trying, though.

Love matches. I didn't really know anyone who had one, so I wasn't sure I'd know what one looked like. Well, there was Pa and Mrs. Ava. He sure seemed in love with her, but I didn't think her feelings were the same, not when she'd lied to him in order to get rid of me. Some folks said love was blind, and that must be what happened to Pa. If that was true, love might be something to stay away from.

My thoughts strayed to Susan. I believed she liked me, but Pa said she was just looking to marry up. I wasn't in the least ready to think about marrying anyone. I was like Lucy, wanting to wait until I was older. Of course, Pa hadn't been in any rush to find me a wife. He kept me too busy working and probably figured he'd have to pay me more if I was going to support a wife. Well, I no longer had to worry about anyone marrying me to move up socially unless I found out what Mrs. Ava had done and convinced Pa. I wondered which would be harder to do.

I rounded a bend, and O'Rourke's wagon came into view. It was stopped at the side of the road. A stream flowed across our path, low water, so we should be able to cross it okay.

O'Rourke climbed down from the wagon seat and pointed to a large flat rock a few feet away. He handed Delia the big pan filled with fried chicken and biscuits. I reckoned it was time for dinner and kneed Butter to move a little faster.

FORTY

Cordelia

We had just set the food out on a large flat rock when Ambrose rode up and joined us. Filling the tin plates Aunt Hannah had included in the supply basket, we ate heartily. After finishing the chicken and biscuits, we each had a cookie and sat silently, resting a few minutes before continuing our journey. I watched the slow-moving flow of water rippling by before turning my attention to the trip ahead and, specifically, to the place we would spend the night.

I flicked a glance at Mr. O'Rourke. "How long until we make tonight's destination?"

"Maybe three hours. It should be almost dark."

"You said these folks are pro-slavery. Besides that, what are they like?"

"They're a family. Reverend Parker, his wife, and children. He had seven two years ago. There could be another by now."

"Or a new Mrs. Parker, if the old one gave out having babies," I said.

Ambrose coughed, and Mr. O'Rourke chuckled.

I frowned at them. "So the head of the family is a preacher. How can a man of God be for slavery?"

Ambrose put the last of his cookie in his mouth and raised his eyebrows, waiting for Mr. O'Rourke to answer.

"You will likely hear the reverend tell you in his own words."

"I thought we weren't supposed to talk about politics," Ambrose said.

"I'm glad to know Cordelia filled you in on the conversation etiquette," Mr. O'Rourke said. "The limits are on what you say, not on what others tell you. Reverend Parker is quite passionate about his position and will no doubt give a long speech about it, especially now, with everyone stirred up about John Brown and the incident at Harper's Ferry. Listen, nod, and keep quiet."

Ambrose and I exchanged looks.

Mr. O'Rourke laughed. "If you plan to travel beyond your own family, you must learn to associate with people of many opinions without ruffling their feathers." He paused before giving a slight smile. "In fact, even within your own family, it is sometimes a good course of action."

I wondered if he was thinking about my family or his own.

O'Rourke pointed to my bloomers. "Those may be all right for travel, but you must change. I hope you brought a dress. Reverend Parker, being a man of God and a Southerner, will expect a young lady to be properly clothed."

"I can't ride Flame in a dress," I grumbled.

"Then you can drive the wagon, and I'll lead your horse and ride Shadow. Go change while I saddle my horse."

FORTY-ONE

Ambrose

Dusk was fading into dark when we arrived at Reverend Parker's place. Pa would have been soaking up every detail of the enormous two-story, white house with a long porch and wooden columns. It smelled of class and money, two things Pa longed to have.

O'Rourke told Delia to guide the team of mules along a drive on the south side of the house. Lights shone through the first-floor glass windows on the front, and another three large windows lined one side. The house was rectangular, like ours but larger, maybe twelve feet longer and ten wider. I figured a family with seven children needed the extra space. Two small, whitewashed cabins sat behind the main house. Several Negro children about Jennie's age played in the yard.

A man called to us from the side of the porch and hurried down the steps. "There you are, Ryan. We've been half-expecting you for days now."

O'Rourke dismounted and strode to our host. The two shook hands and slapped backs. Then the man eyed Cordelia as she climbed down from the wagon. "You've married at last?" he asked O'Rourke.

"Hardly," O'Rourke said. "I'm taking these two young people to visit their great-aunt who lives in New York City. This lady is Cordelia Pierce, and this is her brother Ambrose. Cordelia,

Ambrose, meet Reverend Parker. If you weren't believers already, this man's sermons would convince you."

"Sir," I said, stepping forward and shaking hands.

Delia smiled and held out her hand.

"Pleased to meet you." The reverend lifted her fingers to his mouth and lightly brushed her knuckles with his lips.

His action worried me. What was I supposed to do when I was introduced to his wife and, if he had any, his daughters?

He called to one of the Negro boys who looked about seven years of age. The child ran to stand at attention in front of him.

"Get your pa to take care of my guests' animals," the reverend ordered.

"Yes, sir," the boy said and raced across the yard toward the shack he'd been playing near.

"Come on in." Reverend Parker motioned toward the door of his home. "We've finished supper, but Tillie was getting ready to serve up dishes of apple cobbler with thick cream. Will you join us for dessert?"

O'Rourke laughed. "What do you say, Pierces?"

My stomach rumbled at the thought. "I say yes."

"As do I," Delia said.

We followed the preacher up the front steps of his house and through the front door where a wide receiving area with glowing lanterns allowed me to get my first real look at our host. He was about Pa's age and height, a bit over six feet, but not as muscular, a medium build. His hair was dark blond with graying strands in his sideburns and pointed beard. His gray suit fit him perfectly.

"Mother," he called.

A woman bustled through the doorway, followed by three children under ten. "What is it, Father?"

"Ryan is here with two travelers. Have Tillie prepare dishes of cobbler for them."

"Right away." She turned to the oldest child. "Albert, relay your father's message to Tillie."

"Yes, Mother," the boy said and sped away on his errand.

Mrs. Parker extended her hand to O'Rourke in greeting. "It's good to see you again, Ryan, but you've arrived weeks too soon to photograph what will soon be the latest addition to our family. Perhaps, you'll be back in the spring."

"I will." He took her hand and held it briefly in his open palm.

I relaxed, seeing that I didn't have to kiss any fingers, lightly or otherwise.

O'Rourke reached for Delia's hand and drew her forward. "This is Cordelia Pierce, who is traveling to visit her great-aunt in New York City." He nodded toward me. "And her brother, Ambrose Pierce. They are the niece and nephew of my friend, Hannah True, who runs a well-reputed hotel in Westport."

"Friends of Ryan's are always welcome," Mrs. Parker said, giving echo to her husband's earlier sentiments. "Would you like to wash up before sitting down to dessert?"

We all said we would. One of the older sons led O'Rourke and me to a washroom while Mrs. Parker took Cordelia in another direction, presumably to similar accommodations reserved for the women of the house.

After our ablutions, we all came together in a formal dining room where a Negro maid was placing heaping bowls of apple cobbler around the table. The younger children were served their dessert in the kitchen while the four older Parker offspring, two boys and two girls, joined us at the dining room table. I guessed that the younger of the girls was about my age. The girls were Ruth and Rachel; the boys were Daniel and Samuel. It appeared this family did not believe in nicknames.

After a prayer led by Reverend Parker, a pitcher of thick cream was passed around. My mouth watered as I poured the sweet liquid onto my cobbler. Conversation was mostly limited to comments of 'delicious," and "the best ever" as we all dug into the tasty apple dish. When only a few spoonsful remained in my bowl, I glanced around the table, making sure I was on pace with the others. I didn't want to appear a glutton, but I didn't want to be the last to finish either. While making my survey, I locked eyes momentarily with Rachel, the daughter closest to me in age. Here eyelashes fluttered, and she flashed me a quick smile, lowered her gaze to her bowl, and then raised it, her lashes fluttering once more.

My heart hammered at this display of interest. But maybe I was wrong. I glanced about the table. No one seemed to be paying any attention. But why would they? Her glance had been too brief to be noticed by anyone who hadn't been looking directly at her as I had been. In some ways, Rachel reminded me of Susan. Both were blonde. But where Susan had brown eyes that warmed me, Rachel had blue eyes that sparkled and challenged me. Was I brave enough to return her interest? And to what end? I would be leaving tomorrow. I probably would never see her again. But I might. This is where she lived. I would be coming back this way. But only passing through, I reminded myself, absently spooning some cobbler and hitting my bottom lip, allowing a dribble of thick cream to run down my chin.

Embarrassed, I grabbed for the cloth napkin, my hand hit the water glass, and a few drops of the contents sloshed on the table. Everyone's eyes turned on me.

"Excuse me," I said, my face growing warm.

Delia smiled. "He's a growing boy, still in the awkward stage, like an overgrown puppy."

While I got even hotter, the adults chuckled. Through lowered eyes, I glanced toward Rachel. Her lips were pressed together. Was she laughing at me, too?

Rachel spoke then, not to me but to Delia. "So, Miss Pierce, have you previously visited your great-aunt or will this be your first trip to New York City?"

"My first trip. Until now, my travels have been limited to Westport and Kansas Territory."

Reverend Parker's face shifted from smiling indulgence to a scowl. "Kansas Territory, the lair of abolitionists seeking to destroy our Southern way of life, which was ordained by God, and the late abode of that madman, John Brown, who is now arrested for his assault on Harper's Ferry. About time he was stopped after the havoc he wreaked along Missouri's border with Kansas."

My stomach twisted, the apple cobbler churning, bile rising in my throat. Who would have thought the mere mention of Kansas would bring such a fervent reaction, the kind of thing O'Rourke had warned us about? I pressed the napkin to my lips and breathed.

Knowing Delia's strong opinions, I cleared my throat, which turned attention away from her to my lacking table manners. "Sorry," I mumbled.

Delia, however, didn't need my distraction. She laid her spoon aside, smiled, and pressed on. "Because of our hotel in Westport, and given the pro-slavery feelings there, we've learned to avoid those conversations with our guests. Given that Independence is also a main hub for traffic west, you must get the same mix of opinion here, Reverend Parker."

"We do," he replied, "and our merchants take the same non-committal path in their business dealings, but as a minister of God, I cannot do the same. I must lead my congregation and preach the true word about slavery. It has always existed, and the Bible supports it. Brown thinks he serves God, but by interfering with the God-ordained order of mankind, he really serves Satan."

I sat dumb, puzzled, remembering Reverend Sherwood's sermons about the evils of slavery and how he pointed to the Bible as support for his views. And here was Reverend Parker, another true Christian, pointing to the same Bible, and saying how it supported slavery. How could two devout men using the same book come to such different beliefs? How could the rest of us decide what was right or wrong? Was it all about what the people around us believed and taught us?

The conversation around me swirled, with Reverend Parker doing most of the talking. Tillie cleared the plates away, and we older males retired to the minister's library while the ladies gathered in the parlor for whatever women talked about.

FORTY-TWO

Cordelia

I almost choked at Reverend Parker's use of the Bible to justify slavery. Luckily, the men, Ambrose included, retired to the reverend's library for serious discussions, leaving us members of the gentler sex to discuss the "women's sphere," which was mostly limited to household talk and fashion.

Mrs. Parker picked up her knitting needles and yarn to work on a blanket for her coming baby. The yarn, a pastel blue, looked soft and warm. Seated on either side of her, daughters Ruth and Rachel embroidered flowers on table scarves.

Mrs. Parker rang a bell. When the Negro servant who had waited on us during dessert appeared, Mrs. Parker said, "Bring us some tea."

"Yes, ma'am," Tillie answered. She hurried from the room.

Mrs. Parker turned her attention on me. "You look young to be taking such a long trip with only your brother to look out for you."

"While he makes a suitable chaperone, it is I who looks out for him. I shall be eighteen soon while Ambrose has just turned fifteen." I flicked a glance at Rachel who had been noticeably flirting with Ambrose during dessert. Her eyes rounded in surprise.

"He looks older with that fringe of whiskers on his face," Mrs. Parker said. "Well, some boys mature early." She worked the needles, knitting and purling. "What trade does he plan to pursue?"

"He has several to choose from. He worked in. . . ," I stopped myself in time to exchange *his* for *our*, ". . . our father's blacksmith shop. He is also an excellent builder and stonemason, having apprenticed to one of the best while he was building a two-story home for our family."

"Well, he does sound accomplished," Mrs. Parker said.

"Yes, he also ran the livery stable next to the blacksmith business in Hidden Springs."

Mrs. Parker straightened in her chair and frowned. "Hidden Springs? Isn't that a free-state town?"

Now I'd done it, drawn politics in by accident. "There are mixed opinions all over Kansas Territory," I said, hoping Hiram's confrontation with slave hunters four years before hadn't been a topic of widespread gossip. Surely, something so small and long past would not be remembered here and now.

"True," Mrs. Parker said. "It's just that I heard something about it some time ago. I can't remember what exactly. Well, maybe it will come to me later."

"That's how it works for me. I remember things when my mind is on something else."

Tillie brought the tea tray and set it on a table beside Mrs. Parker's chair.

Mrs. Parker smiled. "Ruth, dear, pour the tea."

"Yes, Mother," Ruth said. She rose from her chair and busied herself with filling the cups. She turned to me. "Sugar?"

"No, plain," I said.

She placed the thin china cup on a saucer and handed them to me.

I raised the cup and sniffed. Chamomile. I touched the cup to my lips and sipped the hot liquid. Conversation buzzed around me about a coming church festival and a Bible study group.

"Are you a student of the Bible, Miss Pierce?" Mrs. Parker asked.

"Oh, yes," I replied. "My Aunt Hilda is married to a minister."

"What denomination?"

"Christian," I replied, hoping there was nothing political about being one. I stifled a yawn. "I'm so sorry, but travel has worn me out. I'd like to retire."

"Of course." She rang a bell, and Tillie entered the room.

"Show Miss Pierce to her room."

"Yes, Missus."

Relieved, I followed Tillie up the stairs to a small bedroom and found my satchel on a bench at the foot of the bed. Tillie turned down the blankets and asked if I needed anything else. I did not; at least, not something she could provide.

FORTY-THREE

Hiram

It was Saturday, late afternoon, almost three weeks since Ambrose had left town. I'd completed an order for axes and packed them for shipping. Rather than start work on a new order, I decided to have pie and coffee at Alice's boardinghouse. Now that Ambrose was gone, I found Susan Hogan less objectionable than I had. Plus, her pies were the best in the Territory, at least as far as I'd tasted.

She was quick to wait on me. When she set a slice of apple pie and a cup of coffee in front of me, I asked, "Is Mrs. Collins in? I'd like to speak to her."

"I'll check," she said in her usual chilly tone before turning her back and marching away. That was fine. I supposed she was still angry about the thrashing I'd given Ambrose. Lots of folks were; Alice Collins included.

I missed Alice's friendship. I realized now that she had been right to turn down my proposal of marriage. With her head for business, she might have tried to run things if we had married. Ava was just right for me. Not only was she young enough to have children, she understood all the social rules and how to build a circle of powerful friends. Still, I wished she had a better head for money. Ava's tastes were excellent, but they were also expensive. I had two successful businesses, but with Ambrose gone, costs for the livery stable and the blacksmith shop were up.

Ambrose had a good head for numbers and always found ways to save money. Willie Hogan came to work for his pay and didn't care that expenses went up because of his carelessness.

I'd tried not to care what happened to Ambrose, but sometimes I picked up a hammer he had used or a tool he had fashioned for the stable, or looked at his horse's empty stall, and I saw him in my mind's eye, pictured the boy who had followed me, proudly shown me his work, bent over sketches and plans with me. He had been my right arm. How could he have turned on me the way he had?

In spite of his betrayal, I still worried about him. If anyone would know where he was and what he was doing, Alice would. Or Susan Hogan, but I'd never ask her.

Yes, Alice was the one to query. She had taken Ambrose in and nursed his wounds.

I took a bite of pie and chewed, reflecting on what I might say to Alice.

"What is it, Hiram?" Alice's voice was brusque. She stood before me, one hand one her hip and a sheaf of papers in the other, her glasses pulled down on the bridge of her nose. Her frown deepened the wrinkles around her eyes, showing her age.

I swallowed the bit of pie and cleared my throat. "I wondered if you'd heard from Ambrose."

"What does that matter to you?"

"He's my son. He betrayed me, but. . ."

She cut me off. "Ambrose never betrayed you. Whatever your wife said he did, she lied. I think in your heart, you know that. You know you tossed out a good son for a deceitful liar."

With that, she turned and stomped from the room.

I had thought she might relent and we might return to our old friendship. But like the others I had counted as friends, Doc. Sloan and Mayor Tompkins, she had sided with Ambrose.

FORTY-FOUR

Ambrose

October 31, 1859

After two weeks on the trail, we finally arrived in St. Louis. If it weren't for O'Rourke's frequent stops to chat with previous clients and drum up business along the way, we might have arrived the previous evening. It was mid-afternoon, a sunny but chilly day because of the blustery north breeze, when we entered the city I'd heard so much about. St. Louis was the biggest town I'd been in, one hundred sixty thousand people.

I rode Butter down a street lined with businesses. O'Rourke rode his horse and Delia, who had changed out of bloomers into a dress, drove the wagon.

O'Rourke came even with the wagon and pointed toward a dry goods store. We stopped in front of it, secured our animals, and went inside. The owner, a tall, thin man, greeted us. I came to his chin, he was that tall. I usually didn't have to look up to see someone's eyes, but I did him. It made me feel younger than I had for some time, like a boy instead of the man I felt I was becoming.

It turned out this man was O'Rourke's cousin although there wasn't much family resemblance beyond them both being tall. Gilbert O'Rourke wore a white apron over his dark trousers and white shirt. He offered us seats by a potbellied stove and poured coffee into tin cups before handing Ryan O'Rourke a bundle of mail that had been gathering for him—for months from the size of the stack.

Gilbert gave directions for stabling the animals. Delia came with me and drove the wagon into the stable behind the store. When we finished watering and feeding the animals, we returned to the store.

"There are sleeping rooms above," Gilbert said. "And there's a party tonight to celebrate Halloween. You won't want to miss it."

Gilbert led us up narrow stairs to our rooms. "There's no plumbing above the first floor," he said, "so you'll have to carry water." He pointed to a bucket on the floor by the door. "There's a well out back."

I offered to get water for both Delia and myself. I was pumping water when a girl of about my age greeted me.

"Hello, have you seen my father?"

I looked into twinkling blue eyes and swallowed hard. When I could speak, I said, "I don't know. What is your father's name?"

"Mr. O'Rourke."

I stopped pumping and stared, the first Mr. O'Rourke coming to my mind being my traveling companion. Then my brain skipped to the second possibility. "You mean Mr. Gilbert O'Rourke?"

She laughed, her eyelids flashed closed and then open again. "Yes, silly. Who else would I mean?"

"I just arrived with Mr. Ryan O'Rourke."

"Cousin Ryan is here? How wonderful. Perhaps he'll take a picture of me in my Halloween dress." She smiled, showing her dimples. "I'm Shauna."

"Ambrose Pierce." Flustered, I went back to pumping water.

"Where did you meet my cousin?"

"In Westport at my Aunt Hannah's." Still pumping furiously, I looked up. A moment later, water spilled over the top of the bucket and landed on my boots and trouser cuffs. "Ahhhh!" I wanted to say something stronger but it would be bad manners. "My sister's waiting," I said. "I'd better get this water to her so she can wash up."

"A sister? You're both traveling with my cousin?"

Her face took on a calculating look, and I figured she was thinking something false. I supposed the Lothario ways Delia said O'Rourke had were not unknown to his cousin. "We both had reasons to travel to New York City. Since Mr. O'Rourke was going there, we each paid fifty dollars to travel with him. Cheaper than the train, but takes considerably longer."

"I suppose."

Hefting the full bucket, I said, "I have to go. Maybe I'll see you at the party. We were invited."

"Then I will see you there."

I hurried away, sloshing water, stopping to pour out enough so I wouldn't get the floors inside wet when I climbed the stairs.

Delia's door was open when I reached her room. She was sitting in a chair by the window, brushing her hair. "So who was the girl at the pump?"

Her voice had a teasing tone, and I knew I was in for it.

"Her name is Shauna, and she is Gilbert O'Rourke's daughter."

"Will she be at the party tonight?"

"She said she would."

"Hmmm."

"What's that supposed to mean?"

She chuckled. "All the girls like you, Ambrose. Lucy told me all about Susan Hogan back in Hidden Springs. Then there was Rachel Parker in Independence. Now here we are in St. Louis for barely an hour, and another girl is sweet on you already."

"She is not. We just spoke. That's all." I poured half the water into the pitcher and turned to leave. "I'm going to wash up."

Delia laughed. "Have to look nice for Shauna. And I thought Mr. O'Rourke was a ladies' man."

My face getting hot, I stomped out of the room.

FORTY-FIVE

Cordelia

Maybe I shouldn't have teased Ambrose, but the way girls seemed to fall for him in an instant amazed me. I spent a few moments trying to see my brother through the eyes of Rachel Parker or this new girl, Shauna. He looked older than fifteen with that stubble of hair on his chin. Beyond his being my brother, part of my difficulty in understanding his appeal to girls was his physical resemblance to Hiram, something he shared with my sister's. Well, there was no use continuing this line of thought.

I put on my one clean dress, a blue calico, and all three of my petticoats. I had nothing for a disguise, save a black lace shawl I had crocheted two winters ago as proof to my sisters that I could perform such womanly tasks if I chose to. The shawl was oblong in shape. I draped it over my head and flung one end across my face. It would have to do.

Changing my mind, I decided to save the mask effect for the party, draped the shawl over my shoulders, and went downstairs to see whether I would have to wait until the party for nourishment.

The first person I saw was Shauna, the girl who had talked with Ambrose earlier at the pump. She was dumping apples into a large wooden tub filled with water.

She looked up as I entered the room. "Hello." She dropped a final apple into the tub and stood to smile at me.

"Hello," I replied. "I'm Cordelia Pierce. I saw you talking with my brother earlier."

Before she could answer, a red-haired woman rushed into the room. "Shauna, have you seen your father? We need to set up the refreshment table."

"He and Cousin Ryan were at the stables earlier."

At that moment Shauna's father and Ryan O'Rourke entered. With two O'Rourke men present, I realized I would have to resort to first names or my thoughts would get tangled. Ryan was carrying two sawhorses and Gilbert a long plank. They went out the front door, and Ryan arranged the sawhorses on the boardwalk in front of the store, and Gilbert topped them with his plank. They came back through, exited the back door, and returned with two more planks.

Mrs. O'Rourke spread a long oilcloth over the makeshift table. As if on cue, a dozen ladies appeared, carrying dishes of food for a pot luck meal, including fried chicken, sliced ham, biscuits, pies, cake, and cookies.

Shauna slipped a sliver of ham from a platter, popped the piece in her mouth, and motioned toward the platter. "Have some."

I looked around and saw a woman take a cookie from a plate. Not able to resist any longer, I reached in my pocket for my handkerchief and selected a small piece of ham. After taking a bite, I covered the remainder with my kerchief and continued walking about, enjoying the games and laughter, occasionally having another bite of meat.

Children showed up in costume, and several women set out a stack of tin plates and called for silence and a blessing before the meal. Gilbert said a quick "Thank you for this food and this good company," and everyone lined up. By the time I filled a plate, folks were sitting along the edge of the boardwalk in front of the stores. Ambrose was standing some distance off with Shauna. The two talked animatedly, obviously enjoying each other's company, so I found a vacant spot on the walk away from them.

Minutes later, Ryan, a patch covering one eye and a pirate's hat on his head, sat down beside me. "What do you think of the family so far?"

"They seem nice, and it looks like Ambrose is getting along well with Shauna."

"She's growing up so fast. It's been two years since I last saw her, but she was a child only that short time ago."

"I feel the same about Ambrose. We saw each other briefly last summer, but before that, it had been four years. My baby brother is growing fuzz on his face. And the girls seem to like it."

"Will you be preaching abstinence to him?"

"I will," I said. I hadn't thought of it before, my brother being physical with a young woman, "knocking boots" as Aunt Hannah would have put it. But now? I took a more direct look at the flirtation going on between Ambrose and Shauna, then thought about Rachel Parker in Independence and of Lucy's comments about Ambrose and Susan Hogan. The proper treatment of a young lady was not something I imagined Hiram had spent much time discussing with Ambrose. My guess was that Hiram's attitude was for a boy to have a good time with any willing female. What might happen as a result would be her problem.

I cast a sideways glance at Ryan. "So you're a pirate?"

"I am, but walking around with one eye covered makes objects appear a bit different. What about you?"

I set my empty plate on the ground in front of me and caught the end of my shawl, flipping it across my face, covering my mouth and nose. "I'm a fortune teller," I said.

"So will you tell mine?"

I sighed. "Unfortunately, I have no cards or crystal ball with which to see the future."

He reached into his pocket and pulled out a deck of cards. "Will these do?"

I laughed. "How do you happen to be carrying around a deck of cards?"

"I thought as the evening went on, some of the men might tire of watching children's games and join me in a game of poker."

"I hadn't taken you for a gambler, Mr. O'Rourke."

"Not with any regularity, but I indulge in a game now and then."

Gilbert and his wife took a seat near Ambrose and Shauna, and I was struck by the lack of resemblance between Shauna and either of her parents. I remarked on it to Ryan.

He sighed. "Yes, what I've heard may be true."

"And what have you heard?"

He frowned. "I shouldn't have said anything. It's a private matter."

"Don't you trust me to keep a secret?"

"I do, but it's nothing of importance to anyone except my cousin's family."

Irritated, I said, "You brought it up, and now I'm curious. I promise not to tell anyone. If it is so inconsequential, I may even forget it."

"You, forget something? I doubt that."

"So?"

"I heard my parents talking about Gilbert and Isabel having been married for almost six years and not having any children. Then Isabel went away for several months. When she returned, she had Shauna in her arms." He smiled. "A gift from God—or a loose woman."

Remembering his Lothario ways, the "loose woman" term set my nerves on edge. It was the sort of thing Hiram said about Ma when he'd called me a bastard. I glanced at Shauna, sitting between her parents, unaware of her possible beginnings in life, her wavy black hair shining in the firelight. I swallowed hard, suddenly realizing the truth—she was Ryan's daughter. The "loose woman" was someone from his past.

Shauna was fourteen, which meant Ryan would have been sixteen or seventeen when she was born. I remembered railing at him for his Lothario ways and asking him if any children had resulted from them. He had said, "Not that I know of." Thinking of the easy, guilt-free way he had revealed her possible adoption, I believed he truly did not know she was his child.

I had no proof except what was before my eyes and knowledge of the way families worked in these situations. Ryan's parents had kept their grandchild close without exposing her to the gossip that had dogged me all my life.

I was silent for so long that Ryan noticed. "You've been staring at Shauna for a full minute. What are you thinking?"

"That the words, 'loose woman,' come off your lips so easily. What about 'loose men,' of which you are one? Men who go about carelessly creating children and then leave them to fate? Lucky Shauna, who has two parents who love her. Unlucky me, to get Hiram for a stepfather." Shaking with anger, I shot to my feet.

Eyes rounding, he realized his mistake and reached for my hand. "I'm sorry. I didn't think . . ."

I jerked my hand away. "Do you ever?" I drew my shawl tight around my shoulders. "I'm tired. Good night."

I stormed away, stomping up the outside stairs to the rooms above the store and hurrying down the hallway. Entering my room for the night, I flung the shawl on the bed and paced the floor for a minute before being drawn to the window, wondering what Ryan was doing now.

I saw him standing with Ambrose, who must have seen my sudden leave-taking. Ambrose looked up toward my window. I stepped back, hoping he hadn't seen me, wondering what Ryan was saying.

What did it matter what he was saying? I dove onto the bed, rolled over on my back, and covered my face with my hands. Why was I so upset about the possibility of Ryan being Shauna's father and his casual attitude about her creation?

The answer surprised me: I was starting to look at Ryan as more than a friend, as a companion, someone I might have a relationship with, that I might even marry if he returned my feelings. Now, that was impossible. I could never marry a man who had so little respect for women. Why was I attracted to unsuitable men? First, there had been Max, who shot a man dead protecting his sister's virtue. I could never make a life with someone who at any moment might be arrested for murder.

There was a knock at the door.

"Delia, are you okay?"

Ambrose.

"I'm fine," I called to him. "I just need some sleep."

What was a lie among family?

FORTY-SIX

Ambrose

Delia obviously didn't want to talk, and I was suddenly out of the party mood and tired, so I went to my room. Halloween celebration sounds drifted up, making sleep impossible. Since it was past time that I wrote to my sisters and to Mrs. Collins, I got out paper and pencil and settled on the bed, putting a thin sheet of wood beneath the paper so I could write. I would ask Mrs. Collins to share the letter with all my friends in Hidden Springs, Susan in particular.

But first, I would write to my sisters.

> Dear Lucy, Ella, and Jennie,
> It is Halloween, and we have reached St. Louis. We entered near the levee and saw dozens of steamboats moored or paddling slowly down the Mississippi, a grand river. When I asked how wide it was here, I got different answers, but most put the width between one-third and one-half mile.
> I went to a Halloween party on the street tonight. Gas street lamps on the corners cast spooky shadows. Ryan O'Rourke dressed as a pirate and Delia as a fortuneteller. I did not have a costume but liked seeing them.

O'Rourke has cousins here, and we are staying in rooms above their store. Delia had a squabble with O'Rourke and left the party. Neither will talk about it, so they'll have to work it out on their own.

The nights are getting cold, but O'Rourke knows people along the way, so we are often allowed to sleep in a barn if there is no room in the house. People welcome him and enjoy his stories. He soaks up news as he travels, but I guess you already know that since he's stopped by the hotel several times over the years.

I hope you are all well and are sending letters to me at Aunt Gertrude's. I am eager to get there and read them, but we have weeks to go before that happens.

Your brother, Ambrose

I folded the letter, addressed it, and sealed it. Hearing a fiddle tuning up, I went to the window and peered out. Couples were squaring off in the street. I thought of going down, but then I saw Shauna and some boy standing together in the dance area. She was tapping her foot, impatient for the dance to begin. I would be moving on in the morning. I might as well try to get some sleep.

FORTY-SEVEN

Cordelia

The next morning, we said our goodbyes to Ryan's cousins. I couldn't help paying close attention to Ryan's parting with Shauna. Seeing his teasing, carefree attitude made me certain that he had no idea he was saying goodbye to his own daughter. But the sudden knitting of Isabel's brows when he kissed Shauna on the forehead and hugged her made me aware of her concern. Or was I imagining it. There were many girls in the world with Ryan's dark hair and blue eyes. They weren't all his children. At least, I hoped not.

Besides, it wasn't the possibility that Shauna was his child that truly put me off. It was that to him the mother who gave her life had to be a "loose woman." Why couldn't she simply be a woman who had let love rule her heart and realized too late that what was for her an act of love was nothing more than "knocking boots" for the man.

In defiance, and since we were leaving, I wore my bloomer outfit, which had Mr. and Mrs. O'Rourke raising their eyebrows. Shauna laughed, her eyes shining, while I explained that riding a horse was much easier this way. I didn't add that I had no intention of driving the wagon, which would allow Ryan to come alongside on Shadow and attempt to strike up a conversation.

We had gone maybe five miles when Ambrose edged Butter up even with me and asked, "What's with you and O'Rourke?"

"What do you mean?" I asked although I knew perfectly well what he meant.

He let out an exasperated groan. "You're not talking to him."

"He's not talking to me either. Hasn't said a word. Not even about me wearing bloomers."

"He looks like he wants to say something but doesn't think you'll receive it well."

"Then, he is being extraordinarily perceptive this morning."

"Does that mean he wasn't very perceptive last night?"

I nodded. "It does."

"What did he say?"

"Nothing that bears repeating."

Ambrose shook his head. "Are you going to keep this up all the way to New York City?"

"And beyond," I assured him.

"Ugh," he responded, slowed Butter to a walk, and waited for O'Rourke in the wagon. Maybe he would have better luck finding out why I was angry with O'Rourke from him. I doubted it though. I wasn't even sure O'Rourke understood.

FORTY-EIGHT

Ambrose

It had been eight days since we left St. Louis, and Delia was still on the outs with O'Rourke. They barely spoke unless absolutely necessary. We had reached the Ohio River and stopped at a farm dwelling. O'Rourke charmed his way into a meal for us and the use of the barn for sleeping as a frigid rain was falling. After we stabled and fed the animals, the farmer's wife served us a good meal of stew and biscuits, and we retired to the barn. Not yet sleepy, I pulled the book of fables from my pack. I hoped I might find some moral that would make Delia rethink her continuing anger toward O'Rourke.

A lantern hanging from a hook cast light and a little warmth in the enclosed area. I carried the book into its circle and drew one of the buffalo robes O'Rourke had pulled from the wagon around me. I settled on a stack of hay and began turning the pages.

"What have you there?" O'Rourke asked.

"A book of fables my mother made me," I said.

Delia smiled. "I remember watching her embroider the cover and draw the pictures for the inside pages."

"Artwork?" O'Rourke held out his hand. "May I see?"

"Sure." I passed the book to him.

He examined the cover. "The stitching is fine. You've taken very good care of this."

"I look at it sometimes, puzzling over the morals to the stories, looking for guidance. Ma always seemed to find the right fable for any occasion. I don't do as well." I pulled my knees up and hugged them to my chest. "Sometimes the story doesn't seem to fit the lesson at the end."

O'Rourke opened the book and his eyes lighted up. "Your mother was a talented artist."

Delia drew her buffalo robe tight, fury in her eyes. "I suppose even a loose woman can have talents."

O'Rourke's face flushed.

My mouth fell open.

"I was only speaking generally about a common situation," he said.

"It's only a common situation because there are men who make it so," Delia shot at him. She drew the robe over her head, turned her back to us, and lay curled on the straw floor, obviously done with us for the night.

"Delia," I said, wanting to somehow ease the tension in the room.

She pulled the robe away from her face long enough to instruct me on fables to review. "Ryan should see 'The Two Frogs' for an admonition to do nothing without regard to the consequences and you, dear brother, should search for a tale warning you to mind your own business." With that she once again covered her head.

O'Rourke handed the book to me, said goodnight, and stretched out on the hay.

I sat holding it for some time, turning the pages, wondering what fable Ma would select if she were here.

FORTY-NINE

Hiram

It was two weeks until Christmas. Ava was excited, ordering who knew what from Fletcher's Emporium and planning a huge party. She'd invited Mayor Tompkins and Doc Sloan, and even Alice Collins, although Ava didn't get on that well with Alice. To my surprise, all three had replied with their acceptances. Perhaps the Christmas spirit had worked in my favor.

I stood in the smithy, pounding metal, the thought of Christmas reminding me that five years before, Mark, my second son to make it into the world alive, had been born. What a wonderful Christmas that had been. Then the crushing blow of his death a week later on New Year's Day. Why?

I put those thoughts behind me. Ava was with child. I would have my new son in May. Surely, it would be a boy. I needed a son to carry on my work. With Ambrose gone, I—.

"Mr. Pierce."

"What is it, Willie?"

"I wondered if I might leave now. All the work is done."

"Bob," I said to Clark, "check to see if he's taken proper care of the animals."

Bob nodded and left his station at the hearth. "Come on, Willie. I'll have a look."

They disappeared into the livery stable. Willie was always

anxious to be gone. That was the difference between a hired boy and a son.

Ambrose.

Once more, I pushed him out of my mind. I would have more sons. Better sons. Sons who would respect me and not try to take what was mine.

Hiram's Boy

PART III

Hazel Hart

FIFTY

Ambrose

I'd thought the Mississippi River was huge, but the Atlantic Ocean took my breath away. A cold breeze blew in off the water, chilling me even though I wore two shirts and two pairs of trousers. Delia had put on all three of her petticoats and was wearing her bloomers underneath them. O'Rourke was wrapped in a huge buffalo robe. With gloved hands, we urged our animals on through the frigid countryside.

It was New Year's Eve when we first saw the gas lights of New York City in the distance. As we drew near Great-aunt Gertrude's home, I wondered what she would be like. A widow in her sixties, Aunt Gertrude was a year older than her sister, my Grandmother True, who had been bedridden for years. By choice, at first, she had taken to her bed after Grandfather True's death, but now she was so weak she could hardly make her way between the chamber pot and her bed.

When we had given O'Rourke the address on Long Island, he said his family lived only blocks from there. We stopped in the street in front of our great-aunt's house, a three-story, gabled home set to the rear of a large lawn. I wondered if there was a shelter for our horses.

"Go knock," O'Rourke said. "I'll wait."

Delia and I slid off our horses and walked up the flagstone

walk, leaving tracks in the fresh snow. Delia struck the iron knocker three times, and we stood shivering in the lightly falling snow.

A middle-aged woman in a mobcap and white apron opened the door. Her eyebrows shot up at sight of us. "I suppose you're the niece and nephew Mrs. Oaks has been expecting."

"Yes, Ma'am," I said. "I'm Ambrose Pierce, and this is my sister, Cordelia."

"Come in, then," she said. "I'll announce you."

Delia glanced at O'Rourke's wagon. "Our friend is waiting. I must let him know we are welcomed so he can continue to his home."

"And we need to get our horses out of the cold," I said.

She frowned.

A tapping noise came from behind her. "What is it, Orna? Why are you holding the door open, letting in the cold air?"

"Your family has arrived," the woman answered. "They want to get their horses out of the cold."

The elderly woman came forward, limping a bit, but stepping quickly for someone with a cane. She peered around us to see O'Rourke's wagon and our horses on the street. "Is that gentleman with you?"

"He is and he isn't," Delia replied. "He accompanied us here, but he is going on to his own family who live on Fifth Avenue."

"That's a fine address for an itinerant photographer," she said. "Very well, let him know all is well here, and take your horses to the stable behind the house."

"Yes, ma'am," I said.

"Aunt Gertrude," she corrected me.

"Go on in and warm up, Delia," I said. "I'll say goodbye to O'Rourke and take care of our horses."

"Tell Mr. O'Rourke thank you for getting us here safely," Delia said.

"I will."

She stepped inside, and the door closed.

I hurried to the street and spoke to O'Rourke. "Delia told me to thank you for getting us here safely."

His smile was pained. "Goodbye, and good luck finding what you're looking for."

He urged his mules forward, and I took our horses' reins and led them around the side of the house to a stable with living quarters above it.

A man greeted me and promised he'd take care of the horses and bring in our saddlebags and other possessions.

I hurried to the house and stopped at the back door, trying to figure out whether to knock when a woman with flour on her apron opened the door. "Are you Miss Pierce's brother?" she asked.

"Yes." I took a deep breath, inhaling the warmth and good smells of the kitchen.

"Come in. Mrs. Oaks is waiting for you in the parlor." She turned and rang a bell.

Orna bustled into the room. "There you are. Come, I'll show you the way to the parlor."

Doors lining the hallway were closed. Perhaps, some rooms were not heated. When we entered the parlor, a fire blazed in the fireplace. Delia was seated on a couch beside Aunt Gertrude.

"I'll take your coat, now, sir," Orna said.

"Yes." Feeling awkward, I fumbled with the buttons, slid my arms out of the sleeves, and let her take the coat from the room, I supposed to hang it on a hook near the main entrance. Or would she take it to my room, wherever that was to be?

I looked to Delia for reassurance. Her eyes rounded. She shook her head and cast a sideways glance at Aunt Gertrude. If anyone needed reassurance, it appeared to be Delia.

FIFTY-ONE

Cordelia

From the moment Aunt Gertrude swept me into the parlor, I felt ill at ease among such luxury. The fireplace was stone with a black walnut mantel topped with white marble. The side tables matched, made of the same dark, chocolate brown wood with white marble tops. Lighted lamps on the mantel and two side tables gave a soft glow to the spacious room.

Aunt Gertrude waved her hand toward a medallion-backed sofa. "Please have a seat." She rang a bell that had rested on one of the tables. Orna appeared.

"Is someone helping Mr. Pierce with the animals?"

"Yes, ma'am," Orna replied.

It took me a moment to realize that by Mr. Pierce she meant Ambrose. I wanted to say he had just turned fifteen and was hardly a mister yet, but I presumed this was all some formal etiquette I knew nothing about. Looking at my lavish surroundings, I realized I was ill-prepared for life in this house.

Just how ill-prepared was about to be revealed.

"Very well then," Aunt Gertrude said. "When Mr. Pierce comes in from his duties, bring him here. In the meantime, bring some tea. Also, check on preparations for the New Year's Eve social."

"A social? A party? Tonight?" I seemed incapable of forming a complete sentence.

"Of course, dear. What's the new year without a party to celebrate?"

For weeks, I had been envisioning Aunt Gertrude as a copy of her younger sister, my grandmother. Except for the white hair, they seemed nothing alike. Whereas Grandmother True had spent the better part of the decade following my grandfather's death in mourning, taking to her bed and filling her life with a persistent whine, Aunt Gertrude's eyes shone with vitality. I breathed a sigh of relief at that, but then, after taking another look around the sumptuously furnished room, my nerves tightened. I knew how to work; I didn't know how to attend socials. Aunts Hilda and May entertained frequently, but I was never invited to their gatherings. Aunt Hannah's informal holiday celebrations at the hotel did not prepare me for upper-class society.

To emphasize my lack of social training, Orna arrived with a silver tea set and fine china. She poured cups of tea. While my aunt and I continued our conversation, Orna set out dessert plates with pastries, apple slices, and cheese.

"Come, have some tea and a pastry," Aunt Gertrude said. And then, "You haven't answered my question about what holidays are for if we don't celebrate them."

I coughed. "What, indeed?" I swallowed and pushed forward, intending to get the obvious in clear view. The most vivid New Year's Eve of my life had been the one on which my week-old infant brother had died. I pushed the memory down and replied, "However, I have nothing to wear to such a fine party as I'm sure you are having. The three petticoats and pair of bloomers I have on are all I have in the way of undergarments, and while I do have a better bodice and skirt in my satchel, I am certain it is not appropriate for formal wear."

Aunt Gertrude's green eyes sparkled. "Don't worry. It may have taken you weeks to arrive, but the mail between here and Westport is much faster. Your Aunt Hannah sent your measurements, and I have had my seamstress make up a complete wardrobe for you, including a lovely gown for such occasions as this evening. I am sure all the young men in attendance will find you quite attractive."

At that moment, Orna arrived with Ambrose. "Here is Mr. Pierce," she announced.

I glanced at Ambrose's flushed face. His gaze caught mine,

seeking some assurance from me that I didn't have to give. I forced a smile.

"Your coat, sir," Orna prompted.

Ambrose shrugged out of the garment and handed it over.

"Do come in and have some tea," Aunt Gertrude said.

Ambrose looked down at his trousers, brushed them, and moved uneasily to a wing chair next to Aunt Gertrude. She poured him a cup of tea and offered a dessert plate of pastry.

"Thank you." He set the cup on a side table, took a bite of the pastry, and shifted his gaze between the two of us.

I spoke up. "Aunt Gertrude says there is to be a party here this evening, and we are *invited*." I put some emphasis on "invited" so he would know it was a command, not an invitation.

Ambrose cast an alarmed look at his clothing. "But. . . ."

Aunt Gertrude interrupted. "No buts, young man. If you are about to plead a lack of wardrobe, as your sister did, I can assure you, as I did her, that there is no cause for concern. I have taken care of everything."

"Oh." Ambrose took a rather large bite of the pastry, either out of hunger or a desire to have an excuse not to speak. He chewed vigorously and swallowed, his Adam's apple bobbing as he did so. "When?" he stammered, "I mean, what time?"

"Guests should begin arriving at eight this evening. About two hours from now. As soon as you finish your refreshments, Orna will show you to your rooms. Each has a bathing room and water is being heated. When you have finished your ablutions, you will find your evening wardrobe laid out for you."

"Oh," Ambrose said and took another large bite of biscuit.

I smiled at his discomfort. Misery really does love company.

FIFTY-TWO

Ambrose

Orna led Delia and me down a long hallway on the second floor. "Here is your room, sir," she said.

I was still having a hard time with being called sir. I smiled tightly at Delia, and she returned the smile.

"Benjamin should be drawing your bath now," Orna said.

"Benjamin?" I asked.

"Your valet," she answered.

"Valet?"

Orna smiled. "Yes, sir." She turned to Delia. "Your room is across the hall. Callie will be assisting you."

Delia stood still and stared at her.

"Come," Orna said when Delia didn't move.

Delia followed and, moments later, was ushered into a room a few feet down the hall on the opposite side from mine.

I turned the knob and entered my room. There was a four-poster bed of black walnut, which seemed to be the favored furniture wood for the house, with a thick comforter and pillows. A chest of drawers and a wardrobe were made of the same wood. A fire blazed in the hearth. I gazed at the thick drapes on the wall and the carpeted floor, and wondered if Pa knew Ma had such a well-off relative. I thought of Ma's hard life and how just a little of the money it took to keep up this place would have eased it. If she had

had such creature comforts as these, would she have lived a longer life?

"Wow, Ma," I muttered.

A door on my right opened, and a freckle-faced boy about my age poked his head out. "There you are, Mr. Pierce. Your bath is ready. If you find the temperature not to your liking, turn the faucet on the left for more hot water. "

"In there?"

"Yes, sir." He smiled. "While you're bathing, I'll lay out your evening clothes. There's a bell pull by the bed. Ring if you need anything."

"Thank you," I said.

We stood looking at each other for what seemed like a full minute.

He finally asked, "Will that be all?"

"Yes," I said.

He went out the door, and I stepped into the room with the copper tub. Beside the tub, there was a stand containing a built-in basin with faucets. Above the stand was a shelf holding a mirror and a razor for shaving. I swiped my hand across my chin, feeling the week's growth of fuzz. Should I continue growing what was now a sparse beard or shave? I'd think about it later.

I stripped off my shirt and trousers and stepped into the tub. The water was lukewarm and settled around my thighs. The faucet on the left would add hot water, according to Benjamin. I turned the faucet. Cool water flowed. I sighed. A modern convenience that didn't work as described. Suddenly the water turned scalding hot. Leaping to the edge of the tub, I swung my feet over the edge, letting the water continue to run. After a minute, I turned off the water and swirled the hot and cold water in the tub, blending the heat to a bearable temperature. Slipping into the tub, I reached for the soap, lathered a cloth, and began bathing, starting with my hair and working my way down. Soon I was clean, but I had no notion of what to do about the dirty bath water.

Stepping out of the tub, I pulled the plug to drain the water, wondering what receptacle it emptied into. I reached for a towel, and after peering at myself in the mirror, I decided to keep the beard. It made me look older, and I might need that in order to get people to give me the information I needed about Mrs. Ava.

Wrapping the towel around me, I entered the bedroom. Benjamin had laid out my clothes, unfamiliar eveningwear. Pa now owned some, thanks to Mrs. Ava, but I had never worn a black tail coat. I stared at it before donning the more familiar drawers and shirt. Next, I slipped on socks, drew the strings at the bottom of the drawers tight around the socks, and then reached for black trousers. Next, came the white linen top shirt and a velvet gray waistcoat. I stared at the tie, a gray strip of silk, and wondered about the proper way to tie it for New York society.

I had never felt uncertain about my appearance and had often smiled at Lucy when she went on a tangent about what was proper to wear for one function or another, shifting from one frock to another, talking to herself about what others would say about a garment or its accessory.

But now, I felt the force of how my appearance might affect others. Delia would be staying on, if all went well, long after I had gone home. Delia. I smiled and wondered what articles of clothing Aunt Gertrude had had made for her.

FIFTY-THREE

Cordelia

I closed the door and looked around at what was now to be my room. *Frills.* The canopy bed, the crocheted coverlet, and the lacy curtains edged by ruffled draperies, the white, light color of the room. Clearly, Aunt Gertrude had decorated for someone more like Lucy. I was sure to be a disappointment.

Expectations.

The word made me think of Quinn, the father I had met for the first time last summer. Before I found him panning for gold in a stream west of Denver, I had expected little. At first, that is what I seemed to have gotten. But circumstances brought us closer, and by the time we parted, I realized he was the best kind of father for me, one who respected me as I was and wouldn't press me to become anything else. When I had chosen a path he considered dangerous, he had given his opinion and left the decision to me.

However, he hadn't known I was going to show up in his life; whereas, Aunt Gertrude had had almost three months to prepare for me, to imagine what I and our lives together might be like.

Corners of the large room held shadows, and the lighted lantern on either side of the fireplace mantel did little to dispel them. I crossed to a dressing table and gazed into the mirror, turning quickly at the sight of a vague form in a dress in the far corner of the room.

"Who's there?" I shrieked, whirling to confront whoever was invading my privacy.

I reached for the closest lantern and turned up the gas to cast a brighter light into the corner. I laughed. My intruder was a dress form clothed in a beautiful evening gown of green silk. From the way the skirt stood out in a perfect bell shape, there was surely a hooped cage crinoline underneath.

A girl's head popped out from behind a door. "Are you all right, miss?"

Startled, I jumped. "Who are you? Why are you here?" I asked.

Her blue eyes twinkled, and her face lit up in a smile. "I'm Callie, your maid. I'm here to help you dress for the party, miss. I've just prepared your bath." She gestured to the room behind her. "The water will cool quickly, so you may want to bathe soon."

She stepped aside, and I entered the room. A round copper tub half full of water sat to one side of the room. A dressing gown and towel hung from hooks on the opposite wall.

"When you undress, you might hand your clothes to me, and I'll put them in the wash," Callie said.

"Yes." Uncomfortable with someone waiting on me, I said, "Please step out."

"Yes, miss."

The door closed, and I disrobed, placing my dress and undergarments on a bench, then collecting them, and as requested, cracking the door open and tossing them out for Callie to launder. Then I stepped into the water. It was cool but not uncomfortable. I used a ladle to scoop water over my head and wash my hair. Next, I scrubbed my skin with a cloth that had been placed on the edge of the tub. A gas flame turned low flickered in a wall holder. The half dark room and water relaxed me. I dozed, my eyelids drooping.

"Miss!" Callie knocked on the door. "Are you all right in there? Mrs. Oaks asks that you come down soon."

My eyelids fluttered. "In a minute," I called out. Rising from the tub, I dried with a towel and slipped my arms into the sleeves of the silk dressing gown. So much silk. I was used to cotton and linsey-woolsey. Serviceable clothes to work in, not luxurious garments to impress. But who would a bathrobe impress when one was alone?

Tying the sash, I entered the bedroom to find the dress had been removed from the form and laid out on the bed. Callie was removing the hoop skirt. Beneath it were a chemise, pantalets, and a corset. I groaned. The last thing I wanted was the tight confines of a corset.

Callie helped me dress, with the white stockings and satin slippers first, then the corset, pulling the strings tight before arranging the hoop skirt. Next, I slipped into the bodice and, finally, the skirt with its yards and yards of fabric.

"Now, let's arrange your hair." Callie took my hand and led me toward the dressing table. I sat on the bench in front of it, and she combed my hair, something no one had done for me since Ma died.

Hair. I stared at my bare neck in the mirror. "My locket! I left it in the bath."

"I'll get it." It took only a moment for her to retrieve the gold necklace with the cameo pendant and return.

"It's special then?" she asked, "a gift?"

"From my Aunt Hannah. There's a lock of my mother's hair inside."

"I see." Her eyes were sad as she handed me the locket, making me feel she truly did understand.

"Now, back to your hair," she said with enthusiasm.

"Is arranging hair a favorite part of your job?" I asked.

"It is." She frowned as she tried to smooth out my wiry red tresses. "But yours is somewhat willful."

"A reflection of my temperament," I said.

She raised an eyebrow. "Then you will have an interesting time with your aunt."

"Are you saying my aunt is willful as well?"

Her eyes rounded. "I would never say such a thing."

She turned her full attention to my hair then. I closed my eyes, not wanting to give advice unless I disliked the outcome. I felt the comb run down the center of my head, the hair parting, the back being pulled up, a twist at the nape of my neck, leaving it bare and cool.

"There," she said at last. "I'll just fasten the necklace and you can open your eyes and tell me what you think."

I shivered at the touch of the cool chain on my skin.

Callie's warm fingers fastened the clasp. "All right, then," she said.

I opened my eyes and stared into the mirror. I barely recognized the woman staring back. I had always thought of myself as the girl who could pass for a boy whenever needed. I was used to high-topped bodices. This one was off the shoulders, my skin feeling the chill of the cool air. I wondered what Ryan would think if he could see me now.

"Your aunt is waiting," Callie prompted.

"Yes." I rose, a bit unsteady on the narrow heels. I was used to a broader sole than the slippers provided. Uncertain on my feet and in my mind, I minced my way to the door, the broad skirt swaying with each step.

FIFTY-FOUR

Ambrose

I was dressed at last, tailcoat and all. At least, I didn't have to put on a top hat.

Benjamin had gone off on some errand. There was a brief knock at the door.

"Yes," I called.

Benjamin slipped inside. "Mrs. Oaks requests your presence in the parlor."

"Very well," I said.

"I'll finish cleaning up in here while you're gone."

I nodded and opened the door. While shutting it behind me, I heard voices and glanced toward Delia's room. A young woman in a green dress was entering the hall. She came toward me, her eyes shining, a broad smile on her face.

"Ambrose, how grown up you look," she said.

"Delia!"

She gave a little twirl, wobbled, and laughed. "You didn't recognize me, did you?"

"I knew your voice, the minute you spoke. But I thought—well—don't I look different, too?"

She stopped in front of me and stroked my chin. "It was that attempt at a beard that gave you away."

I swallowed hard. "I should have shaved, then."

"You're fine. I'm teasing. Sisters are allowed to do that." She let out a sigh. "But maybe I shouldn't tease on such an important occasion." She squeezed my hand. "I'm just so nervous that I'll turn my ankle in these narrow heels and take a tumble in front of Aunt Gertrude's guests."

"You'll be fine," I assured her.

"It's not just the shoes. There's this fool dress to contend with. It's everywhere."

"It certainly is." I stepped behind her as we neared the stairwell. "There's no room for me to walk beside you. Ladies first."

"What? You won't be there to break my fall if I trip?"

"Guess not."

Luckily, we reached the bottom step without mishap and entered the parlor together.

Aunt Gertrude had changed into evening clothes and looked regal in a high-necked gold gown with a brooch. She stretched her arms, her hands palms up, toward us. "Look at what wonders a bath and new clothes make. Cordelia, you look lovely. You remind me of my dear sister when she was your age."

I smiled, knowing Cordelia would not take the comparison as a compliment. She and our grandmother had never gotten along. Grandmother viewed Delia as our mother's "mistake."

Aunt Gertrude continued, "It's such a wonderful time for you to be introduced to society. There will be a number of eligible men here this evening."

I bit my lip and hoped Delia would stifle the complaint she was certain to be holding back.

Aunt Gertrude turned to me. "And you, Ambrose. I can only assume you take after your father, and what a handsome man he must be. How old did you say you were? Fifteen?"

I nodded.

She laughed. "We must find a way to the let the ladies know or your time will be occupied by those too old for you."

I wanted to say that perhaps I was too young to attend this party for adults, but at that moment a man entered, looking dignified and businesslike. "Your first guests have arrived, Madam."

"Very well. Show them in."

I took a deep breath. The party had begun.

FIFTY-FIVE

Cordelia

About a dozen guests had arrived. I was chatting with Aunt Gertrude and a man who was a banker or lawyer or someone considered an eligible bachelor when the butler announced that the O'Rourkes had arrived.

It couldn't be.

But it was.

Standing in the doorway behind an older couple was Ryan O'Rourke, looking splendid but not so different in evening wear. After all, he wore a suit most of the time. He was scanning the room, and I knew he was looking for me. His gaze slid past me and then came back, surprise on his face.

I couldn't help smiling, but I also wondered why he hadn't mentioned that his family was acquainted with Aunt Gertrude.

Beside me, the young man raised his eyebrow and said to Aunt Gertrude, "You invited the Irish?"

"We do a great deal of business with the O'Rourke's," Aunt Gertrude replied.

"Well," he said. "Good evening, Miss Pierce." He nodded and took his leave, giving the impression that Irish wasn't good enough. I remembered that my father was Irish, so I was, too, at least partially. If the Irish were such social pariahs, that lineage might come in handy for getting rid of boorish suitors.

The O'Rourkes approached. The woman sailing toward us in a gray satin dress must be Ryan's mother. The man beside her, surely Ryan's father, had a full head of mixed gray and black hair with sideburns and a beard. He was tall, thin, and impeccably dressed in black except for his white shirt.

And who was the younger woman with them? And why was she clinging so tightly to Ryan's arm?

She was dressed in a pale-blue satin gown trimmed in dark blue ribbons that circled her waist. Her hair ribbons, a shade between the gown and its trim, matched her eyes. She was tall and blond and sure of herself, bending toward Ryan, whispering something while giving me a haughty look as they came to a stop in front of me.

I knew right away I didn't like her.

"Mr. and Mrs. O'Rourke, how nice that you could join us this evening. I'd like you to meet my great-niece, Miss Cordelia Pierce, and her brother, Mr. Ambrose Pierce."

We nodded in recognition.

Aunt Gertrude asked, "Who is this gentleman accompanying you this evening?"

Mrs. O'Rourke flushed. "I apologize for not including our son in the R.S.V.P., but we weren't certain when he would arrive. And you know Miss Melanie Williams, who has long been like a daughter to us." She shot a glance at Mr. O'Rourke, the son, not the father. Ryan had obviously disappointed his parents by not making Miss Williams an official daughter-in-law.

Mr. O'Rourke, the elder, lifted his rather shaggy eyebrows and scanned me from top to toe. "Surely, you are not the Miss Pierce who traveled with my son all the way from Westport."

"The very same," I said, doing my best to hide my delight in seeing the startled look that flashed across Miss Williams' face. "With my brother as chaperone, of course."

Beside me, Ambrose nodded.

Miss Williams flicked him an interested look.

"Her younger brother," Ambrose quickly informed her. He looked around as though seeking an escape route. "I'm probably the youngest person here."

"You've been saved from that distinction," Aunt Gertrude said. "Here are the Millers with their daughter, Blanche." She gave a slight wave of recognition to the threesome that had just entered the room. The O'Rourke's moved on, making way for the newcomers.

"Blanche is also fifteen," Aunt Gertrude said. "This is her first New Year's social. Of course, at her age, she hasn't officially come out yet, but I couldn't bear to think of her parents leaving her home alone on such a special evening."

Once the Millers were formally introduced, Aunt Gertrude said, "Ambrose, perhaps you could get Miss Miller some refreshments."

"Yes," he said. "Would you like some punch, Miss Miller?"

"Yes, Mr. Pierce, I would," she said.

"Well, it's this way." He gestured with his hand.

She glanced toward the table against the far wall and set out a step ahead of him.

"And now, who shall we find for you?" Aunt Gertrude glanced from one unattached man to another. "Ah, there's just the one." She caught the eye of a fellow who appeared to be in his mid-twenties and waggled her fingers.

He smiled and crossed the room, giving me an appraising look as he came.

I pressed my lips together to keep from groaning. This was obviously a planned meeting.

Aunt Gertrude seemed to sense my displeasure. "Now, dear, you must give people a chance. Don't be so quick to judge."

I took as deep a breath as I could, given the corset I was wearing, and forced a smile. The man looked like all the others in his black tailcoat, black trousers, black vest, white shirt, and black tie. The men were like gingerbread cutouts from the same cookie cutter. He was set apart only by the somewhat wiry brown locks that framed his head.

"Mr. Haynes, you must have come in during the crush of arrivals. I haven't been able to introduce you to my great-niece, Miss Cordelia Pierce. Cordelia, Mr. Haynes publishes a periodical, and with your interest in photography, I thought you might have concerns in common."

"Photography!" His eyes widened. "How long have you been interested in the art?"

His question, asked in a serious tone, lifted him a notch in my opinion barometer.

"Four years," I said. "I assisted a photographer with several daguerreotype portraits and want to learn more. I have come to New York to study with Mathew Brady. I hope to be accepted into a class that may start in January."

"Brady. Yes, he has a fine reputation as a photographer. Is this your first visit to the city?" He paused. "Perhaps you'd like a refreshment."

"I would," I said, realizing "refreshment" was a signal for separating from my aunt and having a semi-private conversation.

He made a slight bow to Aunt Gertrude. "Please excuse us." He touched my elbow, and we glided across the room. That is I attempted to glide. My feet hurt, and the tight slippers with their narrow heels had me wobbling. Mr. Haynes' hand on my elbow provided balance and steadiness.

We approached the table where Thomas had taken up double duty to ladle punch. He handed each of us a cup, and we turned to survey the room. As the silence between us lengthened, I wondered if we had used up all of our conversation.

"A periodical," I said. "What subjects do you cover?"

"The political situation," he exclaimed, his eyes shining.

In spite of all cautioning against it, I had to ask. "Are you pro- or anti-slavery?"

"As a journalist, I present both sides."

"Do you cover other topics?"

"The *Postulator* covers all controversial topics. Is there a specific one that interests you?"

"Suffrage," I said. If we were to talk further, he should know where I stood on a woman's rights. Like Aunt Hannah, I saw no use wasting time with someone who did not support my beliefs.

"So you're a suffragette. Do you possess the bloomer dress so popular with those ladies?"

I frowned, his first question being about fashion lowering my opinion of him. "It is in the laundry now. I find the garment particularly appropriate for travel on horseback."

"Apparently, there is more to you than meets the eye."

In the way he said it, the look in his eyes, I felt that his interest in me was more than the pretty presence before him, that he was interested in my mind, so maybe the question had been more about me than my clothing. And certainly, his own worth grew as I talked with him. I had only witnessed society from afar, and those observations were limited to aunts Hilda and May and their circles, which had given me a negative opinion of it and its emphasis on the trappings of wealth, or at least the desired appearance that one had it. Fashion and manners held little interest for me. But conversations about real concerns like freeing the slaves or voting rights for women mattered. Perhaps Aunt Gertrude had given some thought to introducing me to someone I might openly discuss those issues with.

"Who is that man who keeps glancing our way?" Mr. Haynes nodded.

"What man?" I looked about.

"The one with Miss Williams, who seems to be fighting to keep his attention."

I followed his gaze. "Mr. O'Rourke." I slid my eyes in his direction. "He is the photographer I mentioned, a family friend."

"O'Rourke. I know the older couple and three of their sons. O'Rourke Senior advertises in my publication. He owns one of the finest dry goods stores in the city. But I haven't met this son. You say he's a photographer."

"Yes."

"Where is his studio? I should think he needs to advertise."

"He travels throughout the west from St. Louis to California. He has amazing photographs in his portfolio and on the sides of his wagon."

"Really! An itinerant! His parents must be disappointed."

His snobby attitude made my opinion of him fall. "As you said, they have three other sons to run the business."

"Ah, yes."

"Mr. O'Rourke is a talented artist with the pen as well as the camera. A likeness of me is one of many on his wagon, but you might not recognize me. It was four years ago, and I was dressed somewhat differently."

At this bit of news, his eyebrows arched. I smiled and decided not to quench his curiosity. I was thinking of a way to dodge his question when Ambrose and his young lady appeared at my elbow.

Ambrose looked uncomfortable, and the young lady's face was flushed.

FIFTY-SIX

Ambrose

Miss Blanche Miller was a beautiful girl excited at having been invited to attend the social to see in the new year, but we were having difficulty finding common interests. I had little to talk about save the purpose of my trip, exposing Ava's lies, hardly a topic to share with a new acquaintance.

We were standing in awkward silence, sipping our punch, when I spied Delia talking with a man. Thinking she might be as uncomfortable with her new companion as I was with mine, I said, "There's my sister with a gentleman. Do you know him?"

Blanche gave a little sniff and rolled her eyes. "Mr. Haynes. Everyone knows him, and he's hardly a gentleman. He publishes that dreadful periodical touting slavery and a woman's place in a man's sphere."

The messages seemed to conflict. Those who were for slavery were usually against women's suffrage, but the topics sounded interesting and watching Delia try to hold back her thoughts on them would be entertaining.

I smiled. "Let's join them."

"If you wish," Miss Miller said, her tone indicating it was far from her wish.

As we approached Delia and Mr. Haynes, I heard Delia say O'Rourke's name. She sounded in somewhat of a snit.

"Delia," I said, touching her elbow, "introduce us to your companion."

"We've met," Miss Miller said, her brusque tone surprising me.

Delia also seemed surprised at the strong reaction and pressed against her upper lip with her lower one as she often did to keep from making an unsuitable comment. "Well, then," she said, "I will only introduce Mr. Haynes to my brother. Ambrose, this is Mr. Darcy Haynes, the publisher of a periodical with a most interesting name, *The Postulator*. Mr. Haynes, this is my brother, Ambrose Pierce."

As I shook hands with Mr. Haynes, I wondered how to separate him from my sister so I might find out more about his business and what scandals he might be privy to. Beside me, Miss Miller was fidgeting.

Delia glanced between us and then cast a glance about the room. "Some of the gentlemen are leaving, and it's not anywhere close to midnight."

"Retiring to the library, no doubt," Mr. Haynes said, "for serious discussions, while you ladies talk of your sewing circles and the latest fashions from Paris, those so important elements of a woman's sphere."

Delia really had her lower lipped clamped on the upper now, resulting in a far less than attractive expression on her face. She unclamped it long enough to say, "I suppose, Mr. Haynes, we members of the less political sex should leave you men to your important talk." She clasped Miss Miller's hand. "Come, we don't want to miss any news of the current fashions."

Miss Miller agreed, and the two sailed off across the room, their hoop skirts swaying. Halfway across the floor, Delia stumbled and caught herself, and I remembered her fear that the narrow heels might trip her up.

"Based on the speed of their departure, it seems neither young woman was pleased with our company," Mr. Haynes said. "But appearances may well be deceiving."

"I doubt that," I replied. "At least, as far as Miss Miller is concerned. We seemed to have little in common."

"Your sister mentioned she has a deep interest in photography, but she didn't say what it is you do, Mr. Pierce."

"Ambrose, please. Until October, I ran a livery stable for my father in Kansas Territory." Across the room, O'Rourke disengaged himself from Miss Williams and came toward us. "At that time," I continued, "I began serving as chaperone for my sister during our journey with Mr. O'Rourke from Westport, Missouri, to New York City. We only just arrived this afternoon."

"Did I hear my name?" O'Rourke asked as he approached.

"Yes. I was telling Mr. Haynes that Delia and I traveled with you from Westport." I glanced between the two. "Have you met?"

Mr. Haynes laughed. "Only our eyes in glances across the room." He held out his hand. "Darcy Haynes. And I was told by the lovely Miss Pierce that you are Mr. O'Rourke."

The two shook hands as Mr. O'Rourke said, "Ryan."

"Ryan, then. Miss Pierce speaks highly of your photographic skills. Have your images been published in periodicals?"

"Rarely. Most of my photographs have been taken for private clients. The rest are for my personal collection."

"Perhaps you'd consider showing me images of the country between here and California. Miss Pierce said you were an artist as well as a photographer. My publication, *The Postulator*, is often in need of artwork depicting diverse areas."

"Certainly, if you'd like a look. I am always proud to show off my work, as Miss Pierce may have told you."

"We had not gotten that far in our discussion when Ambrose arrived with Miss Miller. The two young women then set off to join the rest of the ladies for more refined conversation."

O'Rourke burst out laughing. "More refined conversation? Cordelia?" Then he cast a look in my direction. "Sorry, Ambrose, I meant nothing untoward about your sister."

"I know what you meant," I said. "That recipes and Paris fashions are generally not attractive topics of discussion for Delia."

Mr. Haynes spoke up. "She did mention she was a suffragette."

"Then her quick exit may have been caused by a sense that you disapproved," I said.

"I was rather ambiguous about my stand. Perhaps I will have an opportunity later to assure her of my support for her cause. What do you say, Ryan? Should I pursue Miss Pierce's good opinion?"

I blinked as I realized the question was deeper than it seemed. Mr. Haynes was asking O'Rourke about his romantic interest in Delia.

O'Rourke gazed across the room at the circle of women. "I think she deserves to know your stand on the matter and your intentions toward her. Surely, Ambrose will make certain they are honorable."

"I will," I said. During our journey, I had wondered about O'Rourke's intentions toward my sister and hers toward him. I must have read them both wrong because he seemed more than willing to give Mr. Haynes a clear path to courting her.

"Yes," Mr. Haynes said. "That is what brothers are for." He turned to me. "I don't believe you mentioned what it is you plan to do in the city. Will you be staying on or returning to Kansas Territory?"

"Staying for a while. I have a personal matter to look into." Since O'Rourke knew about that matter, I wondered if I should continue. Periodical publishers knew a lot about what went on, and Darcy might have contacts who could help me learn what scandal Mrs. Ava had been involved in. "Tell me, Darcy, do you investigate crimes or do you stick with political opinion pieces?"

"It depends on the crime. I don't concern myself with run-of-the-mill thefts and hothead shootings, but if it involves certain levels of society or emphasizes some wrong that needs to be righted beyond the law's reach, I might spend some space on it." He paused at the punch bowl to refill his cup. "Is there a particular crime you had in mind?"

I stood silent, considering what I should say.

O'Rourke spoke up. "Darcy can't help you if you don't give him the information."

Realizing the truth in that, I asked, "I wonder if you have heard of a Miss Ava Carstairs or a Mr. Gerald Ward?"

"Recently?"

"Probably three to four years ago."

Darcy's forehead furrowed. "Hmmm. Carstairs. Ward. I'm not sure. Your best bet is to go over to the *Tribune* and look at their old newspaper files."

"Thank you," I said.

We headed to the library where the talk was all about John Brown and his execution. In the South, Brown was considered unhinged, a madman. Here in New York, many saw him as a martyr who had stood up for the abolitionist cause.

Having now listened to both sides and having heard first hand from family members of Brown's victims in Kansas, I decided to keep my opinions to myself.

Haynes touched my arm. "There's Whitney Armor. He writes financial news for the *Tribune* and the occasional obituary when the regular reporter is out. Maybe he knows something about Carstairs or Ward. Come, I'll introduce you."

Whitney Armor was surrounded by men puffing cigars, the thick smoke drifting our way. I hoped no one offered me one as the smell was disagreeable, making my stomach churn. Still, if I wanted information, the discomfort was a small thing compared to what I might face.

The three of us crossed to the circle of men. "May I have a word?" Mr. Haynes asked of Armor.

Armor nodded at his group and stepped aside. "What is it, Darcy?"

"Are you acquainted with Ryan O'Rourke?" Darcy gestured toward him.

"I don't believe so." He offered his hand and Ryan shook it.

Mr. Haynes turned to me. "And this is his friend, Ambrose Pierce, fresh from Kansas Territory."

Armor gave me a bit more attention then. "So how is the political climate there?"

"Tense," I said, not wanting to get bogged down in the slavery question.

"A short but accurate description, I'm sure." He turned back to Mr. Haynes. "What did you call me aside to discuss?"

"Ambrose is looking for some information, and I thought with your position at the *Tribune*, you might be able to help him."

Armor flicked an impatient glance my way. He obviously thought whatever I wanted was of little consequence in his important world.

It probably was, but this was my opportunity, so I spoke up. "I wondered if there was anything in the newspaper about two people. It would have been three or four years ago. Anything to do with Miss Ava Carstairs or Mr. Gerald Ward."

"Mr. Gerald Ward? An investor in the stock market. Died under questionable circumstances according to his relatives. His doctor ruled natural causes; his heart gave out. Why are you interested?"

My heart hammered with excitement. I'd been in New York City only a few hours, and I already had information. The thought of how I could have been lucky enough to so quickly come across someone in a city of eight hundred thousand people made me feel that Ma truly was guiding me from heaven.

"Because of a connection he might have had with Miss Ava Carstairs, who recently married my father. Have you heard of her?"

"I don't remember that name, but there was a woman who laid claim to some of the Ward fortune, which is the reason family members were crying 'foul play.'"

"Is there some way I might find out who this woman is?"

"I believe there was a court case," Armor said. "You might check city hall."

"Thank you, Mr. Armor. I will do that. And do you believe I might also look at past issues of the *Tribune*?"

"You may. Let me know what you find. This might be news for the society page."

Mr. Armor left us, taking his nasty cigar with him.

I took a deep breath and thanked O'Rourke and Haynes for their help.

"It's been a long day," I said. "I think I'll find my Aunt Gertrude and say good night."

FIFTY-SEVEN

Cordelia

I saw Ambrose enter the ballroom and glance around, not stopping when he came to Miss Miller, his face lighting up when he saw me.

I excused myself and met him halfway. "What brings you to this henhouse?"

"Have you learned anything about Miss Carstairs?" he asked.

"I thought that was your job, not mine."

"And I have a lead," he said, his eyes shining.

"Really? So soon?"

"Yes, I can't believe my luck. Mr. Haynes introduced me to a Mr. Armor who writes for the *Tribune*. He remembers the death of a Gerald Ward under suspicious circumstances. Tomorrow, I'm going down to the *Tribune* and have a look at their back issues."

"Congratulations on your progress. I suppose the quicker you find answers to your questions, the quicker you will leave me to society."

He grinned. "I suppose."

A clock struck eleven.

I sighed. "It's still an hour until midnight. I don't know how much more bodice and sleeve talk I can take."

Across the room, the sound of a violin tuning up caught my attention. Aunt Gertrude approached, a broad smile on her face.

"I've sent Thomas to bring in the men. There'll be dancing until midnight and then a toast to the new year."

Dancing. Another thing I wasn't good at. I'd only done it once, a square dance on the prairie. I'd messed that up, and I was betting this would be more complicated. I was right. The quartet played the first notes of a waltz as the men filed in and chose partners.

I looked desperately at Ambrose. "Do you know how to dance?"

His eyes twinkled. "Are you asking me to be your partner?"

Before I could answer, Mr. Haynes was at my side. "May I have this dance, Miss Pierce?"

"I've never waltzed," I replied.

"Then I shall teach you."

"You must put little value on the safety of your toes," I cautioned.

Ignoring my warning, he held out his hand, and I gave him mine.

He placed his other hand on my waist and whirled me around. My ankle turned. I stumbled and fell against him.

I groaned. "I told you so. And it's not only my lack of dancing skill, but these horrible slippers with the narrow heels."

"Are you injured?" Darcy asked.

"Only my pride."

"Then let us continue at a slower pace."

He showed me the steps, and soon we were moving a bit roughly around the room, but by the end of the dance, I was following his lead without stumbling.

FIFTY-EIGHT

Cordelia

It was New Year's Day. I awoke with a headache and squinted at the light shining in the window. What time was it? Sighing, I reached for my dressing gown, slipped it on, and shuffled to the window. It was full daylight, maybe as late as nine. I wondered what time breakfast was. Surely, I had missed it, and my stomach was rumbling. Well, it wouldn't be the first meal I had ever missed.

The door creaked open, and Callie poked her head around the edge. "Ah, you're awake."

"What time is it?" I asked.

"Nearly noon. I've come to see if you will be joining Mrs. Oaks for the midday meal."

"Of course," I said. "My aunt must wonder at me for being such a lay-a-bed."

"Shall I put out your clothes?"

"I'll select them myself. Thank you, Callie. I won't need your assistance to get dressed."

"If you change your mind, just pull the bell cord."

"I will."

When she was gone, I opened the wardrobe and selected a frock, put on stockings and shoes, my own with heels broad enough to keep me from wobbling, then slipped into my three petticoats. I was not up to managing a hoop skirt, even though I had the feeling that was normal wear. I supposed Aunt Gertrude would be critical, but comfort was more important than fashion this morning. If she had a good opinion of me, I hoped my clothing choices would not change it.

After dressing, I arranged my hair, took a look in the mirror, and frowned at my image. Looking in the mirror was not a habit I wished to form, but in a house where looks appeared to be important, I supposed it was one I should encourage.

As ready as I would ever be to face the day's events, I hurried downstairs. I glanced into the dining room. There were place settings on the long table, but no one had yet assembled there.

Orna came down the hall, her face lighting up at sight of me. "Mrs. Oaks is waiting for you in the parlor."

"Thank you." I hurried to join Aunt Gertrude who was sitting in front of the fire, holding a teacup. "Good morning," I said.

She turned toward me, set her cup in the saucer and placed it on a side table. "There you are. Completely rested, I hope."

"I am so sorry for oversleeping. I'm usually among the first in the house to wake."

"There's no need to apologize. I am the one who should be making apologies, having you attend a party after barely arriving from such a long journey. No wonder you were exhausted."

"What about Ambrose?" I asked. "I suppose he was up hours ago."

"Not hours. Perhaps one. He has gone to the stable to look after your horses." She motioned to a chair near hers. "Have a seat, dear. Would you like a cup of tea? Dinner should be served in half an hour."

I settled into a wing chair and accepted the cup of tea she offered. I took a sip and added a spoonful of sugar while searching for something to talk about.

"What did you think of Mr. Haynes?" Aunt Gertrude asked.

I stifled a groan. This was what I got for not guiding the conversation. "He seems like a nice man. Well informed." What else was there to say about him? "Decent manners," I added.

"You seemed to get on well. And Ambrose appeared to like him, too."

I found Ambrose a more desirable subject than my opinion of

Mr. Haynes, so I asked, "Did Aunt Hannah tell you the purpose of Ambrose's journey to New York?"

She arched her eyebrows. "You mean beyond being a chaperone for you and Mr. O'Rourke?"

I sighed. This was not going in desirable direction. "I mean about his investigation of his father's new wife, Ava Carstairs Pierce."

"So you've never looked on your mother's husband as your father?" Her voice rose a bit at the end of her sentence, making it an obvious question.

"He never looked on himself as my father except in public." I couldn't keep the anger out of my voice. I was not meant for polite society.

"Hannah said as much. It is always difficult in situations such as your mother's to choose the right course of action."

"What choice did my mother have? Grandfather paid Hiram a dowry to take her off his hands, to hide her shame, the family's shame, from society."

Aunt Gertrude set her teacup aside, cocked her head, and looked at me intently. "But she did have a choice. She could come to stay with me and give you to some couple or to an orphanage, or she could marry Hiram and keep you. She chose to marry him and keep you."

I thought of the girl I believed was Ryan's daughter. Her mother had faced the same decision and had given up her child. Was Shauna's life better or worse for the choice? Shauna now lived with parents who loved her. She was their joy. Would I have been someone's joy? That wasn't fair. I was my mother's. I knew that because of every loving word she said to me, the hours she spent holding me and brushing my hair and listening to all my childhood troubles.

Now I realized she had never spoken of making a choice. What I knew of her marriage had come from Hiram. It was his story that my mother had been sweet-talked and abandoned, and he had given her the gift of a respectable marriage in exchange for the pledge that they would build a life and she would give him sons. But he had been cheated when only Ambrose lived. Now Ambrose was cast aside for a new wife and children she had not yet delivered.

"Perhaps Ma might have chosen better for herself," I said.

"And you?"

"I loved her so much, but her life was hard because of me." I set my cup and saucer aside. "Life as an orphan might have been better."

"To make an accurate judgment, you may want to visit some orphanages in the city."

Ambrose appeared and, grateful for the interruption, I smiled. "Ambrose, Aunt Gertrude was just asking about your business in the city. She has some information from Aunt Hannah, but the not full story."

As he came toward us, Orna stepped into the doorway. "Dinner is ready to be served," she said.

Aunt Gertrude pushed up out of her chair. "Well, then. Let's continue the conversation after dining." She touched Ambrose's arm, and he crooked it just so and escorted her from the room. I followed behind, my nose leading me toward the dining room, stomach growling and heart aching.

FIFTY-NINE

Ambrose

The conversation I had interrupted between Aunt Gertrude and Delia had been serious. I knew by the relief on Delia's face and in her voice when I entered the room. Orna's announcement that the noonday meal was ready added to the lessening of tension in Delia's eyes.

We sat down to a sumptuous feast, at least in my eyes: baked ham, sweet potatoes, green beans, green peas, and biscuits with butter and jam. When I thought I was stuffed, Orna brought dessert dishes filled with apple cobbler and a pitcher of thick cream to the table, and I found there was more room in my stomach, after all.

My first bite of cobbler reminded of Susan and her award-winning apple pies. The cobbler was equal but not superior to Susan's pastries. I pushed away the sadness creeping over me and finished my dessert. Little conversation beyond exclamations of "delicious" and "wonderful meal" occurred as we devoured the food.

When the meal was finished and the dished cleared, we retired once again to the parlor and sat in a semicircle of chairs around the fireplace, Aunt Gertrude on the right, Delia in the middle, and me to the left of her. Aunt Gertrude wasted no time returning the conversation to my reasons for coming to New York.

I stared into the fire, gathering my thoughts. "Pa married a woman from New York, Ava Carstairs. After she persuaded Pa that my little sisters had no place in his home and that Ma had been physically and morally weak and had passed it on to her children, she found a way to convince Pa I had behaved in a forward manner with her."

Delia interrupted. "Ma died having his children, and he tossed them away without a care." Tears glittered in her eyes.

Aunt Gertrude raised her hand, palm out. "Delia, let's hear Ambrose's telling of this."

I continued. "He beat me and threw me out, cursing me and disowning me. It took weeks for my ribs to heal and the bruises to completely fade. It would have been worse, though, if Mr. Derryberry, our boarder, hadn't stepped in to stop him. Then Mr. Derryberry took me to town, and Mrs. Collins, who runs the boardinghouse, took me in. The room where I was recovering was next to a fence separating the boardinghouse from Fletcher's Emporium, a business run by Mrs. Ava's cousins. I overheard them talking about having to leave New York because of a scandal involving Mrs. Ava and Mr. Gerald Ward. I've come to discover what that scandal was and warn Pa about what his new bride might have done with or to Mr. Ward." As I talked, my emotions built, causing me to talk faster, and I ended almost out of breath.

Aunt Gertrude closed her eyes, then opened them, a faraway look on her face, as though she were trying to recall something. "Gerald Ward. The name is familiar. I knew a Mrs. Ward several years ago, but I believe she passed on."

"Mr. Haynes suggested we look through back issues of the *Tribune* for possible news articles. That will be my first stop tomorrow."

Delia said, "Once I have applied to Mr. Brady for entrance into his classes, I will help you with the search. There must be dozens of back issues to look through."

Aunt Gertrude smiled. "It may be more like hundreds. The *Tribune* publishes New York issues six days a week. Do you have a time frame?"

"The Fletchers came to Hidden Springs about three years ago, so the events causing them embarrassment must have happened before that, which means 1856 might be a good place to start," I said.

"So you both have plans for tomorrow. What about today, this first day of the New Year? You have an afternoon and an evening ahead of you."

Delia and I looked at each other and shrugged.

"Then you might consider ice-skating. Have you been?"

We shook our heads.

"Of course, I don't skate anymore, but I still love to watch. I'll have Callie and Benjamin get you appropriately outfitted for the activity." She pulled a bell cord.

"Thank you," Delia said.

As we ascended the stairs, Delia shook her head. "Ice-skating? In this cold? What is she thinking?"

SIXTY

Cordelia

Ice-skating was not something I would do again. After three falls, I joined Aunt Gertrude on the sidelines while Ambrose took another turn around the frozen pond.

Aunt Gertrude patted my arm. "I'm afraid I am once again overwhelming you with activity. I so want to show you everything the city has to offer, but I have failed to take into account how exhausted you must be from your trip."

"It isn't the trip I've taken, but my interview tomorrow that keeps me from enjoying our outing." I sought to make her feel better, but the truth was that after several weeks of traveling in often frigid weather, an afternoon on a frozen pond did not appeal.

"Then Mr. Brady is expecting you?"

"Not exactly," I admitted. "I wrote to him last September requesting an interview on my arrival. I had no time to wait for a reply. Tomorrow, I shall simply go and ask for an audience. Mr. O'Rourke suggested I present Mr. Brady with a portfolio of my work, and he helped me take the photographs."

A faint smile touched her lips. "Hannah seems to think you and Mr. O'Rourke might have feelings for each other."

"Those feelings are a combination of friendship and a common interest in photography." I wondered how long it would take to dispel the suppositions of others.

Aunt Gertrude's smile brightened and her eyes gleamed. "And Mr. Haynes? The two of you seemed to get on well."

I sighed, exasperated with all the matchmaking. "Really, Aunt Gertrude! We've only just met."

She folded her hands in her lap and gazed at the skaters whizzing by. "But you'll be seeing each other again."

"Yes. Mr. Haynes has offered to help Ambrose review the *Tribune* files for stories of Ava Carstairs and Mr. Ward. Tomorrow morning, in fact."

To my relief, Ambrose braked to a stop in front of us and suggested we go home and have some hot tea.

Not long after we arrived at Aunt Gertrude's, Mr. Haynes came calling. Orna showed him to the parlor and brought another pot of tea and a cup for him, even though he protested that he didn't need anything.

He spoke to Ambrose. "I wanted to confirm the time for our planned research excursion to the *Tribune*."

"After lunch," Ambrose said. "Delia is going to see Mr. Brady tomorrow morning, and I want to be here to learn how her meeting with him goes."

Tomorrow morning?" He straightened and seemed to be sitting on the edge of his chair as he turned his attention to me. "Would you consider me too forward if I offered to call for you tomorrow morning and transport you to Brady's gallery? My office is near there. I could take care of some tasks and return for you. From there, we might have a midday meal before I collect Ambrose for our visit to the *Tribune*.

I agreed, not bothering to ask Aunt Gertrude's opinion of whether it was proper for me to accompany a man I had just met.

SIXTY-ONE

Cordelia

Once the breakfast dishes were cleared away the next morning, I brought out the photographs I had taken with Mr. O'Rourke's guidance. As I showed each one to Aunt Gertrude, I remembered the circumstances. There was the one of Ambrose standing next to Butter, holding his horse's face still long enough to take the picture. The next was a grisly picture of a dead slave hanged from a tree limb. A third showed the Executive Mansion in Washington, D.C., and a fourth the Independence Hall in Philadelphia. A fifth was of a coal mine and a child curled on the ground, sleeping, waiting for his shift to begin. The last was of a woman waiting to speak before a group, a drawing of children tending machines in a spinning mill on the easel beside her. I wasn't interested in pretty portraits to hang on walls. I wanted my photographs to inspire people to change the laws that allowed mistreatment of others.

Mr. Darcy Haynes was punctual, arriving at the appointed time of nine thirty in the morning. He provided an extra step to make it easier for me reach my seat on the buggy, and soon we were traveling down Broadway toward the Brady gallery. I couldn't help gawking at the many businesses. Brownstones five stories high, and even taller buildings, crowded the sky. I pressed my handkerchief to my mouth, in an effort to block the offensive odors from garbage and animal waste. Pigs ran in the streets.

And yet here were thriving shops and offices. At Tenth and Broadway, Darcy stopped the buggy in front of an imposing building. "Here it is. The Brady Gallery."

My eyes widened at its size, and for a moment, my courage faltered. Who was I to be a student to so great a man? I clutched the package of daguerreotypes to my chest and remembered that Ryan said I was talented.

"Thank you for bringing me, Darcy. I'm not sure I could have found it on my own."

He lifted an eyebrow. "Because it's such a tiny, unobtrusive building?"

I smiled. "Have your fun. No, it's because I'm new to the city and would surely have gotten lost on my own."

"I shall call for you at noon. While your interview may not last long, there is much too see in the gallery. We might have lunch and then fetch Ambrose for the search through the *Tribune's* files."

Darcy helped me dismount from the buggy and waited until I entered the gallery before driving away.

The room was huge, the floor carpeted, the ceiling frescoed, the walls lined with the photographs of famous people. I gazed about at the men and women gathered to look at one photograph, then another. Darcy had been correct in assuming I would want to take my time viewing the images on display. But first, I must locate Mr. Brady.

I approached a man seated at a desk near the entrance.

"Hello," I said. "I wonder if you could direct me to the office of Mr. Mathew Brady. I have written in advance for an interview." Well, that much was true. I hadn't claimed that he'd agreed to one.

The man's eyes narrowed. "Mr. Brady didn't mention any appointment."

I held up the leather bag. "I have brought photographs for his review."

"Well, he's in. Go to the back of the gallery and take the stairs to the top floor."

"Thank you."

Without pausing to view any of the artwork on the walls, I quickly reached the back of the gallery, not wanting the man to have time for second thoughts and stop me. At the top of the stairs, I gazed into a room with cameras and sets, a studio for shooting likenesses. Skylights flooded the interior with natural lights. Farther down, I saw doors.

One was open. I knocked lightly to announce my presence.

The man at the desk looked up from his papers. "What is it, miss?"

"I'm looking for Mr. Brady. I wrote him for an appointment."

"Did you now? And what was his reply?"

So this man wasn't going to be as easily fooled as the one downstairs. Perhaps he was here to keep strangers from taking up Mr. Brady's valuable time.

I straightened, determined to get past this man to see Mr. Brady, to have my chance. "I couldn't wait for a reply. You see, I'm from Westport, Missouri. I had a sudden opportunity to travel to New York, so I took it. My name is Cordelia Pierce. I've learned the basics of photography from Mr. Ryan O'Rourke, a most excellent photographer, but I wish to learn more, all the new processes. Everyone says that Mr. Brady's classes are top notch and the best opportunity for me to learn to use the latest equipment and enhance my abilities."

"Mr. Brady rarely accepts young ladies into his classes."

"But shouldn't talent matter? I have brought samples of my work." I set my bag on the corner of his desk and removed the photographs.

The man gave me a head-to-toe look. "You say you traveled with this Mr. O'Rourke. What manner of transportation was that?"

"He is an itinerant. We traveled in his wagon." Worried that he was making something of my relationship that wasn't true, I picked up Ambrose's picture and held it out to him. "My brother traveled with us as a chaperone."

His eyes skimmed the picture. "A handsome lad. How do I know you were the one who took this photograph and not your Mr. O'Rourke?"

Realizing he had not been dissuaded of the scandalous action he was attributing to me, I felt my face warm. "He is not *my* Mr. O'Rourke. He is a family friend who brought my brother and me to New York to visit our great-aunt, Mrs. Gertrude Oaks."

He cocked his head, interest flickering in his eyes. "Mrs. Oaks is your great-aunt?"

"Yes," I said, realizing that family might get me the interview.

"Is Mr. Brady in?"

"I am Mr. Brady. May I see what else you've brought?"

"Of course." I quickly laid out the remaining five photographs.

Mr. Brady scanned them, barely glancing at the Executive Mansion and Independence Hall, stopping on the image of the lynched slave, his lifeless body hanging. "A rather grim sight," Mr. Brady said. "Were you the photographer, or was it your Mr. O'Rourke?"

Holding back from informing him once again that he was not *my* Mr. O'Rourke, I said, "He advised me about distance, light, and timing, as a mentor does. I operated the camera."

"Hmmm." He moved on to the picture of the child sleeping, leaning against a sign with the words "Mine Entrance" and an arrow pointing the way. "I suppose you saw this boy as a worker in the mine."

"I did."

"And this," he said, moving on to the woman standing behind a podium, an empty hall in front of her, and easel with writing beside her. He peered at me over his glasses. "I suppose I am looking at a suffragette, an abolitionist, or both."

"Both," I said, unsure of whether he meant me or the woman in the photograph. If he was going to reject me on the basis on my beliefs in right and wrong, so be it. "Elizabeth Cady is a friend of my Aunt Hannah's. She was kind enough to let me photograph her before her speech against slavery."

"And what drew you to immortalize these images, Miss Pierce?"

"They tell stories. They show the realities of life and death. They can be a tool to bring understanding to those who have never seen such things. They can be used to change laws for the better. Aunt Hannah says that changing laws is what we must do about the injustices we see."

"How old are you, Miss Pierce?"

"I shall be eighteen in May."

"So you are seventeen. And how long will you be in the city?"

"As long as it takes for me to learn everything there is to know about photography."

"My next class begins on February first. You will present yourself at nine o'clock that morning."

"Thank you, Mr. Brady. I so appreciate the opportunity to learn from you."

"In the meantime, you may want to examine the photographs in the gallery. You can learn much from them."

"I will."

"Now, I need to return to my own work."

"Yes." I hurried to collect my photographs. "I shall be here at the appointed time, ready to learn."

"See that you are."

I hurried from the room, not wanting to give him time to change his mind.

I spent the rest of the morning reviewing Mr. Brady's *Gallery of Illustrious Americans*. When Darcy called for me at noon, I hastened to his buggy, excited to give him my news. I hoped the afternoon would be as successful for Ambrose as the morning had been for me.

SIXTY-TWO

Ambrose

I had never seen Delia in such high spirits. She returned with Mr. Haynes after lunch and immediately started gushing about her meeting with Brady. Truly, I never thought I would use "gushing" to describe anything Delia said; it was more a word for Lucy, but Delia was so overcome with her success that she twirled about the parlor as she recounted the interview to Aunt Gertrude and me.

"He asked about my choice of samples, and he didn't seem to mind when it became obvious I was a suffragette. He didn't voice his approval, but he didn't dismiss me either. When he said he seldom accepted women in his classes, I pressed on, showing him my samples, telling him why the training was so important to me."

I smiled. Pressing on was what Delia did best. Whether it was getting help for Ma or finding her father, once she seized on a course of action, she kept going. Listening to the clock on the mantel ticking away the afternoon, I knew I must interrupt her triumph so I could move on my own goal: to find out what Mrs. Ava had done to shame her relatives so much they moved all the way to Kansas to escape the scandal. Opportunely, the clock struck two.

"Darcy, how late will the newspaper office be open?" I asked.

"Until five. If we are to make a dent in the pile of back issues, we should go."

Delia stopped almost mid-twirl. "Oh, Ambrose. I'm sorry for holding you up. I was just so excited. Yes, let's go."

"You are still helping then?" I asked.

"Did you think I'd change my mind? My class doesn't start until February first, so I have plenty of time. And while I don't give a fig what that woman does to Hiram, the way this Mrs. Ava, as you call her, treated you and Lucy and said horrible things about Ma makes me determined to help you get the truth about her."

Darcy's brows drew together when she called Pa by his first name. She must not have told him we had different fathers. But they had just met, and it wasn't something he needed to know for our investigation of Mrs. Ava.

Delia glanced at Darcy. "So what are we waiting for?"

"Only you." He offered her his arm.

She tucked her hand in the crook of his elbow. "Are you coming, Ambrose?" She turned to Aunt Gertrude. "We'll see you later with a full report."

Aunt Gertrude laughed. "I shall be waiting."

I hurried out the door behind Delia and Darcy, thinking how quickly they had formed a friendship and how she seemed to have forgotten Mr. O'Rourke. But then, he had hinted to Darcy that there was nothing between him and Delia.

With Darcy driving the buggy, we soon arrived at the *Tribune* offices at the corner of Nassau and Spruce. He quickly located Whitney Armor, who guided us to the room where the back issues were kept. Adjusting the gas lights, Armor left us alone to dive into the mountain of print. It would truly be like looking for a needle in a haystack.

"Where should we start?" Darcy asked. "Do you have a month and year?"

"Neither," I said. "But the Fletchers came to Hidden Springs about three years ago. So whatever happened was before that. Let's start in 1856 and work forward."

Darcy found a stack labeled 1856 and put them on a long table in the center of the room. "They are arranged by date, so be careful to put them back in the correct order for the next poor soul who needs to search through them." He divided the stack in thirds and parceled them out to us. "The front pages contain mostly advertisements. Legal notices are generally on page three. Many of those are about settling the estate of a deceased person. With Mr. Armor's information about a child and contested inheritance, there may be something there. News articles also start on that page or the next one, depending on the number of advertisements. The last page also contains police reports and legal proceedings as well as market news."

We settled onto hard wooden chairs and began squinting at the type in the less than brilliantly lit room. Two hours later, we each had a stack of perused papers in front of us with no valuable information. Darcy gathered them carefully in order. "Shall I get another stack?"

I rubbed my eyes. "How can we narrow this down?" Then I thought of Ma, of how I'd carved her birth and death dates on her gravestone. "In what cemetery would Mr. Ward likely be buried?"

"The Green-Wood Cemetery," Darcy said. "It's where all the better families bury their dead."

Delia rolled her eyes. "By better, I suppose you mean wealthy."

"I do," Darcy said. "The cemetery is in Brooklyn."

"Perhaps I can go there tomorrow," I said.

"What do you hope to learn there?" Darcy asked.

"The date of Mr. Ward's death. Surely, it will be on his gravestone."

"I wish you luck then. I fear I can't accompany you. I must wrap up an issue of *The Postulator*."

"I'm sorry, Darcy, we've taken your whole day," Delia said.

"Do not apologize. I had the time and wanted to help, but tomorrow I must work." He turned to me. "However, I shall be most curious to learn of your progress. Perhaps I might call tomorrow evening."

"Yes," I said, suspecting Delia was the real reason for his desire to call. I was his excuse.

SIXTY-THREE

Cordelia

Aunt Gertrude gave us directions and lent us a buggy for our trip to Green-Wood Cemetery the next morning. We huddled in our coats and wrapped blankets around us. The day was bright but cold, wind gusting as Ambrose guided the horses down Twenty Fifth Street. We found the caretaker and asked about Mr. Ward's plot, telling him that we were distant relatives who wanted to visit his grave and pay our respects while we were in the city on business. He showed us a map and indicated the lanes to take reach the site.

As we drove through the park-like setting, it was clear that this was the burial ground for the wealthy. It almost seemed like families tried to outdo each other with their sculptures, tombs, and mausoleums. For the less prosperous, there were catacombs with skylights over each individual family vault.

I studied the directions the caretaker had written for us. "Turn down this lane," I said. "It's the third plot on the right."

Ambrose made the turn and stopped the carriage in front of a tomb built into the side of a hill. We dismounted the carriage. Our boots crunched as we crossed the damp, icy brown grass and read the carvings on either side of the heavy wood door.

Ambrose read the wife's epitaph first. "Lucretia Lyons Ward, Beloved Wife; Born September 5, 1807; Married February 12, 1826; Died July 20, 1846."

I jotted down the dates as Ambrose read them. I wasn't sure that we needed to know about the wife, but in case we did, we would not have to return to the cemetery.

Ambrose moved to the opposite side of the doorway where Gerald Ward's inscription was carved. "Gerald James Ward, Devoted Husband; Born April 16, 1801; Married February 12, 1826; Died December 23, 1856."

"We reviewed the January through April papers yesterday," I said. "Now we can move on to the end of the year."

"It will save us a lot of time." Ambrose rubbed his hands. "Let's get out of this cold and have dinner before taking our next trip to the *Tribune*."

I laughed. "Yes, let's have some of cook's delicious soup and fresh-baked bread. It's amazing how quickly one can get used to bountiful, well-prepared meals. Aunt Gertrude may soon have to instruct her seamstress to let out my clothes to accommodate the weight I am sure to gain. Her desserts alone will have that effect on me."

Ambrose smiled and his eyes got a faraway look. "Her pies don't hold a candle to Susan Hogan's."

SIXTY-FOUR

Ambrose

Thoughts of Susan warmed me as I guided our carriage through the muddy streets of New York toward Aunt Gertrude's mansion. I would write to Susan this evening with whatever we learned at the newspaper office. I knew she would keep my confidence, and I wished she were here with me so I could share events as they happened. Delia was a good partner in my search, but Susan—I would have enjoyed Susan's company more.

There it was. Of all the young ladies I had met from Hidden Springs to New York City, Rachel Parker, Shauna O'Rourke, Blanche Miller, and others along the way, none had captured my affections like Susan Hogan.

I turned onto Broadway. We'd gone only a few blocks when Delia pointed to an immense five-story building. "That's Barnum's American Museum. Darcy says we must see it."

I'd heard of the museum and agreed that it sounded interesting, but what caught me about Delia's words was her familiar reference to Darcy and his opinion. Not so long ago, I thought she cared for Mr. O'Rourke and that, somehow, they'd mend their differences. Now, it seemed he was forgotten. I hoped Susan Hogan would not so easily forget me.

***

After a sumptuous noon meal, Delia and I drove to the *Tribune* office to resume our search of back issues, beginning with Gerald Ward's death date, December 23, 1856. I took the first two weeks, including and following Mr. Ward's passing. I realized there was probably nothing on the exact day of his death, but I didn't want to take the chance of missing something important.

I skimmed the first pages of advertisements and slowed down when I got to page four where the actual news stories began. My eye caught on a story about Kansas and how with Geary as the governor of the territory, Kansas was sure to be a free state. Shaking my head, I pointed out the article to Delia. "Three years and three governors later, Kansas is still a territory." I thought of saying more, about how Pa was working with Colonel Samuel Wood and others to make Kansas a free state, but I figured she wouldn't be interested. Strangely, she and Pa were on the same side when it came to freeing the slaves, but neither would have appreciated anyone pointing it out to them.

Beside me, Delia brushed away tears.

"What's wrong," I asked.

"These death notices for infants and little children up to three or four years old make me think of Ma, of Mark, and the other babies she lost."

"Do you want to quit? I'll take you back to Aunt Gertrude's and continue the search tomorrow."

"No, I'll be all right. Maybe I'll look for something entertaining for a few minutes, then get back to the hunt."

"Tell me if you want to leave," I said before taking up the December 23 issue and the next two. The December 25 issue had two columns of advertisements on the front page; the remaining two contained a poem and a story. The second page took up ads again. Finding nothing on the remaining six pages, I picked up the December 26 issue and turned immediately to the last page where I had come to expect the death notices to appear. And there it was:

> WARD—Gerald J. Ward of this city, passed away December 23, 1856. Relatives and friends of his family are invited to the funeral at the home of his brother-in-law, Mr. Lawrence Laird at his residence of No. 50 Jay Street at 2 o'clock. His remains will be taken to Greenwood Cemetery for internment.

"I have an address." I read the notice to Delia. "We should call on them, see what we can learn."

"I agree. We can always come back here if needed," Delia said.

With high hopes, I copied the information, and we returned the newspapers to the shelf in proper order and left the dim confines of the room.

"Should we go to the Laird's now?" I asked.

"Let's wait until tomorrow. See what Aunt Gertrude and Darcy think is the best approach."

There she was with Darcy's opinion again.

SIXTY-FIVE

Cordelia

We relayed our findings about Mr. Ward to Aunt Gertrude when we returned home that afternoon. In the evening, Darcy came to call, and I told him what we'd found. Then Ambrose excused himself to care for Butter. I realized my brother had spent little time with his horse and missed her; however, I thought it odd he wouldn't want Darcy's advice on how to approach the Lairds.

"What might persuade them to talk to a stranger?" I asked, it being a general question to both Aunt Gertrude and Darcy. We were seated in the parlor, logs blazing in the fireplace, mugs of hot tea warming our hands.

Darcy cast a glance at Aunt Gertrude. "Are you acquainted at all with the family, Mrs. Oaks?"

"I met the Lairds at a charity ball last spring. They were raising money for an orphanage."

Ambrose joined us. "I see you have your heads together. Any suggestions for my visit to Gerald Ward's family tomorrow?"

"Yes," Aunt Gertrude said. "I remember being introduced to them at a function and donating money to their cause. I suggest you introduce yourself as my nephew and then briefly state your business."

"Should I go with Ambrose, or do you think they would talk more readily to one person instead of two?" I asked.

Aunt Gertrude set her teacup on the side table. "Given your negative relationship with his father, he might better plead his case alone."

Darcy raised an eyebrow when Aunt Gertrude referred to Hiram as "his father" and not "your father." I realized the next time we were alone, I must tell him the truth about our family situation. Was he broadminded enough to accept the company of someone with my stained family background?

SIXTY-SIX

Ambrose

Aunt Gertrude advised I call on the Lairds in the afternoon. Before I left at one thirty, she handed me a calling card with her name and address. She had written my name at the bottom. "If they haven't time to see you, ask them to contact you at my address."

"Thank you, Aunt Gertrude," I said.

I retrieved Butter from the stable. She had not been ridden since our arrival, almost a week ago, and I had spent little time with her. I stroked her neck before mounting. She nickered and pressed her head against my cheek. "This is it, girl. This is my chance to find out what scandal Mrs. Ava was involved in."

I mounted Butter and glanced at the map Darcy had drawn showing the directions from here to Jay Street. Twenty minutes later, I arrived at the impressive three-story brick residence. After tying Butter's reins to the post, I shoved my hand in my trousers' pocket and retrieved Aunt Gertrude's calling card. When I reached the front door, I lifted the knocker and struck it three times against the brass plate.

I waited, my shoulders shivering more from nervousness than the cold.

The door opened. A woman whose dress was too refined for a maid stood before me.

"May I speak with Mr. or Mrs. Laird, please?"

"And who are you?"

"My name is Ambrose Pierce. My aunt is Mrs. Gertrude Oaks." I handed her the card. "She met you at a charity ball in the spring."

"And your business with the Lairds?"

"It's personal. If I may speak to the lady or gentleman of the house, I will quickly reveal my reason for calling."

"I am Mrs. Laird. Come in. We can speak in the vestibule."

I removed my hat and entered the hallway. She gestured toward a door on my right. "We'll speak in here."

The room was small and furnished with wooden chairs and warmed by sunlight. It did not appear to be a room where one would spend much time. My time here would be short if the furnishings were any indication.

"Please sit and tell me your business."

I sat and took a deep breath. In my mind, I had gone over a dozen ways to begin this conversation, but now that I must say the words aloud, they seemed locked in my chest. I cleared my throat.

"I'm from Hidden Springs, Kansas Territory. I have come to inquire about a woman you may know, who may have caused some trouble for your brother, Mr. Gerald Ward." I fiddled with my hat brim. "Her name is Ava Carstairs, and she married my father. Her actions have led me to believe that she may have deceived him."

Mrs. Laird's face went from mildly curious and impatient to hardened, her mouth tightening to a thin line. "What makes you think she knew my brother?"

I chose my words carefully, not wanting to get into why Pa had tossed me out of the house and disowned me. "I overheard her talking with her cousin, Agnes Fletcher. I know eavesdropping is wrong, and I didn't set out to do it, but I happened to be in a place to overhear and couldn't leave without making myself known. Anyway, Mrs. Fletcher said her husband was upset about the scandal that caused them to leave New York City and move to our town on the prairie. He didn't want to move again because of Mrs. Ava. I call her Mrs. Ava now because she's married my pa."

Mrs. Laird held up her hand, palm toward me. "That's enough. I don't wish to speak about this matter without consulting my husband. Leave your card. Mr. Laird will send you a message if he wishes to meet with you."

Defeated, I stood. "Yes, ma'am."

She rose, too, and pointed toward the door, then followed me into the hallway.

I stopped at the front door. "Thank you for seeing me. I'll be waiting for that message from Mr. Laird. I just want to warn my father if he has married a woman who may bring him harm."

"I understand, Mr. Pierce. Goodbye."

The goodbye was so final that I had to accept the fact that I might never hear from Mrs. Laird's husband. The only sure path forward was to return to the *Tribune* office and continue searching the back issues in the hope that whatever scandal Mrs. Ava created, it was big enough for the newspaper to cover it.

When I arrived at the *Tribune* and descended the steps to the dimly lit room where the back issues were kept, I was surprised to see Delia and Darcy standing side by side, heads close, reading an article.

Delia looked up. "Any success with the Lairds?"

"No. I spoke with Mrs. Laird and told her I was looking for information on Mrs. Ava. The moment I mentioned Mrs. Ava's name, Mrs. Laird's face changed to a mask, not showing anything but her unwillingness to continue. She said she would give my card to her husband and he would be in touch if he were willing to talk with me. Her reluctance sent me back here." Seeing the twinkle in Delia's eyes and the way her lips twitched, I asked, "Have you found something?"

"Wait until you see." She pointed at one of four newspapers separated from the stack.

I bent to read the article in an issue dated March 28, 1857.

A claim against the Gerald Ward estate has been made by Miss Ava Carstairs, for the minor child known as Daniel Carstairs. Miss Carstairs claims Mr. Ward is the father of said child and is entitled to inherit his considerable fortune and his mansion on Fifth Avenue. Relatives of Mr. Ward are contesting the claim. A court date has been set to review the matter.

"She had a child?" I said. "I bet she never said anything like that to Pa. She made herself out to be a pure, unmarried lady of high morals."

"Well," Delia said, pointing to a second article, "according to this story, the judge didn't see her that way."

I bent to read the second story date June 15, 1857.

> Judge Dobbins finds against the Carstairs claim to the Ward fortune, and Miss Ava Carstairs has been found guilty of perjury when it was ascertained that she lied under oath about the paternity of her child, Daniel Carstairs. Witnesses say it was known that she consorted with one Foley Mann, a disreputable character that frequents the Five Points area. The attorney for the Ward estate reminded the court that Mr. Ward's marriage of twenty years to his wife, now deceased, had not produced any offspring, so there was no reason to believe that even if a relationship that went beyond a maid living in the house existed, a child would be the result. The judge agreed.

"And that's not all," Delia said. "Look at this."
She handed me the third article.

> Baby found on porch. Mr. Laird of this city had quite a shock as he left his house this morning. A market basket had been left on his front steps. On examination, he found a baby with a note pinned to the blanket the child was wrapped in. It read, "Please care for this little one, an American and a child of God who has done no ill to anyone. Like Moses of old, he has been cast adrift in the world. In God's name, do for him what Pharaoh's daughter did for Moses, take him in and raise him as your own."

Mr. Laird immediately called authorities to have the child removed to the Blake Home for Orphans. Mr. Laird believes the abandoned child to be the son of Miss Ava Carstairs, who placed a false claim against the estate of Mr. Laird's deceased brother-in-law, Mr. Gerald Ward, claiming Mr. Ward was the paternal parent. The County Court of New York found no evidence to support the paternity statement, and Miss Ava Carstairs' claim was denied.

Miss Carstairs was located in the home of her cousin, Mrs. Joe Fletcher. She denied abandoning the child but could not produce him for the officers, stating he was staying with friends. She would not name the friends, saying she would not upset them with police visits to their home. Interviews with the Fletchers yielded only their statements that they had no knowledge of the whereabouts of Miss Carstairs's infant.

I stared at the last lines of the story. "The Fletchers were questioned by police. No wonder Mr. Fletcher was so upset. And Pa. He has no idea Miss Carstairs abandoned her own child." I glanced about the room for pen and paper. "Do either of you have something to write with? I need to copy this down so I can show it to Pa."

Delia opened her bag, rustled through the contents, and withdrew a paper and a pencil. "What makes you think your father will believe something you copy on a piece of paper?"

I noticed that Darcy did not look surprised at Delia calling him my father. She must have told him the truth about Ma and her marriage to Pa.

"He just has to, that's all. I'll remind him how quick she was to suggest he abandon our little sisters." I gripped the pencil. "Easy for her to say since she left her own baby on the doorstep of people she must have known didn't want him." I began copying the *Tribune's* date and the page number of the report. A thought occurred to me. "The child may yet be at the orphanage. Perhaps I can learn more there."

Delia said, "I wonder if he will resemble his mother. If he does, we might be able to get a picture of him. We will need a good story to go with our request for the photograph."

Darcy offered his help. "We could say *The Postulator* wants to do an article on the plight of orphans that might stir interest in their being adopted or at least appeal to the sympathy of those wealthy enough to donate to their care. You could take the photograph, Cordelia. A credit for your growing portfolio of work."

Delia's eyes were shining with excitement. "If the article mentions the situation of how Daniel Carstairs became a ward of the home and refers to the *Tribune* articles, it would be added proof of Mrs. Ava's guilt. It would be hard for her to explain away a missing child when she is named as his mother in court and police records."

Excited, I hurriedly began taking down the information. "It won't take long for me to copy this."

"Now that you have what you need, I'll have Darcy drive me home. Aunt Gertrude wants me to return for a dressmaking consultation. Apparently, I need a larger wardrobe. I wonder if she means I am outgrowing my current frocks because of all the good food I've been eating."

She and Darcy stood. I looked up from my scribbling. "Thank you both for helping me. You in particular, Delia. I know Pa isn't your favorite person."

She smiled. "I'm happy to help you, little brother. I'm also happy for giving you the opportunity to show your pa the errors of his ways."

SIXTY-SEVEN

Cordelia

Darcy left me at Aunt Gertrude's. The dressmaker, a free Negro woman with amazing needlework skills, had already arrived. I was led to a sunny room and measured for bodices, skirts, corsets, pantalets, and whatever other items Aunt Gertrude thought necessary in the wardrobe of a young lady of my social standing and prospective work as a photographer. I was sorry that bloomers were not among the items but happy that she wasn't trying to keep me from pursuing my goals. She had said I could come and stay with her while applying to study with Mr. Brady, but I wondered now if she had believed he would accept me as a student.

Once the measuring was done, there was the matter of selecting materials. Silk, cotton, linen—the choices were dizzying, but Aunt Gertrude was there to help, suggesting which fabrics and which colors would be appropriate for which events. It was growing dark, and I was famished by the time the seamstress gathered her belongings and said she would be back in a week with garments to be fitted. She was leaving as Ambrose came in the door.

"Copying took you longer than I expected," I said to him.

He slipped out of his coat and boots, hanging the coat on the stand by the door and changing the muddy boots for slippers.

"I was in the barn with the horses. Caring for them helps me think."

215

Aunt Gertrude said, "Orna is putting supper on the table. While we're eating, you can fill me in on your progress. With the dressmaker here, I was not at liberty to question Cordelia about your success. She said only that you had arrived at the *Tribune* while she and Darcy were examining back issues. Did you find anything useful?"

I laughed. "Oh, my! We certainly did. You'll never guess." I turned to my brother. "You tell it, Ambrose. And if you know, tell us what you will do next."

"Let's eat first," Ambrose said. "It's been a long day."

We sat down to yet another sumptuous meal, beginning with potato bisque. Next came salmon steak, rice, peas, hot rolls and butter, and yet another apple cobbler with thick cream. Thinking about the expense Aunt Gertrude was putting into my new wardrobe, I limited myself to one roll instead of two and smaller helpings of rice and peas.

Ambrose noticed and teased me. "I thought your investigation would have given you an appetite."

I frowned and decided to admit the obvious. "I don't want to outgrow my new wardrobe before the seamstress finishes making it."

Ambrose scraped the last bite of his cobbler from the dessert dish. "I will have to get back to work, or I'll have the same problem."

We finished the meal and retired to the parlor where a cozy fire crackled in the hearth.

After taking what were becoming our accustomed places when gathering there, Aunt Gertrude said, "All right, Ambrose, my curiosity is getting the better of me. What did you find?"

Ambrose drew the copy of the articles he had made and handed the pages to her. "Delia and Darcy had already found the papers with the news stories by the time I arrived. I copied them to show Pa. It tells how Mrs. Ava was a maid in Mr. Ward's house. After he died, she let his family know she was having his child. They didn't believe her, so she went to court. The court found against her."

I interrupted, still so angry with what the woman had done that I couldn't contain my opinion. "She left her baby on the Laird's doorstep, and they put him in an orphanage."

Aunt Gertrude studied the papers Ambrose handed her. "You write a fine hand, nephew," she said.

"I was careful to write clearly. I wanted Pa to be able to read it. Even so, he might not believe me. He's so besotted with her. He believes everything she says. She may tell him I made up the whole thing, even though he could hire someone to check the back issues for him. She might say it is someone with the same name, although I don't see how that would work since the Fletchers are named, too. That would take coincidence too far. We discussed going to the orphanage to see the child, maybe taking a photograph of him if they will let us." He looked at me. "Do you still think that is possible?"

Aunt Gertrude asked, "You don't have equipment for that, do you, Cordelia?"

"No, and there are so many new items coming out that I don't wish to purchase any until I begin my studies with Brady."

Ambrose sighed. "Well, then, I guess we can't do it."

"I'll speak to Mr. O'Rourke," I said. "He spent three months listening to your plight. Surely, he would like to know the outcome and would even help if asked."

Ambrose smiled. "Yes, he very well might if you asked him."

So in order to help Ambrose, I must settle my differences with Ryan O'Rourke.

***

I sent a note to Ryan the next morning, asking him to please call. He did so in the afternoon. After being seated in the parlor, he leaned back in the chair and studied my face.

"Well, Sam," he said, using the name I had given him when I was disguised as a boy four years before, "what do you need?"

I flushed at his assumption I had asked him to call because I wanted something. He was correct, which made it that much more embarrassing.

"Ambrose has discovered what Mrs. Ava did." I gave a brief summary of the woman's horrendous actions, realizing as I did that she truly was a loose woman if ever there was one. "Ambrose fears his father won't believe him and wants to present proof. He thinks a picture of the child might help, particularly if the boy happens to resemble his mother. He wondered—we wondered—if you might take the photograph or allow me to use your camera."

Ryan shifted his gaze to the fireplace, stared into the flames. Silence reigned as the clock ticked the seconds away.

No longer able to take his silence, I said, "Don't make Ambrose suffer because of disagreements between you and me."

He fastened his eyes on mine. "And what, exactly, is our disagreement? I've never been clear on that."

My hands clenched into fists in my lap. I did my best to keep my voice down though fury was rising in me. "You used the same words I've heard from Hiram's mouth dozens of times. *Loose women*. What about loose men? I asked you once if you had any children. You said 'Not that I know of.' But maybe you have."

"You say that with some conviction. What do you think you know?"

"That your cousin's adopted daughter has a strong resemblance to you. What 'loose woman' did you know around the time Shauna was conceived?"

His face paled. Eyes rounded, he stared at me, and then looked back in the flames.

I immediately regretted my accusation. I may have sabotaged Ambrose's ability to get the picture he hoped would prove his claims about Mrs. Ava, and who knew what grief I might have brought on Shauna and her family, whether I was right or wrong? Had I destroyed a close family with my impulsive talk?

"I'm sorry. I shouldn't have said that. I'm probably wrong. Please don't hold my temper against Ambrose. From all accounts, Mrs. Ava is a bad person. She has stolen Ambrose's birthright and the house and business he helped build. She must be stopped."

Ryan studied me. "Ambrose wishes to save his father from harm. Knowing how you feel about Hiram, I can't believe you care for his salvation."

"He is a despicable man, and the news can damn him to hell for all I care. But Ambrose and my sisters, who have also been cast aside, deserve better. This woman called my mother physically and morally weak, when she is the one with atrocious morals."

"You speak with such hatred about a woman you've never met."

"I don't have to have met her to know what she is. Neither do you. You saw Ambrose's bruises from the beating he received because of her false claims. He was still in pain from broken ribs,

218

his face still swollen and discolored." My breath was heaving. "Then there is her own son. She left him on a doorstep. Now he is in an orphanage. Who comforts him when he falls? Who tucks him in at night? How can a mother walk away?"

"All right, you may take the wagon. In the event Ambrose he can arrange for the photograph, you may use my equipment to take the picture. Ambrose can bring the wagon and plates to me for development as soon as the photographs are taken." He stood. "Goodbye."

He turned and strode from the room. His "Goodbye" echoed in my mind and had the sound of forever.

SIXTY-EIGHT

Ambrose

After talking with Mr. O'Rourke the previous day, Delia drove his wagon to Aunt Gertrude's. He had agreed to allow her use his photographic equipment. Beyond that, I could only guess at how contentious the conversation had been since Delia frowned when I asked and refused to give any particulars beyond the fact that I would be returning the wagon to him.

When morning came, Delia spent a considerable time buffing the plates in hopes that the head of the orphanage would allow us to take photographs. During that time we talked of the best way to succeed in our mission, and we decided to take Aunt Gertrude's carriage to the Blake Home for Orphans. We thought it best to look as prosperous as we could, hoping Mr. Julian Blake, the founder and overseer of the orphanage would deem us worthy of his time, so after Cordelia finished with the buffing, we transferred the camera, tripod, and other equipment to the coach.

It was a cold bitter day when we set out. Eldon, who cared for the horses, was our driver. He stopped the carriage in front of a three-story brick building devoid of outer decoration. A high fence surrounded a side yard. The snow of the past week had melted, leaving a muddy area of ground without a speck of grass, worn away possibly by the many feet that trampled it during good weather. Delia and I stood for a moment taking in the building before climbing four steps to the front door. I struck the knocker on the iron plate.

There was a stirring inside, and the knob turned. A severe-looking woman in a gray dress with a white apron appeared in the doorway. "Please state your business," she said.

"My name is Ambrose Pierce, and this is my sister, Cordelia Pierce. We should like to speak with Mr. Julian Blake about a child who may be in his care."

The woman eyed me. "To what purpose? You look young to be taking one to raise."

"We believe we know the child's mother and that she might be convinced to claim him. When she left him, she was in difficult circumstances," I said.

She responded, "Aren't they all?" But the words sounded more like she was stating a fact than a question.

Seeing her resistance, I said, "Our aunt, Gertrude Oaks, donated money for a charity ball put on to benefit the Blake Home some years ago." I handed her Aunt Gertrude's card and the note of introduction.

"Very well, then. Come in."

We entered a high-ceilinged hallway with bare wood floors. A winding staircase provided passage to the upper stories.

The woman pointed to a wooden bench along one wall. "Sit," she said. "I will announce you to Mr. Blake."

When she disappeared down the maze of hallways, I looked at Delia. "Do you think he will see us?"

"He has the possibility of gain in two ways: get rid of a child and receive a donation. Certainly, he will not pass on those opportunities."

Minutes later, the woman returned. "Mr. Blake will see you. Follow me." She led the way, stepping quickly down corridors. We passed a large schoolroom where children were seated at long rows of tables. Dressed in the same dull gray as our guide, they hunched over slates, chalk in hand.

"They have no hair," I said.

"No hair, no lice," the woman said.

Delia and I exchanged glances. Her clamped lips told me she was holding back an opinion that would probably get us tossed out if she didn't succeed in keeping her mouth shut.

A few more feet, and we came to a door that was cracked open. The woman tapped on it.

"Come," a man's voice called out.

She entered ahead of us. "Sir, here are Mr. and Miss Pierce, who are inquiring about one of our charges."

He stood. "Thank you, Hester. That will be all."

After she left, Mr. Blake indicated chairs in front of his desk. "Please sit. Which child has your interest and why?"

I framed my words carefully, not wanting to give away too much. "Daniel Carstairs. He should be almost three years old. He was placed here by the Laird family whose doorstep he was left on when he was an infant."

"Yes, the child is still with us, and the initial donation for his care has long ago been spent with no follow-up funds." He paused. "What is your interest in the child?"

"I believe his mother might want him back. She now resides in better circumstances in Kansas Territory. I heard her mention him with some regret to her cousin, Mrs. Fletcher." I felt bad for lying, but after the whopper Mrs. Ava had told Pa about me, I figured God would forgive my untruth.

Mr. Blake tapped a pencil on his desk. "Parents do often claim their children when their lives improve. And he will soon be of an age to do productive work, another year of two and he can be weeding in the garden. In four years or so, he could work in a factory. We have seen him through the time when he is the greatest drain on our time and efforts."

Beside me, Delia's fists were clenching at her sides. I remembered the picture of the boy sleeping under the sign pointing to the coal mine.

Before she said something to get us thrown out, I spoke up, "Perhaps a donation to lessen the expenses you have had so far would be in order."

Delia spoke up. "If the child is indeed Daniel Carstairs. May we see the boy?"

"Of course." Mr. Blake stood. "He is still in the nursery. We will move him to the dormitory with the younger boys when he is three—if he is still with us. This way."

We followed him to the front hall and up a flight of stairs to the second floor. The first room was a dormitory. "The three-to-six-year-old boys sleep here. The next room is occupied by the older boys. The nursery where the Carstairs child sleeps is after that."

I caught a glimpse of the rooms as we passed by: they were narrow with two rows of beds and a chest of drawers after every four beds. I supposed one drawer per child. The windows were small and high, allowing light in but giving no view of the outer world. We stopped in front of the closed nursery door.

Mr. Blake warned, "You must be quiet. We have four infants who may be sleeping."

He opened the door.

This room was not so narrow. The beds were cribs with wood bars on the sides to keep the children from falling. All except one child was imprisoned in these multipurpose pieces of furniture. That child appeared to be the oldest. He was sitting on the floor along the outside wall with a pile of wooden blocks in front of him. He was putting a fifth block on the top of his stack when the tower weaved and fell. He looked up, startled, almost fearful when he saw us, like he expected to be punished. When nothing happened, he picked up a block and began building another tower.

Mr. Blake motioned us back to the hall and closed the nursery door. "Now you've seen the child, do you suppose his mother will claim him?"

"He has a sweet face," Delia said. "How could a mother resist if she saw it?"

"Will she be coming to visit then?" he asked.

"No, but there is another way. My sister is a photographer." I looked to Delia, hoping she would continue the explanation.

She picked up where I left off. "I have borrowed a camera from the photographer who has been teaching me. If there is a room with enough light, I can take the likeness in a few minutes. His mother is already regretting her decision. The picture of her child would melt her heart the rest of the way. We will mail the photograph to her and await her reply. My brother will be returning to Kansas Territory in the spring and could take the child with him."

I swallowed hard on hearing this lie and nodded in agreement.

Mr. Blake's eyes narrowed. "A photograph," he said, his voice flat. He clearly did not like the idea.

"Yes," Delia said. "And my aunt, who has such a warm heart

when it comes to children, has said she will make a donation of ten dollars immediately and another ten next month if you will allow us to send a picture that will make his mother unable to forget her child. And," she added, "Kansas Territory is a long way from here. If she should change her mind once she takes him, he would not be returned here."

The mention of money and one less mouth to feed got Mr. Blake's attention. "Very well, I'll show you to the parlor. It has southern exposure, so there is good light. Do you have this equipment with you?"

"In our carriage," I said.

"Follow me." He turned and went quickly down the stairs, past the schoolroom where children were spelling words aloud, and opened a door where a fire crackled in the hearth. He pulled back velvet draperies to let in the light. "Will this suffice?"

"It will," Delia replied.

"Then set up the equipment, and I'll have the boy brought down." He rang a bell, and Hester entered the room.

"Yes, sir," she said.

He gave his instructions. "Have one of the older boys help Mr. Pierce with the photographic equipment."

"Yes, Mr. Blake." She squinted at us. "Come along. I'll have Hal help you."

Hal was a boy about my age. Bald like the other inmates of the orphanage, his ears quickly reddened in the cold. Eldon, our driver, had retreated to the inside of the carriage for warmth. Dressed for the weather in a heavy coat, hat, scarf, and gloves, his eyebrows shot up at the sight of Hal's light clothing.

Hal seemed to ignore the reaction as we set about retrieving the camera, tripod, and other equipment.

"What is this?" Hal asked, picking up the Jenny Lind headrest.

I explained its use. "I wonder how Daniel will react to it."

"You won't need it," Hal said. "Just tell him to be still. He won't move."

"It's a considerable long time for a child—or anyone—not to move," I said. "How long depends on the light. Lucky that the sun is bright today even though it is freezing out here."

"Then we should stop talking and get inside before Mr. Blake gets after me for taking too long."

I decided it was best not to remind him that he was the one who started this conversation with his question. I carried the camera and let him take the less breakable items.

We arrived in the parlor to find Delia arranging a chair in the best light for the photograph. She indicated where we were to set up the equipment. Having watched her take photographs while traveling with O'Rourke, I knew how to assemble everything.

"Thank you, Hal," I said.

Mr. Blake said, "We'll call you when it is time to transport these items back to their carriage."

"Yes, Mr. Blake." Hal left the room.

After setting up the camera, Delia had me take a seat on the chair she had chosen so she could make some adjustments. After a few moments of back and forth between me and the camera, she said, "I'm ready for Daniel now."

Mr. Blake rang a bell.

Hester appeared.

"Bring the child."

She nodded and stepped out to do his bidding. Minutes later, she led Daniel into the room.

It was our first good look at him. He wore the long-sleeved gray shirt and gray trousers that made up the school uniform and sturdy but scuffed shoes that were probably handed down from boys who had outgrown them. The clothes appeared freshly laundered, and I supposed the matron had him change for the photograph.

He stood stiff, serious, wide-eyed, as though wary of what might happen.

Delia approached and took his hand. "Hello, Daniel. My name is Cordelia. I've come to take a likeness of you with my camera." She pointed to the equipment. "To do that, I need you to sit on this chair." She took his hand, led him to the chair, and lifted him onto the seat.

"Now, sit still while I make adjustments."

Delia did her usual back and forth, arranging the boy and adjusting the camera angles just so. When everything was to her satisfaction, she said, "Now for the headrest. I hope it doesn't frighten him."

"That won't be necessary," Mr. Blake said. "He will follow my command."

225

"Very well." Delia made one more trip to Daniel, pressed his back to straighten his posture and pointed. "Look right there."

She returned to peer through the lens. "Now."

"Mr. Blake turned his cold eyes on Daniel. "Daniel, attention! Don't move until I say you may," he commanded.

The boy's eyes rounded. His back straightened, and he sat stone still.

The seconds ticked. I fidgeted and wondered at the boy's rigid posture. At last, Delia said she was done and removed the first plate. "I will take one more to be sure. Ambrose, I should like you to be in the picture with him. Hold him on your lap if he will permit it."

"He will do what he is told to do," Mr. Blake said.

I had no doubt of that. I crossed to the chair and knelt in front of the boy. "Hello, Daniel. My name is Ambrose. I'm going to be in the next picture with you. I'm going to pick you up and put you on my lap." I stood, lifted him, and sat down, arranging him on my knee.

"Delia, I can't play statue nearly as well as Daniel. I think I will need the headrest."

She smiled as she began arranging us and adjusting the camera. When all was to her satisfaction, she attached the headrest.

Returning to the camera, she nodded to Mr. Blake. "Now," she said.

"Daniel, don't move until I say so."

I felt his body stiffen. I hoped I could be as still. As we sat for those few minutes, him on my lap, I realized this was my stepbrother. Not a blood relative but still a part of my life. I should do something for him, even if Mrs. Ava never claimed him. And where was his father in all this? Maybe Mr. Ward really had been his father. Just because a court ruled he wasn't didn't make it so. Well, the truth would never be known. I was so lost in my thoughts that when Delia called that we were finished, the statement surprised me.

Delia said, "I have one more prepared plate. Mr. Blake, would you like to sit for a photograph? I could deliver the developed picture with the donation we discussed."

"Well, I am not dressed for such an event."

"You look very distinguished just as you are," Delia said.

What almost passed for a smile faintly glimmered at the compliment.

Delia pressed on. "Would you prefer to sit or stand for your portrait?"

The man who had been all brusque and business faltered. "Well, I…"

"I see you have a full bookshelf. Perhaps, we might have you sit, an open book in your lap. Yes," she said, her voice building enthusiastically, "we will show your intellectual side." She fairly floated across the room, her full skirt swaying, and selected a clothbound book with gilt letters on a leather spine. "Mill's *On Liberty*. This will do nicely." She motioned toward the wing chair she had used for the earlier photographs. "Come. I'll get you in position."

He crossed to the chair, frowning as he sat, and accepted the book from Delia.

"Do you wear reading glasses, Mr. Blake?"

"I wouldn't want a photograph of me wearing glasses." He was suddenly all firmness again.

"I understand. But they aren't for you to wear. They are a prop. Something we might place on the table or you might rest on the book as though you had just removed them. They would add to your scholarly, learned appearance."

His objections melted away. "They are in my office."

"Would it be all right for Ambrose to retrieve them? Or would you prefer we asked Hester to bring them?"

"Hester," he said. "Pull the bell cord." He pointed to it.

I pulled the cord, and Hester appeared. Upon receiving her orders, she bustled from the room, returning a minute later with the spectacles in hand.

Soon, Mr. Blake, legs crossed, the open book resting on one, the stem of the eyeglasses held by his fingers laid on the pages, was being minutely positioned with such careful attention one would have thought she was photographing nobility.

Delia stepped back and surveyed her work. "Perfect," she said at last. "Now, do you prefer the headrest or should I proceed without it."

"I have been a soldier, Miss Pierce. I assure you I can maintain a position for as long as necessary."

"I did sense that about you, Mr. Blake. I shall proceed." She stepped behind the camera and bent over the lens. "Now."

All was still except for a grandfather clock ticked the seconds and minutes.

"We are done," Delia said.

Mr. Blake let out a breath and shrugged his shoulders. "When can I expect to see the finished product?"

"Tomorrow if the weather holds." She turned to me. "Ambrose, you can pack the equipment now." She offered Mr. Blake her hand. "Thank you for seeing us. I realize your time is valuable, and we've taken a great deal of it."

"My pleasure, Miss Pierce. I look forward to tomorrow's visit, weather permitting, and to seeing the finished photograph."

After we were packed and on our way, I said, "He seemed quite taken with you at the end. I'm not sure you should go back there alone."

SIXTY-NINE

Cordelia

When we arrived at Aunt Gertrude's, we quickly transferred the photographic equipment to Ryan's wagon, and Ambrose continued on to Ryan O'Rourke's so he could develop the pictures, which he had agreed to do if he didn't have to see me.

When I entered the house, Aunt Gertrude was waiting for me in the parlor. She had Orna bring us tea and biscuits. Once we were settled on the sofa, teacups in hand, she said, "You look upset. Tell me."

I described the horror I had witnessed: the children's shaved heads, the dormitory rooms bare of personal possessions or cheer of any kind, the boy frightened into stiffness for as long as Mr. Blake said he must not move.

"Wait until you see the photographs." I frowned. "If they turn out well. It would've been better if the plates had been developed immediately, but that wasn't possible."

Aunt Gertrude lifted an eyebrow. "Your mood tells me there's more than that on your mind."

"All the while I was there, I couldn't stop thinking of what you said about Ma, about how she had a choice. She could leave me in a home like that one or keep me. She chose to keep me. I have often thought that might have been the wrong decision for both of us. Hiram is a tyrant. But after what I saw today, what my life might have been like, I am thankful I had Ma's love. Those children have no one."

"That's not completely true." Aunt Gertrude set her cup aside. "Many of the children do have relatives, even parents, who cannot care for them. They stay at the orphanage for a while and then return to their families when circumstances permit."

"Or when they are old enough to work and earn money."

"You sound grim. What makes you so pessimistic?"

I placed my teacup and saucer on the side table and folded my hands in my lap, thinking of how much to tell her. "Last summer I traveled to the gold mines west of Denver to find my father, Justin Quinn. He told me his father died when he was a child. His mother contracted with a farmer to care for him in exchange for his work; then she remarried and took her two younger children to California with her new husband. My father never heard from her again. He did go in search of her years later and found that she and his brother and sister were all doing well. But he didn't speak to them. He said that, unlike me, he hadn't the courage to be rejected."

"Will you see your father again?"

"I don't know. He's somewhere in the west looking for gold. I received a letter before I left Westport. I should write and tell him of my arrival here and my prospective studies with Mr. Brady." I paused, studying my hands. "Why are there so many unwanted children in the world? Why don't people care about them more than they care about money or whether the children are boys or girls?"

"What do you mean?"

"Hiram cares about boys. He tossed my sisters aside without a thought in the hopes that his new wife would produce sons. Maybe the news that she's had one son already will be a plus for her instead of the negative Ambrose thinks it will."

"Hiram Pierce does not sound like a man who will take well to having been lied to," Aunt Gertrude said. "She's made a fool of him. Once he realizes that, I think he may put her out."

"Maybe. But she's clever. Look at how she convinced Hiram that Ambrose had paid some improper attention to her. She could easily say that the child was Mr. Ward's, even if the judge refused to rule in her favor, and that, as you say about other children abandoned by their parents, she had no way to care for him. If he is as besotted with her as Ambrose claims, she could easily gain his sympathy."

Aunt Gertrude tilted her head to one side. "Given your feelings about your stepfather, what outcome do you hope for, Cordelia?"

"Whichever is the best one for Ambrose. I sense he wants to go home to Hidden Springs. There is a girl he likes very much and wants to see again, perhaps to court her. But how can he live in a small town like that with such division between him and his father?" I shook my head. "But there is nothing more I can do, so I must simply wait."

SEVENTY

Ambrose

I sat in the near darkness inside O'Rourke's wagon as he developed the photographs Delia had taken. When he finished the first, the one of me with Daniel on my lap, I sat staring at it, the feeling of connection I'd had when I held him coming back. He was only a stepbrother, but I had that sense of family.

"What are your plans now, Ambrose?" O'Rourke asked as he began work on the second photograph.

"To take what I've learned to Pa."

"What do you hope he will do with that information?"

I stared at the candle flame. "I don't know what he will do about Mrs. Ava. I just hope he will believe me, so we can be father and son again. If Mrs. Ava stays, I can never live in his house again, but if I can convince him I did nothing wrong, I could work with him in the stable and smithy."

"It sounds like you have strong ties to Hidden Springs if want to stay that much. Is all this just about your father?"

I clutched the frame containing the picture. "There's a girl."

O'Rourke chuckled. "Isn't there always at your age? But I'm surprised. You met several pretty girls on our journey to New York. What makes this one special?"

I laughed and tried for a joke. "Her cooking. She wins every pie-baking contest in the area."

"And?"

Since joking hadn't worked, I decided to be serious. "She's pretty and smart. She helped take care of me after the beating Pa gave me. When I visited Ma's grave and was talking about my problems, Susan showed up. She had come to visit her sister who had passed away. She talks to dead people too. She understands me." I paused, wondering if I should ask the question. Well, he was almost finished with the plates, so I may as well.

"At the beginning of our trip, I thought you might be attracted to Delia. Both Aunt Hannah and Lucy hinted as much."

"My feelings about your sister are complicated," he said. "I suppose those complications began with my being fooled by her all those years ago when she passed as a boy and I didn't detect her." He busied himself encasing the second photograph in a frame.

"But I thought you got past that," I said.

"So did I. In fact, I'm almost sure I did, but she won't get past what I said that offended her. As I see it now, we were people with the same interests thrown together over an extended period of time. Being confined in close quarters will either bring two people closer or show them they are not meant to be. We were shown the latter."

He handed me the photograph of Daniel. "So," he said, changing the subject, "you are taken with a young lady named Susan who bakes pies and understands you. Aren't you young to be making promises to her?"

"That's what Pa said. Well, not exactly. He said she was trying to catch a fellow with money and good social standing. That her affections were all about what I could give her and that she didn't have any true feelings for me." I sighed. "Seems to me he got what he warned me about."

I paused, remembering that Delia had advised me that one did not get answers by avoiding questions, so I plunged ahead. "I feel like Susan is meant to be my life partner. Is there no one you have felt that way about?"

He was busy now with the third plate, his back to me, so I couldn't see his face. "Once, long ago. I was about your age, I think. I suppose that is the age when we first begin thinking of our futures and who might share them. My father thought I was too young and inexperienced in the ways of the world. He sent me on a tour of the British Isles—to visit our relatives who had remained in

Ireland. When I returned, the young lady and her family had moved away. She left no message about where her family was going. My father pointed out that I must not have meant much to her if she could leave without a word."

There was a strangeness in his voice, a shakiness. "I've come to believe my father wasn't telling me the truth, not all of it at least. In the end, he was the one who lost because I disappointed him. During a short stay in England, I learned photography. I returned home knowing the routine life of a merchant was not for me. I worked until I saved enough to outfit my wagon and travel the country. For a while, I carried the romantic idea that my young lady would, through destiny, come to sit for a picture and we would be reunited. A single trip across the entire country, from New York to California, dissuaded me of that notion."

We sat in silence for a moment. Then he said, "If Susan is still there when you return to Hidden Springs and you are both of the same mind—or should I say heart—then do not lose her."

I knew from the sound of his voice that his heart had never been truly available to Delia. It was for the best that she had found Darcy Haynes.

SEVENTY-ONE

Cordelia

Ambrose returned with the photographs and came into the parlor where I was sitting with Aunt Gertrude. He held out a package wrapped in brown paper. I quickly removed the wrapping from the frames and laid them on the table in front of the sofa.

Aunt Gertrude bent for a closer look. "Oh my! The poor child's eyes are so bleak, so without hope."

I glanced at Ambrose. "Aunt Gertrude said sometimes relatives take them out of the orphanage. Do you think his mother will want him?"

"Even if she did, Pa probably wouldn't. As you know, he doesn't like extra mouths to feed unless they are his own."

"True, and Daniel's too young to earn his keep. Plus, he's proof Mrs. Ava duped him. Men don't take kindly to that." I thought of Ryan when I said the last. It was so true. They couldn't take being fooled.

Aunt Gertrude picked up the picture of Ambrose holding Daniel. "You look so solemn. What were you thinking as this was taken?"

Ambrose blinked and then looked down at his hands. "I was thinking that as much as I didn't like Mrs. Ava, this child was my stepbrother, a part of my family, and he needed help, and there was nothing I could do."

I leaned forward, grasped Ambrose's fingers, and squeezed. "I know how bad being helpless feels. I once felt the same way. When I was taking Daniel's picture, I thought of Gabe."

"Who is Gabe?" Aunt Gertrude asked.

"A ten-year-old Negro boy I met when I ran away to Aunt Hannah's, hoping she could help Ma."

"I haven't heard this story," Ambrose said.

"I was traveling with Miz Wilma, a healer. One night we were awakened by someone rustling around our wagon. It turned out to be Gabe. His mother had been sold to someone headed west, and he had run away trying to find her. He didn't have any other family. Miz Wilma fed him and gave him some ship biscuit to take with him. Later, after I reached Westport and was traveling back to Hidden Springs with Aunt Hannah, I saw Gabe again. The slave hunters had caught him. They had him walking behind a horse with a rope tied around him. Every few steps, the rider would tighten the rope, jerk him off his feet, and drag him a foot or two before letting him stand again." I shuddered, remembering. "We didn't do anything, just looked away and hoped the men wouldn't bother us. By the time we were half a mile down the road and safe, I felt so bad I was crying. Aunt Hannah asked me what was wrong. I told her we should have done something. When she said, 'What?' I said 'shoot 'em.' She told me why that was a bad idea, and that the law was on the slave hunters' side. Bad things could happen to us if we tried to help Gabe. The best we could do was change the law."

Aunt Gertrude patted my hand. "She gave you good advice."

Still shaking, I stood and paced. "That was four years ago, and nothing's changed. The law is still the same. No one should be able to treat a child like that, no matter the color."

"Changing a law is a slow process. Trust it will happen," Aunt Gertrude said.

"Meanwhile, Gabe and Daniel and hundreds of children will be beaten and neglected, and the law will be fine with that." I stopped pacing and stared at the flames licking the almost burned-out logs in the fireplace. "Their hearts will crumble and disintegrate like the ashes of those charred logs."

I whirled to face Aunt Hannah and Ambrose. "If only taking photographs didn't take so long and require such stillness, I could show people what happens to children who have no one to look out for them, no one to love them and protect them. That's why studying with Brady is so important to me. I need to know the latest methods that may speed up the process. Not only that, but I am practicing sketching. Ryan showed me some techniques. The trouble, of course, is that others may debate the reality of a sketch, but a photograph shows truth."

"I shall do what I can to help you in your quest," Aunt Gertrude said, her eyes misty as she turned to Ambrose. "What about you? What will you do now that you have gathered the story and have the photographs to show?"

"I must leave for Hidden Springs, possibly tomorrow. It's a long journey, but with just Butter and no wagon, I can make the trip in less time."

"It's winter," I protested. "Use some common sense. You'll freeze. You must wait for spring."

Ambrose smiled. "When have you ever let common sense keep you from doing what you felt you must?"

"But Ambrose. . . " I sputtered.

Aunt Gertrude raised a hand to silence me. "Just as I will help Cordelia fulfill her mission, I will help you with yours, Ambrose. You and your horse may travel by railroad or riverboat. The trip will take days instead of months, and while conditions are often described as uncomfortable, they are soon over without the dangers involved in solitary travel. We will begin searching for accommodations tomorrow."

"But I have no money," Ambrose said. "There hasn't been time to work."

"I shall be happy to pay your passage, but I do ask that you write and tell me what happens and what your future plans are once this mission is completed."

Joy lit Ambrose's eyes. "Of course, I will write. Thank you, Aunt Gertrude, for all you have done and are doing."

"It is my pleasure to help you and Cordelia reach such worthy goals."

SEVENTY-TWO

Ambrose

The next day was filled with activity. In spite of Delia's protests, I accompanied her when she took the photograph to Mr. Blake at the orphan's home.

He was not pleased to see me in company with my sister, making me certain his intentions toward her were not honorable. Still, the meeting went well enough. Mr. Blake was pleased with his image, as well he should be. Delia had positioned him perfectly within the frame. He looked just as scholarly and dignified as she had promised. To that, O'Rourke had added a touch of flesh color to his face and hands and silver to his buttons and cufflinks.

"You do excellent work, Miss Pierce," he said. "I wonder that you even need classes with Brady. You seem quite skilled enough in the art to proceed on your own."

"Thank you for your fine opinion, Mr. Blake. However, the photographic field changes quickly. New camera and developing equipment are being invented almost daily. I aim to begin with the latest knowledge." She opened her reticule and withdrew a gold coin. "My aunt was so taken with the pictures of Daniel that she wanted to help your cause, so she has doubled her donation to twenty dollars." She handed him the gold piece. "And now, my brother has business to look after, so we must leave. But I wonder, would it be permissible for me to look in on young Daniel from time to time, perhaps even take him for an afternoon excursion."

"Well," he said, considering.

"There are many educational opportunities in the city, and possibly, we might meet other philanthropists who might be encouraged to donate to your orphanage."

"That does sound promising. Send round a message when you would like to take the boy on an excursion, and we will arrange it."

The minute I got Delia in the buggy and we were driving away, I said, "What are you thinking? I won't be here to protect you."

Delia laughed. "Oh, Ambrose, I love you, but I can protect myself. I keep a loaded derringer in my handbag."

***

I let Delia off at Aunt Gertrude's and went in search of travel accommodations, checking both railroads and boat lines for possibilities. I learned I could take various trains from New York City to Philadelphia and Pittsburgh. Switching from one railroad line to another, I could get as far as St. Louis. From there, I could get passage on boats on the Missouri River to Westport—if the river wasn't frozen. If it was, I would have to ride Butter the rest of the way, almost a thousand miles to Westport and another hundred and fifty to Hidden Springs.

I learned I could travel with Butter in a stock car. I would not have put her in one without me by her side. The cars with livestock were normally behind the engine, which provided a smoother ride than the passenger cars farther back. However, they were made of slatted wood that allowed cold air to come in, so many layers of clothing would be necessary to keep warm, and Butter would need a blanket.

On returning to Aunt Gertrude's, I found Delia in front of the fireplace in the parlor. She was reading letters from Aunt Hannah and Lucy. "There's one for you from Hidden Springs," she said, holding out a letter.

It was from Mrs. Collins. "Is this all?" I asked.

"Yes," Delia said.

Eagerly, I opened the letter. The next best thing to getting a missive from Susan would be to read about how she was doing in a letter from Mrs. Collins. I tore it open and scanned the single page of her careful handwriting, conveying her concern for me and her hope that I was doing well. No word at all about Susan.

SEVENTY-THREE

Ambrose

Snow and ice prevented me from leaving New York City until the last day of January. Cordelia wanted to see me off at the train station, but Darcy and Aunt Gertrude convinced her she shouldn't risk illness when her photographic studies with Mathew Brady beginning the next day.

The trip, which should have taken two to three weeks at most, ended up taking four to get as far as St. Louis, what with blocked tracks and frozen sections of rivers from ice storms. The railroads were a patchwork of short lines across the country. Missing one train sometimes meant waiting a day or more for another one heading to the same destination, so it was the end of February when I stepped off the train in St. Louis with Butter. I thought of stopping by Gilbert O'Rourke's store and saying hello to his family but decided against it. They would ask for stories of our travels to New York, which would probably last long into the night. Needing rest and an early start, I found a stable for Butter and paid an extra dollar to bed down there for the night. As was my plan, I was up early the next morning, had a quick breakfast at a nearby restaurant, and, with the river icy and no other public transportation going my way, saddled Butter and began the two-hundred-fifty mile ride to Aunt Hannah's.

Twelve days later, I arrived in Westport. I sat on a hill and looked down at the town, relieved to at last be nearing the end of my long ride. I followed a well-worn trail into town and was soon in front of the hotel just as my little sisters were walking home from school.

I slid off Butter's back, tied her to a post, and stepped onto the boardwalk.

Ella saw me first and let out a whoop. "Ambrose! You're back," she shouted as she broke into a run.

I caught her in my arms and swung her around. I set her down so I could hug Jennie and Lucy in turn.

"We're so glad you're back," Lucy said. "We were all worried about you traveling alone. Not that we don't trust your abilities, but if anything did happen, we might never know."

"Well, I'm here and safe now."

"With plenty of stories about your adventures, I should think." Lucy's eyes searched mine. "Come inside and tell us."

"I have to stable Butter first. She's had a hard trip and could use some fresh hay and water."

"We'll see you inside then," Lucy said.

I mounted Butter and rode around the hotel to the stables. After caring for my horse, I picked up my saddlebags and went in the back door and through the kitchen, inhaling the smells of fresh-baked bread and stewing beef, my stomach growling. I was hungry, but I'd hold off eating until I had properly greeted Aunt Hannah and the girls and given a quick accounting of my trip.

There'd be time for details later. And, of course, I'd want to hear all about what had been going on with them since I left.

They were waiting for me in the big dining hall at one end of the long plank tables where travelers were served. The room was nearly empty now, being late afternoon. In an hour or so, it would begin filling up as the evening mealtime approached.

I put my saddlebags on the bench seat. Aunt Hannah brought a cup of hot coffee and set it on the table in front of me.

Lucy was bursting to know what I had learned. "You didn't give any details in your letters, Ambrose. You just said you found out Mrs. Ava was a liar and a con artist who tried to bilk a rich man's family out of their inheritance. Tell us the whole story."

"Aunt Gertrude was the key," I said. "Without her and her New Year's Eve social, I don't know how long it might have taken."

Lucy's eyes lit up at the mention of the social. "Was it beautiful?"

"Yes," I said. "Many well-off members of society were present. The most important one for my purposes was Darcy Haynes, the owner and editor of a periodical call *The Postulator*. He was quite taken with Delia, and that attraction made him amenable to helping me."

Lucy shook her head. "First, I thought Delia was interested in O'Rourke, and second, she's such a mouse. How did she attract a refined city man so quickly?"

I laughed. "To quote some of the New York shop owners, it is all in the packaging." I cast a sideways glance at Aunt Hannah. "It seems someone sent Delia's measurements to Aunt Gertrude, and she had her dressmaker prepare a ball gown for Delia. Our great-aunt had hoped we would arrive before Christmas, but when we showed up on New Year's Eve, there was still time for the dress to be useful."

Lucy's eyes widened. "A ball gown?"

"Yes," I replied. "Complete with that unmentionable some refer to as a hoop skirt. I have to say I didn't recognize Delia with her hair all done up and her skirts swirling, taking up the entire hallway." I enjoyed teasing Lucy with Delia's appearance, but I wanted to get on with my own story. "Anyway, Darcy suggested we look through back issues of the *Tribune*, and we found this."

I produced the handwritten copy I had made of Mrs. Ava's claims against the Ward estate for her child. When I finished reading my notes aloud, I looked up into the stunned faces of my aunt and sisters.

"We have a stepbrother." I reached into my saddlebags, withdrew the photographs, and laid them out on the table for all to see. "This is our stepbrother, Daniel Carstairs."

Jennie's eyes widened. "He's bald."

"All the children at the orphanage are," I said. "Their heads are shaved to prevent bugs."

Aunt Hannah picked up the photograph of me holding Daniel. "You look sad. What were you thinking?"

"What his life must be like. He was so frightened. When Mr. Blake, the owner and overseer of the orphanage told him not to move, he stiffened like a block of wood. I could scarcely feel his breath. See his eyes in the picture, how round and fearful they are? I can't imagine what happens to make the child so afraid. And then there was how little he weighed. He's almost three, and I swear, he was no heavier than any of you girls were at a year old."

"What will you do with the pictures?" Ella asked.

"Show them to Pa as proof the child exists. Together with the stories I copied from the newspapers, he might believe me when I tell him Mrs. Ava is the boy's mother, and maybe he'll see her for the liar she is."

"I wish you luck with that, Ambrose," Aunt Hannah said, "but your father may not be willing to see any truth beyond the one he believes."

"But it isn't the truth he believes," I insisted. "It is her lies."

She sighed. "Everyone has a different truth. But it can change in a moment. Perhaps it will for your father when he sees these pictures."

Something about her sad face drew me out of my own problems. "What's wrong, Aunt Hannah?"

"We're homeless," Jennie said.

"What?" I looked from Jennie's tearful face to Ella, Lucy, and Aunt Hannah.

"Truthfully," Aunt Hannah said, "It is I who will be leaving. Lucy will be living with Aunt May, and Ella and Jennie will move in with Aunt Hilda."

"But why?" I asked. "I thought they were going to stay here with you."

Aunt Hilda said, "While you were traveling, your Grandmother True passed away. That means my father's will leaving the hotel to my sister's husbands gave them the right to sell the business after my mother's death. The new owners take possession on the first of June. At that time, I must find a new place to live."

"But where will you go?" I asked.

"I have friends in the East who suggested I might hold discussions for ladies' groups. I have written articles that have been published, and perhaps there is work for me in that area. I have saved some money over the years, so I'm not destitute. Still, I don't have enough to keep your sisters with me."

Ella spoke up. "We don't want to live with Aunt Hilda. She's mean and stingy, and she doesn't like us."

"What she doesn't like is your backtalk," Lucy said.

Jennie stuck her tongue out at Lucy. "You don't care about us because you get to live with Aunt Hilda and wear all the latest fashions."

"Girls, that's enough about us," Aunt Hannah scolded. "I'm sure Ambrose has more to tell us about his journeys."

I had thought so, too, but now that I had heard my sisters' lives were about to be changed once again, I couldn't think of a thing to say.

Lucy gave me a direction. "Tell us about Delia and this Mr. Haynes. And whatever happened to Mr. O'Rourke?"

I gave them a quick summary of the falling out between Mr. O'Rourke and Delia followed by the New Year's Eve social and Mr. Haynes's attraction to Delia. "He publishes *The Postulator*, a periodical that discusses both sides of important issues. He didn't even blink when Delia told him she was a suffragette."

By the time I finished telling my stories, the room was filling with hungry travelers and dishes had been set out. We got in line and filled our plates. After the meal, I yawned and stretched. "Is there a room for me, or should I sleep in the stable with Butter?"

"I have a room for you," Aunt Hannah said. "How long will you be here?"

"I leave in the morning. The sooner I give Pa the news, the better."

Aunt Hannah sighed. "Not soon enough, I'm afraid. Mrs. Ava is with child. The little stranger should arrive as early as the end of May. My understanding is that preparation for the child is one reason your father was in such a hurry to sell the hotel. His new wife is not as thrifty as your mother. A finely furnished house and a fashionably dressed wife are expensive."

My heart sank. Mrs. Ava was having Pa's child. He still deserved the truth, but he would never be free of her—not if the child was a boy. I reckoned he wouldn't blink twice about losing another girl. He hadn't when it came to forgetting about my sisters.

Later that night, I lay in bed with a heavy heart. No matter how Pa took my news, nothing good would come of it. Well, maybe something. If he believed me, I could work with him again and make plans for a life with Susan Hogan.

SEVENTY-FOUR

Ambrose

I left Westport shortly after breakfast the following morning. At Leavenworth, I took the military road toward Ft. Riley. Five days later, nearing sunset, I reached Hidden Springs. My first stop was the cemetery and Ma's grave. Throughout the trip from Westport, I had gone back and forth on whether to go straight to the house and confront Pa or to talk with Mrs. Collins or Susan first to get a sense of how thing were going for Pa. Maybe sitting beside Ma's grave and saying a prayer would show me the way.

I knelt and traced the inscription on the stone with my finger. "I made it back, and Ma, you won't believe what I found. Well, I suppose you already know, looking down from heaven and all. There were times I felt like you were guiding me, and now maybe you can help me figure out the best way to tell Pa what I know."

The earth was cold and damp beneath my knees. The grass had greened in patches and the trees were budding. "I'm sitting here remembering the last time I visited. It was after Pa had beaten and disowned me. Thinking on that now, it seems like the best thing would be to talk to him away from the house. Maybe I should have Mrs. Collins ask him to come to the restaurant. He couldn't do much in public. There'd be someone to stop him."

I sighed. "I don't want to fight with him, Ma, but when he thinks he's right, he doesn't see reason. Then there's Mrs. Ava. I don't care about her, but it turns out she's with child, a half-brother or sister for me. What if Pa gets mad and hurts her or the baby?"

Another possibility came. One I hadn't considered. "I could tell Mrs. Ava first, but it would give her a chance to fix up some story to make me out a liar. Pa believed her before, so he might this time, as well. If he does, has my trip been a waste? Will Pa or Mrs. Ava give Daniel the home he deserves?"

"Ambrose, is it you?"

Susan.

At the sound of her soft voice, my heart swelled with gladness.

I stood, tears in my eyes, laughing. "Yes, it is." Then I looked down at my ragged trousers and thought about my beard and shaggy hair and was embarrassed. I had shaved before leaving Westbrook, but my beard was back, and my last haircut had been in New York, almost two months before. "How did you know?"

The corners of her mouth twitched. "Butter. I recognized your horse."

Remembering my sisters had done the same, I said, "I'd better never change horses. That seems to be how everyone knows me."

I reached out to hug her, but she sidestepped away. "Did you learn anything about Mrs. Ava?"

"I did. As soon as I found out what she had done, I started for home. I'm sorry I didn't take time to write." I frowned. "But I received only one letter from you the whole time I was gone, so I wasn't sure you wanted to hear from me."

She glanced at me and then away. "I will explain, but not this minute." She raised a finger and swiped a tear from the corner of her eye. "What will you do now?"

"I'm trying to figure that out. That's why I'm here talking to Ma. When and where should I tell Pa that Mrs. Ava has a son who is three years old this month?"

Susan's eyes widened. "She's been married before? She told everyone she was a single lady."

"She is a single woman. She had an out-of-wedlock child with Gerald Ward, a wealthy man. At least, she said the child was his. When Mr. Ward died, she tried to claim his fortune for her son, but Ward's sister and nephews went to court, and the judge decided the boy was not Ward's offspring. So she left the baby on the doorstep of Ward's sister. They turned him over to an orphanage."

"Oh, Ambrose! How awful." She shook her head, her eyes more sad than shocked. "She left her child. How could a mother do that?"

"I guess it happens a lot. Delia and I went to the orphanage. It was full of children. Mr. Blake, the director, let us take two pictures of Daniel. They're in my saddlebags. Who should I talk to first, Susan? Pa or Mrs. Ava?"

"I think you should come to the boardinghouse and get cleaned up. Then ask Mrs. Collins. Or Reverend Sherwood."

I stood. "Getting cleaned up first sounds like a good idea." I glanced toward the road and for the first time noticed the buckboard stopped beside Butter. "Did you drive that here?"

"I did. I was coming back from delivering a cake when I saw your horse."

"Well, go on then, and I'll see you in town. Tell Mrs. Collins I'll want to rent a room. I can pay this time."

"I will." She took off, quickly wending her way through the graves, which seemed to have increased in number at an alarming rate.

Once Susan had driven away, I crouched beside the grave. "Susan seemed distant, Ma, like there was something she didn't want to tell me. Maybe she likes someone else now."

SEVENTY-FIVE

Hiram

I heard it first from Bob Clark when he came back to work from his noon break.

"Ambrose is back," he said.

I laid down my hammer and plunged the hot iron in water. "Did you see him?"

"Just his horse over in front of the boardinghouse."

"I'm surprised he'd show his face around here after what he did." I began washing up. Ava was coming by after choir practice. Our plan was to eat at the boardinghouse café.

Bob removed his leather apron from a hook and put it on. "You never said what he did, exactly, that you can't forgive him for."

"And I won't. It's not something for the gossips to talk about."

"But they talk anyway, Hiram. Everyone likes Ambrose. They think he is a good person. No one can imagine what he did that turned you against him."

"Imagination is all any of them will get unless Ambrose breaks his silence." Maybe that was why he was back. To tell everyone his story. Not the truth—he wouldn't want anyone to know he made improper advances on his stepmother—but something that would stir up his friends against me.

Ava came in then, standing inside the front door. "Is that Ambrose's horse in front of the boardinghouse?" she asked.

"Bob says it is. Do you still want to eat there today?"

"I do. People will talk if we vary our habits. We have a meal there every week after my choir practice. No need to give gossips any scraps to talk about."

"I agree." I took her arm, and we stepped outside. "I don't see the horse."

"If it's gone, perhaps Ambrose is, too," Ava said.

We crossed the street and entered the café door. Our usual place by the window was open, so we seated ourselves and waited for Susan Hogan to come take our orders.

She brought plates to travelers near the counter and refilled their coffee, then brought us water. "What can I get you today?"

"Chicken noodle soup," Ava said, "and a biscuit." She pressed her hand to her waist. "The time I can eat without feeling ill can't come soon enough."

"I'll have the meat loaf dinner," I said. "Bring coffee." I wanted to ask the girl about Ambrose. If he had told anyone his plans, I figured it would be Susan Hogan. But he didn't know about her yet, about what had happened, or at least, what she claimed happened. I watched her head for the kitchen to turn in our orders, trying to determine if she were putting on weight in her belly. Her story was she'd been attacked by three men on her way home from work four months ago. Her brother Willie had found her in a grove of trees by the river, passed out. I wasn't sure I bought the part about her being attacked. The way I saw it, she probably got too friendly with some fellows and gave them the wrong idea. Before Ambrose had turned on me, I'd warned him to stay away from the little gold digger. A lot of good that had done.

"What are you thinking?" Ava asked.

I turned to Ava. "Just that I'm hungry. Why's it taking so long to bring our food?"

Ava nodded in the direction of the kitchen. "It's on the way now."

Susan hurried toward us, a tray of food in her hands. "Here you go," Susan said, placing the dishes in front of us. "Will there be anything else?"

"Not now," I said, "but I'll have pie later. What about you, Ava?"

"Pudding," she said.

"Very well," Susan said.

I studied her walk and spoke my curiosity aloud. "Do you think she is with child?"

"Could be. There was all that talk about her being attacked." Ava bent toward me. "A fine way to cover loose morals."

From behind me, a man said, "If anyone would know how to cover loose morals, it would be you, Mrs. Ava." The voice was deeper, but I knew it was Ambrose's.

I started to stand, but Ambrose's hand gripped my shoulder and pushed me down. "Let's not disturb Mrs. Collins's customers. I have something to show you."

He placed two pictures on the table, one of a bald child alone and another of Ambrose holding the child.

"The child I'm holding is Daniel Carstairs, Mrs. Ava's son, the one she tried to use to bilk a family out of their inheritance. When that didn't work, she abandoned him on their doorstep and never looked back. He's in an orphans' home in New York City now."

Ava was breathing hard, her eyes wild. "You liar. I have no idea who this child is. How dare you make such accusations?"

Ambrose dropped a sheaf of handwritten papers beside my plate. "I copied these news articles from the New York City *Tribune*. I included the issue dates for each one. Mrs. Ava is named in the stories."

Ava's voice shook as she declared, "Someone with the same name. It's why I had to leave New York. Ugly stories about someone else with the same name," she repeated. Then she pressed her hand against her waist and moaned. "Oh! Oh, no!" Her face paled and her eyes widened.

"What is it" I asked, alarmed.

"The pain of being caught," Ambrose said.

"Our child," Ava sobbed. "Oh, it's too soon."

Fear filled me at the thought of losing another child. This couldn't be happening again.

"Leave us," I snapped at Ambrose. "If my son dies, I'll have your hide."

SEVENTY-SIX

Ambrose

Mrs. Ava was an expert actress, for sure. Plus, she knew how to play into Pa's fears of losing another boy—if she was a carrying a son. If it was even his. After all, there had been the question about Daniel's parentage.

"Leave," Pa said. He grabbed the papers and thrust them at me. "Take your lies with you."

I shook my head and refused to take back the evidence. "I have brought you the truth. Do with it what you will."

I had done all I could for Pa, and, once again, he had rejected me.

Around us, diners stared. Mrs. Collins appeared in the kitchen doorway, demanding to know what was happening. Doc Sloan got up from his table and rushed toward us as Mrs. Ava clutched her belly. Only she knew if her pain was real.

I turned, knowing it was the last conversation I would ever have with my father.

***

Hours later, I lay in the dark in the room I had rented, thinking about all that had happened. Mrs. Collins had come by half an hour ago to tell me that Mrs. Ava was next door with the Fletchers, in bed and apparently not in labor, so the child she carried was safe for now. Doc Sloan had ordered bed rest, which meant she would be staying with her cousins for some time. Pa was hovering at her bedside.

I was glad for that news. I wouldn't want to be responsible for the loss of Pa's baby, but now that all hope of reconciling with him was gone, I wondered what I should do next. During my journey to New York and back when I sometimes thought all was futile, that Pa would never believe me, I had kept going. I'd had a purpose. Now what was there?

My thoughts turned to Susan and how she'd said she could explain why she hadn't written. Given how bad the day had been, I expected she would have bad news, whatever it might be.

I opened my saddlebag and removed the book of fables. I didn't open it, just lay back on the bed with the book on my chest and wondered what story moral would best guide me.

There was a knock at the door, and then Susan's soft voice calling, "Ambrose."

I put the book aside and hurried to the door. "Come in."

I turned up the lantern flame.

She went to the window and looked out, her mood pensive. "I promised to tell you something, so I'm here to do that. You don't have to say anything after. I'll just leave."

I stood still, wanting to reach for her, but remembering how she had sidestepped my embrace earlier, I held back. "Go on." My chest tightened. If she didn't say something soon, my heart might stop.

"I'm surprised your father or someone else hasn't told you," she said.

"I was too busy telling Pa things for him to say anything about you, and you're the only other person I've really talked to."

She had clasped her hands now, was wringing them. "Four months ago, I was attacked by three men." Her shoulders were shaking. She pressed one hand to her mouth and the other to her stomach.

That gesture, hand to stomach, was one I was familiar with, had seen so many times from my mother and others, that I knew before she said the next words.

"And I—I'm with child. One of those awful men is my child's father."

I stood, numb, trying to think what say, to get my mind around what she told me. I thought of my mother and Delia and their pain, of Daniel Carstairs and the fear in his eyes. I thought of how Mrs. Ava had labeled my mother weak in body and morals. I knew what people, including Pa, were probably saying about Susan.

"Well," Susan said, jolting me out of my thoughts, "now you know." She sniffled and turned toward the door.

"Susan, wait." I reached for her, caught her hand. I couldn't let the sweetest, kindest girl I'd ever met walk out of my life. "I know we're both young, and I don't have anything, not even a job or a place to live, but I love you, and I want to marry you, and raise a family together."

"You want to marry me?" Her voice shook as though she might not be able to believe me. "After what I just told you? What about the child?"

"We are having a child, ours from now on until forever—if you say yes."

"Oh, Ambrose, yes."

"Then I'll walk you home tonight, and tomorrow Reverend Sherwood will marry us."

I knew what my father would say when he learned of my marriage to Susan. Darkness had claimed Pa's heart. I would not let it claim my own. I was more than Hiram's boy. I was a man, and tomorrow I would have a family of my own.

A NOTE TO MY READERS

Thank you for reading *Hiram's Boy*. I hope you enjoyed the novel. I'd love your comments on this book or the previous books in the series, *Cordelia's Journey* and *For Want of a Father*. I'd also like to know what members of the Pierce family you'd like to see as main characters in future books. Leave your comments at piercefamilysaga.com, and I'll get back to you.

In the meantime, if you haven't read the previous books in the series, you may want to check them out.

Cordelia's Journey

A brutal stepfather . . . A dying mother. . .

A loving daughter who tries to save her

Kansas Territory, 1855

In this coming-of-age story, thirteen-year-old Cordelia endures her stepfather's abuse until she learns her ailing mother is pregnant again. Fearing her mother will die in childbirth, she runs away, heading for Westport and her aunt, the only person who might be able to save her mother. She disguises herself as a boy and sets out on foot to make the 150-mile trip. Following the Kansas River, she hitches rides with a variety of travelers going east, facing setbacks along the way while learning lessons about the world and her place in it.

Cordelia's Journey is the first book in the Pierce Family Saga, a series of historical novels that follow Cordelia and her family through the latter half of the nineteenth century.

For Want of a Father

Fathers, daughters, and expectations

In 1859, half-sisters Lucy and Cordelia travel by stagecoach from Westport, Missouri to Kansas Territory. Since their mother's death four years ago, both have lived with their aunt. Now Lucy's father wants her home. For Lucy, 13, it is a dream come true. Cordelia, 17, chaperones Lucy on the trip home, then continues on the stage to Denver to search for the father she has never met. Her expectations are low, but she can't stop the occasional dream. Will either father live up to his daughter's expectations, or will each break his daughter's heart?

ABOUT THE AUTHOR

Hazel Hart, a member of Kansas Authors Club, has won awards for her short fiction, including "Amanda Marie," published in *Kansas Voices*, and "Confessions," printed in *Words out of the Flatlands*. She has three contemporary suspense novels and one young adult novel available in paperback and e-book formats.

Hiram's Boy is the third novel in the Pierce Family Saga series. *Cordelia's Journey*, the first book, is set in Kansas Territory in 1855. The second book, *For Want of a Father*, takes place in 1859. She is currently working on the fourth book, which occurs during the Civil War and continues the stories of the Pierce siblings: Cordelia, a photographer and journalist, Lucy, a nurse, and Ambrose, a soldier in the Union Army. For updates on the progress of the fourth book and to learn more about the characters, visit piercefamilysaga.com

Printed in the USA
CPSIA information can be obtained
at www.ICGtesting.com
LVHW022139300924
792598LV00035B/594